The
DARK BLUE
WINTER
OVERCOAT

Born in Reykjavik in 1962, SJÓN is a celebrated Icelandic novelist and poet. He won the Nordic Council's Literature Prize (the Nordic countries' equivalent of the Man Booker Prize) for his novel *The Blue Fox*, and the novel *From the Mouth of the Whale* was shortlisted for both the International IMPAC Dublin Literary Award and the Independent Foreign Fiction Prize. His novel *Moonstone – The Boy Who Never Was* (2013) received every major literature prize in Iceland. Sjón's biggest work to date, the trilogy *CoDex 1962*, was published in its final form in autumn 2016 to great acclaim and will be published in English by Sceptre. He has published nine poetry collections, written four opera librettos and song lyrics for various artists. In 2001 he was nominated for an Oscar for his lyrics in the film *Dancer in the Dark*. Sjón's novels have been published in thirty-five languages.

TED HODGKINSON is a broadcaster, editor, critic, writer and Senior Programmer for Literature and Spoken Word at Southbank Centre, Europe's largest arts centre. Formerly online editor at Granta magazine of new writing, his essays, interviews and reviews have appeared across a range of publications and websites, including the *Times Literary Supplement*, the *Literary Review*, the *New Statesman*, the *Spectator*, the *Literary Hub* and the *Independent*. He is a former British Council literature programmer for the Middle East, North Africa and South Asia. He currently sits on the judging panel of the Royal Society of Literature Encore Award for the best second novel and the selection panel for the Rockefeller Foundation's Bellagio Fellowship. He has previously judged the BBC National Short Story Award, the British Book Awards and the Costa Book Awards.

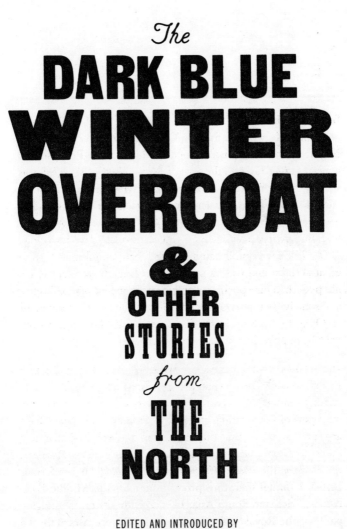

The
DARK BLUE
WINTER
OVERCOAT

&

OTHER
STORIES
from
THE
NORTH

EDITED AND INTRODUCED BY
SJÓN AND TED HODGKINSON

PUSHKIN PRESS

Pushkin Press
71–75 Shelton Street
London, WC2H 9JQ

First published in 2017

Introduction © Sjón and Ted Hodgkinson 2017

Published in partnership with Southbank Centre as part of Nordic Matters.
With support from the Nordic Council of Ministers and NordLit

3 5 7 9 10 8 6 4 2

ISBN-13: 978-1-78227-382-0

Designed and typeset by Tetragon, London
Printed and bound by CPI Group (UK) Ltd, Croydon CRO 4YY

www.pushkinpress.com

Contents

Introduction

TED HODGKINSON AND SJÓN

T HE NORTH CONJURES epic storytelling. It is the birth-
place of the saga, where stories of human survival
have long been sculpted by the region's raw elements, as in
turn they have shaped its varied landscapes, from sheltering
forests to islands lashed by unforgiving seas. The ancestry
of this tradition can be found in many-volumed novels that
detail struggles against the headwinds of the modern-day
elements, and also in the vicissitudes of Nordic noir, which
keep us in suspense, season after season. More than recounting feats of endurance, the storytelling of the region is also
alive to the possibilities of human transformation, rooted
in the metaphysical world of folklore and fairy tale. The
contemporary Nordic short story is a crucible in which
these properties are fused together, capturing a quest for
survival while prising open, in the space of just a few pages,
potential for radical change. These are timely qualities in
a world on the brink, in which we need to find ways of
reimagining our relationship to our natural surroundings,
ourselves and each other.

Sjón is an author uniquely attuned to these storytelling
frequencies, who in his own writing across many forms creates
historical epics in miniature, focusing on moments of pro-
found transformation, through an often surreal lens. A priest
hunts a mysterious blue fox across the stark winter-scape of

nineteenth-century Iceland. Or in his most recent novel, a young boy captivated by cinema awakens to his true identity as Spanish flu ravages Reykjavík in 1918. Sjón has brought his own distinctive vision to this first ever selection of short stories from the Nordic region in English, published to coincide with the Southbank Centre's Nordic Matters series and the London Literature Festival. Our selection encompasses writers from across generations of each literary culture, to present a prismatic perspective of each place, refracting a broad range of literary styles and human experience. The overall balance of genders reflects a region which has produced some of the finest writers of either gender at work today, though it's also especially notable that many of those from the younger generation are women breathing fresh life into the literature of their homelands, including Dorthe Nors, Linda Boström Knausgaard and Niviaq Korneliussen. While in recent years many Nordic novelists have found their way into English translation, relatively few of those writers who have focused on the short story have made that same journey—this anthology aims to help close those gaps and create openings into a revelatory world of storytelling.

To introduce the selection, I begin by asking my co-editor Sjón what he sees as the cultural and literary connections between the eight distinctive Nordic lands of Denmark, Norway, Sweden, Finland, the Faroe Islands, Åland Islands, Greenland and his native Iceland.

*

*Sjón, the Nordic region covers a vast and varied terrain, both geograph-
ically and culturally. What are the things which bind it together? What
are the elements that make up a Nordic identity? And after editing this
anthology, what have you discovered about the literary links between the
writers of the North?*

The Nordic identity question is one Nordic authors are repeat-
edly asked in interviews or on the panels of literary festivals;
especially abroad and especially in the context of the Nordic
Council's Literature Prize. Their usual reaction to it is to be
annoyed at hearing it again, before they answer that there is
no common identity; that the literatures of each country have
developed in their own specific ways; and so on. But as I take it,
the question is really not about our own contemporary literary
output but the deeper currents that run under the whole social
make-up of the North. So I always try to answer it positively.

The fact that we share history, both cultural and political,
that goes back more than a millennium means our societies—
which in the beginning seem to have all been Germanic and
heathen, and speaking variants of Old Norse—have been
introduced to great historical changes at the same time and
had to react to them from that common ground. So the
region's movement from the Norse religions to Catholicism,
from Catholicism to the Protestant Reformation, from the
Reformation to Enlightenment via the Renaissance, from
monarchy to democracy and then on to twentieth-century
trends in ideologies, art movements and empowerment of
social groups, could therefore be seen as one, making us a
single culture with regional variations.

The long shared political history is, of course, also a story
of wars, invasions, defeats, colonization and the fight for

independence among those countries—and thereby of narratives about individuals and communities caught up in those events at the same time while in different parts of the North.

By editing this anthology with you, Ted, I have become even more sure than ever before of how deep the common Nordic roots lie and how consistent authors in the North are in collectively nurturing and feeding from them.

From Johan Bargum's haunting story in which a father believes he is a dog, to Hassan Blasim's fierce and funny tale of a tiger who is writing a crime novel and drives the 55 bus in Helsinki, to Dorthe Nors's spooky story of a man with an injured ankle waiting by a deer stand as darkness falls, many of the stories here capture a moment of transformation, or characters caught on the threshold between worlds. Your writing is also deeply alive to the possibilities of transformation. What makes Nordic writers so imaginatively drawn to the metaphysical, or even the magical?

I think that within much of Nordic literature there are two main tendencies at play—the naturalist school and the folk tradition or diverse common-folk's belief systems—and since the beginning of modernity one can see them used together or combined in different measures in most of the best short stories and novels from the region. The naturalists' legacy of writing socially relevant stories—and their faith in the author's power to be a voice of change by revealing society's ills with literary means—is still there and responsible for the strong humanist foundation shared by the stories readers will find in this anthology. A part of that humanist worldview is respecting what folk stories have to offer as literature and as the means to understand the universe and man's place in it. And, as you know, once you are there—in a forest of stories, on an island of too many tales, in a city of sorrowful rhymes—you are in a world where metamorphosis and transcending the borders of the "real" and the "true" are more than just possible, they are tools of survival in harsh natural surroundings or a failing community. Today this can be seen in narratives about changing identities or new sexualities.

Another strong factor in Nordic literature is the early input of the avant-garde in most of the countries—surrealist poetry and the modernist novel—which on the one hand has resulted in a relentless questioning of the realist method, and on the other in renewing the ways authors can use elements from folk culture in their writing. Add to all of this the influence of diverse strands of Protestant and radical political thinking on Nordic authors and you have a heady brew. I'll stop here, but I am glad you mentioned Hassan Blasim as he and other authors who have come to our countries in the North from faraway places around the globe are already creating new challenges for Nordic literature and moving it forward with their own stories from abroad and within, with references to shape-shifters we couldn't even dream of.

Why do the stories we tell matter in a world on the brink?

Even though our Nordic welfare states are today as modern/ post-modern as they can possibly can be, the great works of twentieth-century Nordic literature makes us keenly aware that we are just a generation or two—maybe three, four, I tend to forget as I get older—away from life lived in hardship brought on by unjust and unforgiving societies. This is a literary and social heritage I don't hesitate to insist no Nordic writer can escape from and which can be found at the root of all the stories in this anthology, even when it is not directly noticed; no matter if their authors are born sixty-one years apart, in 1929 like the Norwegian Kjell Askildsen or in 1990 like Niviaq Korneliussen from Greenland.

But what they also share, apart from this grounding in social awareness, is the need to tell a good story (melancholic, absurd or grim as it may be) with means both tested and newly invented. Because who has the patience to read a tale from small places at the edge of the globe or on the margins of communities if it isn't told with wit—dark and dry, of course, we are Nordic—precision and restrained empathy for its characters?

The Dark Blue Winter Overcoat travels with diverse stories in its pockets and even in its linings. It comes to its readers from the affluent North that tops every global survey of happiness and equality, but on closer inspection it will reveal itself to be worn at the elbows, patched up here and there. In our present world of conflict and climate change, it offers what literature has always had to offer—the few moments of warmth that come from sharing a story, a chance for people to compare their fates, to discover their common humanity and to ask for stories in return.

SUNDAY

NAJA MARIE AIDT

I T WAS COMPLETELY STILL ON the terrace in front
of the house where Iben was sitting on a bench with
her back against the wall, enjoying watching the children
bounce on the trampoline. She could hear Peter shouting
something, making the children squeal with delight. It was
such a beautiful day. The September sun crashed down
from a cloudless sky. The cat snuck under the bench. They
had all sat there eating breakfast a little while ago, and now
Kamilla was inside doing the dishes with the girls. Iben
closed her eyes and leaned her head back. She remembered
a sad and pretty song that had always made her cry with
joy when she was young. She whistled the opening lines to
herself. Then someone was pulling on her sleeves. It was
her son wanting to go down and throw stones into the pond
at the far end of the yard. She got up and took him by
the hand.

Mosquitoes swarmed over the water. She threw a stick
in and told the boy that it was now sailing out into the wide
world. But the boy replied that it would never come up from
that mud-hole again. The girl bounced light as a feather up
and down on the trampoline. Peter stood near them smoking. Then Kamilla came out on the balcony with a camera.
"Smile!" she shouted. Iben and the boy went over to the
others, and then all four of them looked up at her. Peter made

the children say *cheese*. Kamilla suggested that they go to the bakery to get some pastries.

They put both children in the pram. The neighbourhood was abuzz with Sunday and late summer; people were busy with garden work and afternoon coffee, a group of teenagers played ball, and some younger boys sat in an apple tree and threw rocks at a small group of girls playing hopscotch. The strong orange afternoon light made everything look clear and almost surreal. Peter's brown eyes shone like illuminated stained glass, and she began to wonder about the yellow spot she thought he had in his left eye, which he definitely once had, but that she hadn't noticed in a long time.

"What a day!" he said, pushing her to the side so he could take over the pram. "And here we are taking a stroll," she said. "Yeah," he said, "here we are taking a stroll."

The bakery was closed so they had to go to the petrol station at the other end of town. They walked in step, side by side. They talked a little about the older girls. Iben said they should probably start thinking about birth control for the oldest one. "For Christ's sake, she's only fourteen!" Peter said, raising his voice. Iben told him that the youngest one was still lagging behind in school and was getting terrible grades. "You have to go over her homework with her more," she said. Peter snorted, "Birth control!" She looked up at a poplar tree and caught sight of a squirrel. She counted to ten slowly to herself. A large BMW was parking in front of them. "They've got too much fucking money around here," said Peter, stepping testily to the side as the car backed over a large puddle. "We'll never have that problem," she said. Then he stopped at the hotdog stand and got the children hot dogs with ketchup and relish. He bought a hamburger for himself. She had a bite, and he wiped ketchup from her cheek. They shared a pint of chocolate milk. "Like the old days," he said, with his mouth full of relish, "before we learned how to cook." "When we lived on fried cod roe," she said. "With mushy potatoes," he said. "Yeah, and that was because you insisted on cooking them in the duvets, like your mother taught you, but you can only make rice pudding that way." Then the girl began to cry and he pulled her out of the pram and swung her around. That scared her and she gulped down most of her hot dog. Iben hurried to walk ahead. It was such a beautiful day.

They stood in the convenience store at the petrol station, each with a child in their arms—he wanted a lemon pound cake and she, a marzipan cake. They ended up buying both. On the way back, he wanted to have a cigarette. "Why didn't you buy some yourself?" she asked. "I didn't think of it," he answered, as she rooted around in her pocket for a match. She sighed. He began to hum an old pop song, and soon he was screaming it at the top of his lungs. People in their gardens turned to look at them. The girl fell asleep. The light grew deeper in colour, redder, and she said she'd heard that at some point people who are dying blaze up, become their old selves again, full of energy, so that their loved ones almost think that they're about to come round, and then suddenly they die; this feels unexpected and so it comes as a big shock. Peter threw his cigarette over a wrought-iron gate. "That's what they deserve," he said. "Did you hear anything I said?" she asked. "Rich bastards!" he yelled. The man passing them on the path in a polo shirt and tan trousers stared condescendingly, first at them, then at the worn pram, which they had bought for the older girls.

When they got back to Kamilla's house, the girls came bounding up the garden path. The eldest smacked the garden gate into Peter's stomach. Kamilla came walking across the lawn with a coffee pot. "They're going down to get the dog at Madsen's," Iben said. "What the hell is the dog doing at Madsen's?" Peter asked. "They used to have a dog salon, Peter. You know that Mum and Dad always got Bonnie trimmed there." Peter looked at Iben with an expression that made her laugh hysterically. "Peter! It's a terrier," she said, miffed. "It needs to be trimmed once in a while, and Madsen does it on the cheap." Iben took the boy out of the pram and walked a little way away. "A terrier!" she heard him say, and she began to titter and pushed herself forward in order not to laugh outright. She could feel that Peter was watching her. She heard him laugh loudly. "You two!" said Kamilla, who was disappointed about the pastries. She had been looking forward to cream puffs. And it was cold now, even though all three of them were wrapped in duvets. Iben still didn't dare look at Peter. Laughter stirred in her throat; for a moment she was afraid she'd begin to cry. The boy stuffed a large piece of lemon pound cake in his mouth. The girl sighed in her sleep. Peter said, "Can you take the girls next weekend? Dorte's parents are coming to stay with us." "Poor you," said Iben, wiping the boy's mouth. He was busy pulling apart a dead flower. A cold wind blew the petals onto the grass. She had finally got control of herself. "I thought you were coming to Aunt Janne's birthday on Sunday," said Kamilla. "Sorry," said Peter, shooting Iben a look, who suddenly had to put her hand to her mouth to hold back the laughter. Kamilla leaned back in the chair. "How long have you two been divorced?" she asked. "Seven years in November," said

Iben, looking at Peter. "Isn't that right?" He nodded. "Seven years in November," he repeated. The sun shone right in his eyes, and she finally caught sight of the yellow spot in the brown. She felt strangely relieved. She knew it was there somewhere.

TRANSLATED BY DENISE NEWMAN

THE MAN IN THE BOAT

PER OLOV ENQUIST

T HE STORY, as I recounted it to Mats . . .

This all took place the summer I was nine. We lived by a lake called Bursjön, a fine lake, large, with small islands. I was nine and Håkan was ten. A river passed through the lake, entering at the northern end and flowing out at the southern. It came from far up in Lappmarken, and in spring timber was floated downstream. In May I could see it all from our window: the lake filling with logs, lumps of ice and ice floes, the timber slowly drifting southwards, and then, one day that same month, finally disappearing.

But not all the timber went. Some of it strayed off to the side, got stuck on the shore, stranded. They were top-quality logs, thick and impressive; they were buoyant, riding high in the water. We knew what would happen to them. After a week the log drivers would come, nudge the logs out from the shore, manoeuvre them together and shove them off in the wake of the others. The log drivers walked along the shore, or some of them rowed in boats; they could clean up the lake in a day, removing everything. They were called the "rear crew". When the rear crew left, the lake was empty once more.

That was the reason Håkan and I hid the three logs. There was a ditch running into the lake, at the very spot where we lived. We hauled the logs into the ditch and up twenty metres, and then we laid them all in a long row, stashed away in the grass at the side, which covered them up, camouflaging them. It took a whole day. We knew very well it was forbidden, but Håkan said that it didn't matter, because it was only the company who would lose out, and they had enough money anyway. They could wait a year or two for their timber.

Håkan knew all about it. The day the rear crew left, we lay low at the edge of the forest, watching the log drivers. They were walking along the shore, while a rowing boat was out on the water. Now and then one of them found a log and dragged it into the water, and then the men in the boat took over. We could hear their voices. It was still spring; we heard them talking, but we couldn't hear what they said. And I remember how Håkan and I lay there in the undergrowth at the edge of the forest, out of view and motionless, watching the log drivers draw nearer as they talked to one another. When they reached the ditch where we had hidden our three logs, they stopped for a while and had a smoke, and I can still remember how clearly I could hear Håkan's breathing and my own heartbeat—as distinctly as if they were echoing in the cool spring air.

But they walked on. And they didn't see the logs. The next day the lake was empty of timber and log drivers, and the rear crew had gone for another year. But we still had the logs. And the lake was ours. We alone had command of it now, for the whole summer.

We waited two days, just in case. But I remember being woken early on the morning of the third day by someone knocking on my window. It was Håkan, who had climbed up the fire escape to the first floor and was hanging there, making faces and sticking out his tongue and tapping on the pane of glass. I got up and walked across the floor, which was comfortably cool under my feet, and I could see that Håkan was holding something in his hand: a hammer. We were going to do it today. Right now.

I threw on some clothes. I must have eaten breakfast as well, but it couldn't have taken long. I ran out. Håkan was sitting behind the house, by the wall, wearing his red shirt and blue plimsolls, holding the hammer and a packet of three-inch nails, and smiling at me as I approached.

"Now, damn it," he said, "we're going to start building!"

That morning we began constructing the raft. We dragged the logs out into the water again, placed the longest in the middle and the other two on either side, and whacked some struts on top. One cross plank at the front, which we nailed onto the logs; three planks in the middle and two at the rear. We used three-inch nails, except at the back, where we used six-inch ones that Håkan had got hold of somewhere.

"When we don't need it any more," he said in a thick voice, his mouth full of nails, "we'll chuck the planks away and pull the nails out. If we leave the nails in, it's really bad for the saw blade. And it ruins the old boys' piecework rate."

He worked in silence for a moment, and then he said, "You mustn't forget the piecework rate."

Håkan was only a year older than me, but he knew a huge amount and he taught me lots of things. I remember that summer very well: we built a raft of three logs; it had a sail on it; Håkan was there. It was the summer I was nine and he was ten. It was 1943.

It only took a day to finish it.

*

Håkan weighed thirty-eight kilos and I weighed thirty-five. The logs lay deep in the water. Generally, only a tenth of the log sticks up. It depends partly on how green it is. Some are pretty much sunken timber, while others float high in the water. Together, we weighed seventy-three kilos. When the wind blew, the waves nearly always splashed over the deck and came up in the gap between the logs. The water was quite cold to begin with, no more than 14 to 15 degrees; we were wearing wellingtons. Apart from that, the raft was well kitted out. For the most part, we pushed ourselves along. The pole was exactly three metres long and reached quite a distance out. Two pieces of plank were supposed to be paddles (but it was almost impossible to paddle; very slow at any rate). We had provisions in a small food container right at the back (secured with a one-inch nail to the rear platform). They consisted of: 1 bottle of water, 1 piece of sausage (10 cm long), 1 half-loaf, 8 biscuits, 1 knife, 100 grams margarine, 20 sugar cubes, 1 small tin of treacle (a kind of dark syrup that the cows were given, but Håkan maintained it was better than ordinary syrup; I didn't like treacle myself, but he wanted to take a tin with us and I didn't argue). Those were our provisions. Our armoury on the raft was a wooden crossbow with six arrows, a willow slingshot for pine cones plus ammunition (thirty-five cones) and Håkan's old catapult with spare elastic and ten smallish stones.

There was no doubt, we ruled the lake.

However, the day I have to tell you about, when everything ended and everything began, we went out quite late. It was after seven in the evening; we had said we were going fishing, for which we were given permission. It was August. For the last two days, we had been experimenting with a sail on the raft, stretching a sheet between two long sticks. Sometimes we held onto the sticks ourselves, at other times we tried to lash them down. Neither way really worked, but this evening there was a good wind, coming straight off the land. After we had secured the provisions and ammunition, we set out. The sun was just setting on the other side, the wind was strong and we could see we were skimming along nicely, being blown out into the middle of the lake. It was all rather lovely; I didn't want to mention it to Håkan, but as the sun went down, it was beautiful. Whenever I confided to him my thoughts about that kind of thing, Håkan would laugh.

It is at this precise point that I find it hardest to recall exactly what happened—but I'll try to explain it all the same. Håkan was sitting in front and said he had just spied an enemy skiff we needed to ram. He ordered full sail, commanded the crew to stand by with the grappling irons, and he went astern to fetch the crossbow, which was lying in the middle of the raft. By this time, the waves were fairly high and it was dusk as well. Now I remember better: darkness had started to fall, except in the direction the sun had set, where the sky was still red—and Håkan stood up and walked astern to fetch his crossbow. The whole surface of the raft was quite slippery and slithery, and I saw him stagger and step to the side; and then he lost his balance. It all happened right in front of me. Håkan's silhouette swaying and toppling over against the deep pink horizon. I remember it clearly. And I remember equally clearly his face in the water; I could see he was scared and embarrassed at the same time (scared because he couldn't swim very well, embarrassed because he had been so clumsy).

There was a heavy swell on the lake. I held my hand out to him. It was just as the light was fading; poor visibility, extremely cold water, a deep pink streak where the sun had set. Håkan's face, down there in the water, smiling, as if he were thinking: Damn it, how stupid of me! And I stretched out my hand to him.

The next thing I remember must have been quite some time later. An hour perhaps, probably more. I was sitting aft. Håkan was sitting at the bow end, on the forward platform. He was sitting with his back to me, huddled up. Huddled up, as if he was freezing cold. When I looked around on the raft, I realized we must have lost a lot of our things in the confusion when Håkan fell in. The sail was gone. The bits of wood that were supposed to be paddles were gone. The pole to push ourselves along with was gone. The entire raft was empty, apart from the nailed-down food container with emergency provisions, because I was sitting on that—and apart from Håkan and me, sitting hunched up, at either end of the raft.

And yet the most remarkable thing was something else; and I have thought long and hard about this since, and come somehow to the conclusion that there is a gap in my memory somewhere. The remarkable thing was that the wind had stopped, totally. It was utterly calm: the waves had subsided, the water was like a mirror. It was completely still and completely dark. It felt like the middle of the night, but the moon had risen. It was shining. The moon was almost full, the night was black, the water flat; but the moon was shining. It looked so strange. In the shimmering path of moonlight reflecting on the lake was a silent raft, almost a wreck, and on it two boys crouched; the water was like silver, still and absolutely soundless.

23

We must be in the middle of the lake, I thought. When I turned, I saw the lights from home, small white dots, far away, like tiny white pinpricks in black velvet. I looked at the moon. Then back at the water, at the curious white moonlight and the raft in the middle of the shimmering moon path, at Håkan's rigid back. It felt like a dream, so strange, the quietness so deep I didn't dare to break it. I wanted to speak to Håkan, but instead I said nothing.

We sat in silence, for a long, long time.

I don't know what I was thinking about. I know I tried to work out what had happened, how Håkan had fallen in, how he had climbed back up, why he was sitting there, so silent. Why the wind had stopped. Why the waves had dropped. Why the moon was shining. I must have thought about how we would get home. We had nothing to row with, no sail, no wind.

I must have felt cold, but I have no recollection of that. I remember the peculiar stillness, the motionless black water, the moon, the raft in the middle of the moon path, the silence, the pitch-black night around us.

An hour or so passed, perhaps. Then I heard the faint sound, as if from an immense distance, of oars. The sound didn't come from home, but from due east, which was odd, because there were no houses in that direction. But it was the stroke of oars, no doubt about it. I sat with my head turned to the east, staring straight out into the inky blackness, but could see nothing.

The stroke of oars came closer and closer. He was rowing slowly. Splish. Splash. I couldn't see anything. Nearer and nearer. Then, all at once, a boat appeared against the reflection of the moon on the water, the silhouette slowly slipping into

24

the moon path. As it came towards us, I could see the back of the man who was rowing.

I stood up and could see that Håkan was on his feet too. We stood still, staring at the boat gliding towards us.

"Hello," I shouted, over the water, "please, come and help us!"

The man in the boat didn't turn round. He didn't look at us. He simply let the boat glide silently up to us and lifted the oars. Water dripping from the oars, the boat gliding, as in a dream, the man not turning round—I remember it so well. Why didn't he answer?

And then he reached us. Came to rest beside the raft. And only then did he turn around.

I saw his face in the moonlight. I didn't recognize him. I had never seen him before. He had dark hair, a thin face, he didn't look at me. He looked only at Håkan. He was not from these parts, but he had come to help us. And he stretched his hand out to Håkan, and Håkan took his hand and stepped carefully into the dinghy and sat at the stern. Neither of them said a single word. And I stood still and watched them.

The rowing boat then slowly moved off, so imperceptibly I didn't understand what was happening at first. But the man had sat down, sat down at the oars. And started to row. Håkan sat in the stern, his back to me, and he didn't move, didn't look at me. The man started to row, and the boat slowly disappeared in the darkness.

I couldn't call out. I stood still, turned to stone. I must have stayed there like that for a long time.

What I remember of this is so confused, it's difficult to recount. I must have sat down on the platform at the back. I must have been extremely cold. I know that I opened the box with emergency provisions, I ate. I lifted out the tin of treacle, the syrup I didn't actually like; I ate it. I dipped my fingers in and put it in my mouth; it tasted sweet. I sat on the platform at the back and watched dawn breaking, watched the light creeping in over the lake, the morning mists rising and lifting, until finally it was light.

And then the boats came.

It was Grandfather who arrived first. Later on, they said they had been searching and calling for a long time, but I hadn't answered. I told them I hadn't heard their shouts. Grandfather arrived first. I stood up, my face sticky with the treacle that had run down my chin. Grandfather took my hand and lifted me into the boat; my face was covered in treacle, but I was perfectly calm. I remember I lay down flat on my back in the bottom of the boat, lay still, staring straight up, while they wrapped blankets around me, and Grandfather started to row, very fast, as if in a great hurry. I was lying in the bottom of the dinghy. My lips and chin were sticky with the treacle that had run down my neck. Grandfather was rowing. I lay there, looking at his face.

I must have been very ill after this. I remember being in bed with a fever, dreaming such strange dreams. Sometimes I was bathed in sweat; other times I slept and was woken by my own screams. They came in and sat with me: Mama was there, Grandfather and Grandmother, and Annika. Many days must have passed; I don't know how many.

Until one day I was well. It happened so quickly, it was like switching on a light. First very ill. Then—all at once—I woke one day and was completely well.

Grandfather was sitting with me.

"What happened to the raft?" I asked. "Did you bring it ashore or is it still out there?"

"We brought it in," he said.

"Is it moored now?"

"No," he said very calmly, "we broke it up and got rid of the timber. I did it myself the same day."

"Oh," I said. "Did you take all the nails out?"

"I did," he said.

"That's good," I said. "Otherwise the chaps at the sawmill would have caught the nails on the saw and it would have ruined their piecework rate."

"Yes, I know," he said.

"What was the name of the man rowing the boat Håkan went in?"

But Grandfather didn't reply; he just sat there, looking pensive.

"He wasn't from round here," I said. "He looked like Eriksson who works the barking drum at the sawmill, but it wasn't him."

"No," Grandfather said softly. "Now you have to get some more sleep."

He was standing at the door, looking at me, and when I started to tell him what had happened that night, he looked slightly irritated, or something else—he looked odd—and he just turned and left, quite abruptly. The next day, the first day I was allowed to get up, he came back and asked me to tell him. And I told him everything.

He just sat there, looking pensive, as he often used to do in the chapel; whenever things became slow and boring and serious, he would sit and think about fishing. He looked pensive

27

then. He was looking exactly the same now, so I assumed he was thinking about fishing again.

I said, "It's a good job you pulled all the nails out. It would have ruined their piecework rate."

Then he said, straight into the air, "Well now, about Håkan. He didn't come back."

That summer I read a great deal. The book I liked best was the story of the Flying Dutchman. He had once committed a dreadful crime: he had not reached out his hand to some drowning sailors—he had thought only of himself—and he had let them drown. So he was damned: whenever he and his ship came to a port, a headwind blew up and he was unable to enter the harbour. He had to continue to the next one, and the next, and the next.

And there he sailed, year in, year out. Sailors would see him coming in his ship, in the middle of the night, in a fierce storm, and in the moonlight they saw him standing on the deck, lashed to the wheel, doomed to sail for evermore. An unknown man.

I told Grandfather about it.

"Do you understand?" I said. "That's the *only* time you see him, in the middle of the night. He comes sailing along in the moonlight. Isn't it strange? An unknown man, who never speaks to anyone, but just arrives, at night, in the moonlight. Do you understand, Grandfather?"

"No. What about?" Grandfather asked.

"Well," I said, "an unknown man, a stormy night, and you see him in the moonlight. *He just comes gliding along in the moonlight!* Do you see? There must be a connection, mustn't there?"

28

"I don't understand," Grandfather cut me short.

"He came rowing from the east that night," I said. "You know as well as I do that there's no one living in the east. Not here by the lake. Not even a tourist. *But he came from the east.*"

In July I began a systematic exploration of the lake's eastern shores. I didn't tell the others what I was doing. The grown-ups had already taken me aside for long talks, long, serious talks, about what, I don't recall, don't want to recall. They would never understand, they would only ask me to do something else, to help out in the cowshed, to think about something else, something else, something else.

I decided to explore the lake's eastern shores.

It was in July 1943, a very warm summer. Håkan always used to call the eastern part of the lake "the cesspool"—it wasn't very pleasant, there were lots of tree stumps and rubbish in the water, the bottom was mucky and slimy, the shore was scrubby and in some places cleared of trees in that barren kind of way that made you thirsty just by looking at it. I took some water in a bottle and I began to search. I started furthest away down by the shore and then walked up a hundred metres. Then diagonally down to the beach again, then up. In this way I would be able to comb the entire area.

I walked for several hours, got very thirsty, drank some water. When my water ran out, I went home.

In July I searched the eastern part of the lake, and I found nothing. The only thing I came upon was the remains of a half-rotted boat, a dinghy. It had been pulled a long way up on land, with its hull in the air. It must have been there for years.

29

I sat down on the boat. The sun was shining and it was very warm. I cupped my hands around my mouth and shouted, loudly, out across the water, "Håkan! Håkan! Håkan!"

But no answer came. No echo. Nothing at all. And then I knew, finally, that there was no trace of Håkan in the eastern part of the lake, and no trace of the man in the boat.

In September that year I searched for the last time.

September was the month I liked best. In Västerbotten's coastal regions the cold arrived quite early, the autumnal colours started appearing in the middle of the month, and in the last two weeks you could break a thin layer of ice on the puddles every morning. The entire lake seemed embedded in a band of dark green and golden red. All the forests looked like that. Green from the conifers, golden red from the birch trees. Mist lay over the lake, and it was cold.

On one of the last days of that month, I took Grandfather's boat and rowed out. I didn't have permission, but I did it. It was the day of my ninth birthday.

I rowed around the whole lake. There was a thin mist everywhere, a mist that was almost transparent and only a few metres high, but which nevertheless made me feel as though I were rowing in an empty, forsaken world. As if I was completely alone. And it felt good.

I rowed around the whole lake. And then I rowed out into the middle. I pulled up the oars, settled down and waited.

It was lonely in the mist, in a very strange way; it felt safe. I thought about everything that had happened and, oddly, I no longer felt despair when I thought about Håkan's disappearance. I just didn't understand how it had happened, who the man in the boat was. Why had he left me behind? Where was Håkan now? Why didn't he come back?

I must have sat there for an hour. Then I saw a boat coming towards me, out of the mist.

It was a dinghy with a man rowing. Someone was sitting in the stern with his face turned towards me.

There could be no mistake. It was Håkan. The dinghy glided slowly towards me, without a sound, straight through the mist, and I wasn't in the least bit afraid. Håkan was sitting in the stern, looking right at me, and he looked exactly the same as before. And he smiled at me.

It was utterly silent. I sat still and watched the other dinghy glide slowly towards me, next to me, past me. The whole time Håkan was looking at me, a peculiar expression on his face. With a slight smile, he was looking right at me. As if he wanted to say: Here I am. *You don't need to search any more.* You've found me. And now you've found me, you have to stop searching for me. I'm fine. You must understand that. You have to stop searching for me, because you've found me. And now you need to be yourself. You need to be grown up.

We didn't say a word, but we looked at one another. And we both smiled. And then the dinghy slid away, and they were gone. And since that time I haven't seen my only friend Håkan again.

I sat still for a long time, thinking, before I took up the oars to start rowing; but at that moment I saw something floating in the water. It was a long pole. It was the pole we used to push ourselves along on the raft. I thought: Håkan wanted to give it back. That's good. I'll pick it up.

I picked it up. And then I rowed back.

When I returned, Grandfather was standing on the shore. I saw him from a distance. He looked furious, which always makes his body go rigid and weird, his shoulders drop and he glares directly in front of him. I wasn't afraid, though. I steered the boat straight for the shore, lifted the oars, picked up the pole and threw it onto the beach.

He looked at it and said, "Where did you find that?"

All I said was, "I've got it back."

I climbed out of the boat and we dragged it out together. Before he had time to tell me off, I said, "And I'm just going to say, I'm not going to search any more. I'm not going to look for Håkan any more. It's over now."

He stood in silence, staring at me, as if he couldn't understand what I was trying to say.

"No," I said, "it's over, Grandfather. Now I know."

I set off up towards the farm, over the meadow. It was September, frost on the grass and brittle underfoot; it crunched where you walked. Grandfather was still standing down there by the boat. And I thought how odd it all is: you get knocked back, but nothing is ever hopeless. Sometimes you just want to die, but when everything seems at its worst, there is still a way out. You get knocked back and it feels bad, but you learn a great deal. And if you didn't learn, you would never grow up, never understand. I thought about the Flying Dutchman and the story about the Snow Queen and all the other stories I'd heard. And I thought about the man in the boat taking Håkan away from me, and never again would I be ill like I'd been that summer.

I wouldn't play in the same way as before, not believe the same kinds of tales, not try to *avoid things*; nothing would be the same as before. It was September: Håkan would have been ten years and one month, if he had lived. I walked up to the farm. Grandfather stayed by the boat. I remember I was crying, but at the same time I felt very peaceful. The air was cold. It was the last time I went out searching. I finally knew who the man in the boat was. I walked home. It was crunching under my feet. It was cold. And that was it, the whole story.

TRANSLATED BY DEBORAH BRAGAN-TURNER

IN A DEER STAND

DORTHE NORS

I T'S A QUESTION OF TIME. Sooner or later, somebody will show up. Even dirt tracks like these can't stay deserted forever. The farm he walked past when he entered the area must be inhabited. The people who live there must go for walks sometimes, right? And the deer stand is probably the farmer's, and it's just a question of time before it starts raining. The vegetation down on the ground is dry. Some twiggy bushes, some heather too. To the right, a thicket; to the left, the start of a tree plantation. The sunken road leads in there for some reason, so it's just a question of time before someone comes. Take him, for instance; *he* came this way. Just yesterday, even if it feels longer. The circumstances make it feel longer. It's likely that his ankle's broken, though it's also possible that it's just a sprain. The pain isn't constant, but there *is* some swelling. Now he sits here and he has no phone. She must be in pieces back home. He can imagine it. Walking around with his phone in her hand, out in the utility room. She's standing there with it in her hand. She stands and curses him for not taking it with. And it's only a question of time before the police are involved. Maybe they already have been for some time now. It's probably been on the local radio; that he's forty-seven, that he drives a BMW, that he left home in a depressed state. He can't bear the thought of them saying those last words.

34

He isn't depressed, it's just that she wasn't supposed to win every battle.

Last night there was screeching from inside the forest. Some owls, foxes perhaps. There was someone who'd seen wolves out here, and no doubt Lisette has come by the house. She's probably sitting on the couch with her wide eyes, eating it all up. He's so tired. His clothes are damp, and last night he froze something terrible. There are some black birds overhead, rooks he thinks, and his wife's pacing around in the yard, restless. He painted the eaves last spring. It's a nice house, but now she wants to sell it. He really likes the house, but now she wants something else. When she wants something else, there's nothing he can do. He's lost every battle. As recently as the day before yesterday, he had an urge to call his brother, but he's lost that battle. She doesn't like his brother, though Lisette's welcome to visit. Lisette often stands in their kitchen-dining area and calls up her network. Lisette's got a big network, but mostly she hangs out with his. And in principle, he's only got the kids left. It's a long time since his wife stopped taking part in the gatherings on his side of the family. There's something wrong with both of his parents, she says. Something wrong with his brother's kids, his brother's girlfriend and especially his brother. She says that his brother sows discord. That's because his brother once told him he ought to get divorced. And because he loses all battles, he went straight home and told her: *My brother thinks I should get divorced.* So this isn't the first time he's driven out to some forest. He's done it a fair amount over the years. Sometimes to call up his folks on the sly, or his brother. He also calls them when he's down washing the car. He doesn't dare call from the house. Then she'd find out, or Lisette would, and he's pretty sure that Lisette tells tales.

He's sitting in a deer stand, his ankle is definitely sprained, and something's happened to the light. A mist is rising. It creeps towards him across the crowberry bushes. Which means that evening is closing in on the deer stand again. Perhaps he should try to crawl down, but she wins every battle. He no longer calls his brother, for instance. The distance between them has become permanent, and when he drove off, he deliberately didn't bring his phone with him. He wanted to be alone, so that's what he is now. He stepped on a tussock wrong, in the strip between the wheel ruts, some seventy metres from the deer stand. First the pain, then off with the sock; he was pretty sure he could already see it starting to swell. Did he shout for someone? Well, he shouted a bit the first hour, then darkness began to descend and he set about reaching the deer stand. Now he's inside, and from up here he can see the plantation, some undergrowth and withered heather, mist.

He tots up the distances between towns. It must be about seventy-nine miles home. That's how far he is from the utility room, where she's standing and staring at his phone, though no doubt Lisette's there. Lisette's playing the role of comforter, co-conspirator and slave, yes, Lisette's her slave too, but a slave with privileges. While he sits somewhere deep inside a West Jutland tree plantation. He heard something shrieking in the forest last night. Probably a fox, but wolves have been sighted here too. The hunters set up game cameras to get a glimpse of the animals they hope to shoot. Or else it's farmers wanting photos of whoever's eating their turnips, usually red deer, he supposes. Then one morning this wolf is standing there, staring straight into the camera. He's seen it in the newspaper, but wolves can't climb, and he managed to haul himself up into the deer stand last night before darkness fell. The pain isn't too bad, and it's just a question of time before she sits down next to the washing machine. Her hands cupped over her knees, and he hasn't seen her cry in years. She didn't cry when her mother died. Her face can clap shut over a feeling like the lid of a freezer over stick insects. He had some in eighth grade, stick insects, in a terrarium. They weren't much fun, and then his biology teacher said that putting them in the freezer would kill them. He peered at the insects for a long time before he placed them in the freezer. They stood there rocking, looking stalk-like. When he took the terrarium out the next day, they stood there stiff. They didn't suffer, he supposed, they just stiffened in position. Thinking back on them now, they looked like someone who's achieved complete control over their own stage illusion—and she's been successful that way too. Maybe she doesn't have any feelings at all. She's got lots of hobbies, but it isn't clear that she has feelings. She's got Lisette, but she has no feelings, at least not for him. She hates his brother and the rest of his family, but even though hatred's a kind of feeling, it doesn't count. He told her one time that he missed his brother. He shouldn't have said that, and he'll never say it again; he's lost all his battles, he knows that. He also knows that this is retreat. He has the clear sense, for instance, that Lisette's standing in the kitchen area at this very moment. Lisette's become more and more a constant presence—driving their daughter to handball, joining them during the holidays and attending the kids' graduations; sitting in the bedroom on the edge of the bed. Lisette's her representative, a subject like himself, but with privileges. Lisette's got short legs and a driver's licence, and by now the police must have been brought in. He's right here, of course, half lying, half sitting. It's been more than a day since he drove off. In a depressed state of mind, though that's not true. He just wanted the feeling of winning, and now he has a view of a landscape at dusk. His trousers are green from moss and something else, extending high up his legs. The boards he's sitting on have been attacked by algae. If she saw this sort of algae on the patio, she'd have him fetch the poison. What *hasn't* he done on that house? And now she wants to sell. She wants to move into something smaller, though it'd be good to have an extra room. *An extra room?* he asked. *For Lisette*, she replied, and then he took the car and left his phone behind. His family's grown used to his absence, and besides, he isn't the same any more. Actually, he's sensed that for a long time. How something has clapped shut over him. First she won all the battles, then he positioned himself squarely on her side. In that way, he stopped losing, and she tired of scrutinizing him. That was the logic behind it, but now he's sitting here. In a deer stand, deep in the forest. A mist has risen, the night will be cold, and a wolf has been sighted.

TRANSLATED BY MISHA HOEKSTRA

THE WHITE-BEAR KING VALEMON

LINDA BOSTRÖM KNAUSGAARD

T HE HOUSE I LIVED IN with my parents stood on a dingy
piece of land at the edge of the forest, between the forest
and the road leading to the city. The road construction was
still going on, advancing steadily, consuming the earth bit by
bit. Men wearing headlamps toiled in the night with crowbars
and pickaxes. In the daytime they burnt everything away
with their fire cannon. There was always something ablaze
somewhere nearby and the soot got in everywhere, sticking
to the walls and windows, the glasses from which we drank.

Mother cleaned from morning till night. Scrubbing, wiping
cloths over panels and windows, tables and chairs. All the way
up her arms she was covered in the soot. The sheets could no
longer be washed white. Hers was the generation of cleanliness
and poverty. She battled the dirt and counted the money we
received for giving up our land and supporting the expansion
of the city, as it said on the certificate that hung in a place of
honour in our front room.

Father lay in his room, drinking and smoking the cigarettes
he rolled. He called for me on occasion whenever he wanted
company. It wasn't often, but when he did he would talk about
the olden days. He got the albums out. His photographs and
autograph book. He'd been an autograph hunter once, later

a tank driver in the northern regions, where mantles of snow covered the firs, the roads, the boglands.

If he was in a good mood, he would take out the maps. He kept them rolled up under the bed and would spread them out on top of the army blanket that was stiff with dirt and coffee stains. Mother never ventured to his room with her cloths and cleaning.

Here I wallow in my shite, he would say, inhaling and then blowing out the smoke that filled the cramped space like a fog, as if to give atmosphere to the stories of his army days. He reconstructed various operations, his ruler passing over differently shaded areas on the map.

Not getting lost, that was my talent, he said with a laugh. Burträsk, he went on, jabbing a yellow-stained finger at the spot. Burträsk, Råneå, Jukkasjärvi. And that dump Karesuando. He laughed again, a mouthful of brown teeth.

Sometimes I went with the workmen into the city, climbing up into the cab of the orange earthmover and drinking the alcohol they passed around. It was like death itself, they said. Better than death. We drove with the windows down and took potshots with rifles, or let rip with the fire cannon, setting the ditches aflame, the sprawl, dogs.

My name is Ellinor.

You were born lucky, my father said.

You slid out of me like a seal, my mother said. You stared at me all night. You didn't sleep like other infants. Your eyelashes were curled together. I saw the way they dried and unfolded like the petals of a flower stretching out to the sun.

My name is Ellinor and I have a wish. The crown of gold I see in my dreams at night. I want it.

It's the only thing I want.

*

I heard his voice all through my childhood. It was a voice I knew as well as my own. It could speak from the drinking glass when I brushed my teeth, seep down through the ceiling crack in the front room or mingle with my mother's voice when she asked me to wash the dishes. It was a hum in the walls and a whistle in the wind when the trees swayed and creaked. A dark and yet immaculate tone that fluttered and tingled inside, wrapping itself around the bones of my body, as substantial and nourishing as the food I ate. Wordlessly it told me I was taken care of, provided for, protected. It made my steps more intrepid than they ever would have been. I knew all this inside. The way you know you breathe and live on in the night when you're asleep, without ever giving it a conscious thought.

I remember the first early winters when the sea froze at the shores and the children congregated like dark little birds on the grey slabs of ice that scraped their open edges against each other, forcing us to quickly shift our weight from one slab to another so as not to fall into the freezing water. I could run across the cracking ice without being afraid. I didn't think about it much, the tone that kept my back straight and put a spring in my step.

The ice disappeared, and the cold of winter. Summer came, and the sun warmed up the earth, the soil breathed out its smells, its innermost aromas. I climbed the trees and looked out across the land, at the machinery waiting in the turning area. All the children and their parents who had ridden the machines into the city with their pots and pans, clothes, shoes and armchairs, departed in their little flocks, there to split up and be spread like flower seeds, absorbed by asphalt and buildings, installed in flats to live new and better lives by new, metropolitan principles. I sat in a tree and watched their worldly goods being driven away and those I had called my friends vanish, and the abandoned properties and emptiness that spread in their absence became mine alone.

I woke up early in the mornings. I drifted around the house and read the books on the shelves, buttered sandwiches I piled up like towers and took outside with me, my mother's fur coat over my nightclothes. I pottered about barefoot in the dirt and soot as I ate. Here and there I paused and thought about what I saw in front of me, or about my sandwich and the way it dissolved between my teeth, or I would let my imagination wander into the landscape and turn itself into wild grunting animals that chased me back and forth across the terrain. I took tobacco from my father's room, rolled cigarettes and breathed the smoke in and out of my lungs, with the unpleasant sensation and clarity that followed. Father slept with his mouth and eyes open. His troubled breathing and the room's rank odour were smeared across the walls in all the years he inhabited that tiny space. One morning when I went in to get tobacco, he awoke at once, sat bolt upright in the bed and gripped my hand, pulling me down towards him and shrieking into my face never to accept advice from a woman, before returning quite as abruptly to his slumbers, once more to wander through sleep, his skin a brittle, yellowed shell about his flesh.

I was fond of my mornings alone, though I paid for them with evenings of fatigue. I was asleep in my bed even before the first entertainment programmes came on the television

42

and filled our house with images of life from a world far beyond our own. Mother arranged the TV tray, with buns and marmalade, and put out teacups for herself, for me and for my father, although he only ever emerged from his room to eat his evening meal. All the solitary evenings she sat there with her teacup in the glow of the television set saddened me immensely, but my fatigue and the urge to wake with the first light were stronger. I slept in my bed and awoke to the new day as if to a celebration, even if everything lay desolate about me. My room was pleasant: the intricately carved wood of the bedstead, the chair next to it with its pile of books, the clock that ticked and the lamp whose shade was decorated with boats sailing on a sea, the picture on the wall of elves dancing in meadows of flowers. And in all the life, I lived his voice was so familiar to me, so deeply a part of me that I was often unable to tell if the thoughts I listened to were his or mine.

One day I went along the path into the forest to catch tadpoles. In one hand I held a plastic bag containing sandwiches, a bottle of milk and some biscuits. In the other a washing-up bowl in which the tadpoles could swim, and a scoop from the time we had the boat.

The scoop still smelled of the sea, of kelp and old wood from the shed. The yellow washing-up bowl knocked against my leg as I walked, and on the way I sang a once popular song about dying honourably on the battlefield, feeling the sun scorch my neck, its warmth soaking into my back and bare shoulders. Inside the forest the light was dimmer, slanting down between the leaves and branches of the trees, the pond with its inky waters appearing, like a black jewel, on the other side of a moss-covered bank. I dropped to my knees at its edge, sinking down into the saturated earth until small pools formed at my sides. Water lilies floated on the glassy surface, stalks descending, sinewy and strong, towards the bottom. Pond skaters skittered across the water. Dragonflies flitted in the air. The pond was teeming with tadpoles, little heads and tails milling at the surface. I filled the bowl with the murky water. It smelled of iron. Some of the tadpoles that came with it had already grown tiny legs that kicked as they swam.

The forest was as quiet as sleep, the stillness of sleep before opening one's eyes and peering at the pristine day. I stood up, lifting an arm to my brow to wipe away my perspiration, and looked straight into a pair of dark eyes. I'm not sure how long we stared at each other like that, our gazes entwined without blinking. My chest filled with joy and my body shivered in the heat. His gaze reached into my core, it wandered through my organism as if through some uncharted land, stopping now and then to consider what it was he saw. When he lowered his eyes and drank from the tadpole-infested water, it was as if it were my blood he drank, as if it were my flesh he touched with his tongue. And then he was gone, vanished into the forest.

I grew up. The piece of land on which we lived shrank. The road into the city was blocked and the mines sensed the soil's slightest vibration. In the floodlit night the beams of the searchlights glanced off our faces as we sat around the table, eating the dinner mother had so painstakingly prepared from scratch. The fire roared. My father's hollow face was drenched, beads of sweat emerged on the backs of his hands like tiny mushrooms, his moisture staining the table. Mother's hands trembled. I rose to speak.

I told them they had to choose there and then whether they wished to die in the flames of all that was familiar to them, or to grow old as wanderers and face an uncertain fate in the forest. Father's yellow eyes blinked and mother wept.

They won't let us die here, she said, and gestured towards the diploma. We get money every month. We live a decent life.

I went and got the hunting knife Father kept under his mattress. When I returned I kissed my parents goodbye, went out of the door and strode towards the forest.

He was waiting for me at the pond. I climbed onto his back and after we'd come a fair way he asked: Have you ever sat on anything softer? Have you ever seen anything more clearly?

No. Never.

The sight I beheld made tears well in my eyes. The luscious green, the darkness of the forest pools, the glittering sky. The animals that moved among the trees. The song of the deer and the gleaming eyes of the lynx. For some time they walked at our side, leading us deeper into the forest that was his and theirs and—so it occurred to me the further we went—mine too. I cried like the child I once was, until the night closed around me and his movements beneath me rocked me to sleep.

I would live much of my remaining life in darkness.

He wasn't always the way I saw him then, he told me. I've been living under a witch's spell, he said. In the day I'm a bear, in the night a man. Can you promise me something? You must never see me as a man.

I stared into the forest. I saw its lush abundance, the great moss-covered standing stones that topped the curve of a hillock. How they ever got there had long since vanished from any living memory, only the forest itself knew. My gaze wandered up the thick trunks of the trees, onwards into the blue expanse of sky, and then, for the first time, he put the blindfold over my eyes.

To begin with, my time in darkness was like constant waking. My body would seek him out and the fire that burned within me flared at the slightest touch. All through the day I would live in the excitement of approaching night. Each hour took me closer to him, each morning bound up with the night that had passed and that to come. I woke up wanting it to be night. Could a person feel more elated?

Through days, weeks, years we wandered. I aged in the forest. Eventually we neared the fringes. The trees became more scattered, abandoned houses began to appear. First one, then another, then another still. I realized we were wandering towards death. It was the only thing that awaited us, there was nothing else. My chest ached at the thought.

Do you think about dying too? I asked him. About which of us will be first? About who will be left behind, and who gone forever?

No, he said. I don't think about it.

I gave birth to a girl. A magnificent girl who thrust herself from my body with a victory cry. Her blood-smeared eyes opened and we looked at each other for the first time. I became someone else. The mother of this girl. She would draw nourishment from me and I would cherish giving her life. The first night, snuggled up. The smell of the forest pools on her body and mine. All of a sudden I felt a will had come to me. The will to live with this child. All of a sudden there was a future beyond the now in which we existed. It was the child's future. Her life, held in my arms, feeding so hungrily from my body. I existed for her sake. Only for her sake. She was the innermost circle. He was outside, though close. He would never be closest again. It frightened me more than it frightened him.

One night I dreamt about my parents. I was sitting in the kitchen eating my mother's food. Father and Mother watched me eat in silence. Then Mother asked me how I was. I told her about the girl, about the beauty of the forest and the man I loved who was a bear during the day and whom I was forbidden to see as a man. Mother looked at me for a long time, then went out and brought back some candle stumps she wrapped in a tea towel and handed to me.

So you can see the one who makes you happy.

Father chewed on his food and said: Don't do it. It's good the way it is.

When I awoke I was holding the candle stumps in my hand.

What until then had been so easy, so taken for granted, became impossible. I lit the first candle.

I saw you. How could I not, I tell myself in an effort to explain. It was inevitable. The betrayal was there from the start, implanted in our history, perhaps its very premise.

It's my fault that we wander now on separate paths, each in our own landscape. It's my fault that we may never find each other alive. Perhaps I am a mother who failed her child. Perhaps I will never see her again. Perhaps there is no way back. Perhaps you are already dead.

*

I walked alone in the forest. I no longer know how many nights followed the days.

I saw a light between the trees. A cottage. Little windows and lamps burning inside. It was night. My fists pounded at the door. Is anyone there? Open up. Help me.

Rain battered down.

Was this the last of my strength I mustered?

My lungs expelled the scream from my chest. The earth rumbled and shook. The mountain, suddenly rising up, emerging before my eyes. The eternity of darkness in front of me. Smooth rock reaching into the sky.

The door opened. Shadows steeped in lightless murk. A shuffle of footsteps. A person without the will to lift their feet, passing through the dark.

I peered inside. The fire burning in the open hearth. The golden rings hanging on the wall. A narrow bed. A figure lying outstretched upon it, face hidden beneath a newspaper. Hypodermics littered about the floor.

Ellinor?

A voice from under the paper.

My name. My name. Someone spoke my name.

I stepped forward to the bed. Did I not? I sat down on a stool beside it. I heard the sound of breathing.

Yes, I replied. You know who I am?

Laughter. I waited. I heard his breathing dwindle, a gentle whistle.

I think I slept too. I was exhausted.

When I awoke on the floor, the man was up making coffee. He turned with a mug in his hand and gave it to me as if we were old friends. The radio was playing. A song I heard once, a long time ago. He was handsome this man. He touched something inside me and it must have shown in my face because he laughed at me and straight away I felt angry and restless.

I want you to do something for me, he said. His eyes were blue. He turned back to the fire and heated up some powder in a spoon. He filled a hypodermic, knotted the tie around his arm and stuck the needle deep into his vein.

I have something you need, he said.

I didn't want to watch him, so I went over to the wall where the golden rings hung. They sparkled in the light of the fire.

That knife you carry. His voice again. So aggravating. Have you used it?

Once I had seen you I couldn't get enough of you. I had to see you again. Every night I said it would be the last. But each time you put the blindfold over my eyes, I knew I would soon see your face again and the moment you slept I took it off. What is it about beauty that draws us so? I wanted to show you to the world. To the girl. This is your father, I would say. This man looks after you. Looks after me.

I felt so strong. So happy. I snuggled up to you and smoothed my hand over the shapes of your body. Studied you in the light of the candle stumps. Your hands and lips, your closed eyelids. Your allure kept me awake and I thought to myself that it wasn't right the way we were living. That it wasn't fair on you to keep you hidden. Dazzled, I absorbed myself in thoughts of your grandeur. I wanted to lift you from our hiding place and stun the world. I became obsessed. The thoughts became a truth. They said the life we led wasn't good enough, there was another life waiting for us somewhere, and all we had to do was reach out and take it.

Was it my thinking out loud that woke you?

You opened your eyes and looked at me. You looked at me and I saw in your eyes what I had done. We came together there in that look. In the grief of realizing that life as we knew it was over.

Do you see the mountain over there? Can you see beyond it to the other side? The world is small, Ellinor. It's not like you think. He laughed. The world's a little dungheap.

Do you see the mountain?

I think back on the night that passed. The tumult and the silence that followed.

He indicated a door at the rear of the house. That way. But I want to give you something first. Don't you think it's sad, Ellinor? My having what you need. The only one who has. He took my hand and drew me close. Drew me to the face into which I did not wish to look. His rugged face, the eyes that beguiled me. It was as if he were shouting, though his voice was a whisper.

I've been working on them as long as I can remember. You can have them, Ellinor. The iron claws are yours that you may climb the mountain. I shall give you all you need, to do what no one else can. Do you see the mountain, Ellinor? That steep face? Its smooth and endless rock? He laughed again. That's where your future starts.

Claws of iron.

The needle that sought my blood. My innermost self. His voice inside me there, and all around.

The sudden cold and heat.

Have you ever seen anything more clearly?

No. Never. Never as now.

The exquisite night. The smell of the mountain.

He attached the claws to my outspread fingers. I laughed. The night and the warmth of his body. The dream of who I was, which I was now living out. My laughter rose and echoed back. It came out again as weeping. His face there in the night, in front of me. He was floating. Expanding and diminishing.

Now, Ellinor.

I laughed as he took the knife. The knife I had carried so long I had forgotten what it was. What it could be used for. Now suddenly it was all I saw. The way it shimmered in the dark.

Do it well. He looked at me. I fell silent. The thick taste of metal in the mouth. The taste of fear.

Do it well. The words were like blows. Nothing less. Not now, not since.

I took the knife. Gripped it there as it danced in the air. I held the shaft. My hand, with the claws closed around it.

I followed the knife into his body. I touched his heart. Again and again.

So easy it was to die, I thought, and turned towards the mountain.

All that night, all the day after and the night after that, I climbed the mountain. Scaled the steep face with my claws. I was too scared to look up or down. Too scared to turn my head to the side. I stared straight out in front of me, my hand searching for the next crack that might offer purchase, the next little ledge on which to set my foot. The cold issued from the rock and felt like breath against my face. Fatigue racked my body, wormed its way into my thoughts and settled like a fog behind my eyes. Onwards. Onwards and upwards. I inched my way, claws gouging the rock. Climb the mountain, Ellinor. I saw myself from a distance, a tiny dot moving almost imperceptibly upon the vast surface, the rock, the mountain. I could not think about the girl. I had abandoned all thought of her when I fled from the house in the night. I had left her. If I were to think of her sweet smell after a night in sleep, or of how she would come running towards me when there was something she had done that she wanted to tell me about, the radiance in her eyes, my delirious joy at her existence, I would not have been able to leave her there all on her own. The choice of her or him could only ever be her and her alone. Why, then, was I here? With blood trickling down my arms?

My anger at this now being my life, the anger that rose up in me when all else was erased, was what made me go on, though my strength was long gone, had seeped away, shed onto the senseless rock.

When the second night became a dawn, when I could no longer manage to lift a hand, I found myself at the summit.

The wind buffeted me, blowing warm, dry air into my face. He's here, it said. The one you love is waiting for you. You've arrived now. You must find the hall where he lies in a casket. Go past the planes and the hangars, pay no heed to their gaping mouths through which the people surge and vanish.

I got to my feet and looked out over the airfield. The enormous planes, so big as to almost defy belief, were lined up in a row with stiff and shiny wings.

People on the ground, milling all around them. Lorries driving up the ramps into the bodies of the aircraft. The sound of the engines. A thunderous clamour that caused the earth to tremble.

One of the planes detached itself and taxied away, accelerated and heaved itself into the air. I watched it climb into the sky and vanish.

I crossed the airfield, at the perimeter of the world, and went towards the light, so bright I had to look down at the ground so as not to be dazzled. Somewhere inside me I knew I was dead.

TRANSLATED BY MARTIN AITKEN

THE AUTHOR HIMSELF

(from My Encounters with the Great Authors
of Our Nation: A Hall of Mirrors*)*

MADAME NIELSEN

I SAW PETER HØEG from the back seat of my parents'
car, a sudden perception, like a revelation, an abruptly
descended prophet, as I leaned forward between the seats in
front to take the piece of blue SorBits chewing gum that my
father, hidden behind his headrest, was holding out in the
palm of his hand while we sped northwards through Jutland
on the E45 motorway. He (the author, my future real self)
was actually concealed behind a half-mask of leather, and his
intensely, almost insanely bright, eyes were gazing up at the
sky from above an article on page 4 of *Politiken*'s arts section,
which my mother, in the passenger seat next to my father,
held in her lap. "Who's that?" I asked, and my mother, who
didn't have the courage to take her eyes off the road for fear
that my father would steer us into a head-on collision with an
oncoming vehicle, handed back the newspaper between the
two headrests, and I took it and laid it out on my bare knees
and read what from then on would be a holy scripture, a kind
of personal genesis penned by the author himself and recalling
the moment in his life at which he had become an author.
Until then it had never occurred to me to write as much as a
single line outside the confines of my school exercise books or
my reports in physics or social studies, but from that moment

on I wanted to be an author too, or rather I wanted to be Peter Høeg, a person of multiple talents and personas who would never need to decide, because he could do everything all at once: study drama in Paris, trek through deserts, speak Swahili, fence, ski, dance ballet, climb mountains, write novels, sail the seven seas (simultaneously!), give talks, and meditate and look like a monk, and *be* a monk, and play Johannes V. Jensen, and *be* Johannes V. Jensen with the aid of only a half-mask, and marry an African and have beautiful children, and live like a saint in ten square metres of space in an oasis in the middle of the city, and write his books on his lap in only two hours a day, in the evenings even, when he's feeling at his most exhausted, and breast-feeding, even though he's a man! I wanted to meet him. But where? How do you meet a person who seems to be everywhere all at once?

The only thing I had to go on was the novel that the article claimed was the centre of everything, and which the caption said had been published earlier that year. But since I was only twenty-five or twenty-six and had read little more than adventure books, Troels Kløvedal's travel writings, and *The Clan of the Cave Bear*, the title *Conception of the Twentieth Century** sounded like it might be heavy-going. So to begin with, I simply tore the page out of the newspaper, folded it up and put it in the back pocket of my sister's cut-off jeans (which I was wearing, and which she would end up giving me a few years later, because, she said, "Those boxer shorts you go around in aren't shorts at all, they're underpants, and I don't want people seeing me out with a brother in his underpants!"), and after that I leaned back in my seat and

* The English-language version of Høeg's novel would later be published under the title *The History of Danish Dreams*.

looked out through the window at the Danish summer flashing by as I sank deeper and deeper into my own *Conception
of Peter Høeg*.

It wasn't until a few years later, after I had gone back to
the house by the sea and had finally got round to visiting the
library in the little town that I discovered *Conception of the
Twentieth Century* on the shelf, alongside the librarian's rec-
ommendation, and borrowed it and took it back home with
me to read at once, while lying on the coir mat in the shady
living room. After that, everything happened so quickly. I
was only six years younger than he, but the only thing I had
achieved in my life at that point was . . . nothing. As soon
as *Tales of the Night* appeared in Arnold Busck's bookstore, I
took it down from the shelf and slipped it inside my anorak
and hurried out again, pregnant with significance. I had read
neither Márquez nor Karen Blixen, and so I found it to be
both brilliant and unique. I enrolled immediately in a drama
school in Vordingborg and stole *Miss Smilla's Feeling for Snow*
from the local bookstore there. At the same time, in a kind
of parallel life—or rather two, ten or twenty parallel lives—I
was accepted into the School of Journalism, attended ballet
lessons at Det Fynske Balletakademi, worked out at the gym,
took a course in Spanish, went to Alpe d'Huez to become
a skiing instructor, played the flute, toyed with the idea of
applying to the Academy of Music, studied psychology at
Aarhus University, Spanish at Odense University, played in
a local band, took guitar lessons from Svend Staal, practised
t'ai chi under the guidance of Tal R, and applied to work
on a development project in a village outside Managua in
Nicaragua (a motor scooter came with the job), all *at the
same time*. I was everywhere, doing everything I couldn't, and

without success, but most importantly: without meeting him, the revelation around whom my life revolved.

But then at last, one day in the spring of 1993, the twenty lives converged into one:

I step through the door of the meeting room of the Danish Authors' Society at Strandgade 6, and in the midst of what looks like the entire teeming congregation of Great Authors, along with their mothers and stepchildren and publishers and worst critics, all with wine glasses in hand and faces turned towards the man giving the award speech, there he stands among them, the only person in the room *without* a wine glass in his hand, seemingly unaffected by all his success and the leading of so many hectic lives in recent years, wearing sandals and airy, loose-fitting cotton trousers that are unrestrictive of the genitals, undamaging to precious eggs, and a casual, unironed, flax-coloured smock, his tousled hair bleached by the sun, his skin golden brown as though, quite unlike any other Great Author, he has not stepped directly from a taxi cab but from a circumnavigating wooden schooner, an engineless vessel that almost silently, with only the gentle glug of water under its stern, slipped into the harbour with the first blush of rising sun to moor at the quayside some fifty metres away behind the Ministry of Foreign Affairs. He stands as one sits, or more exactly *stands*, in a saddle: back straight, legs apart, knees slightly bent, anus thrust forward into alignment with the spinal column so as to allow the free flow of energy and inspiration and to permit the soul to plume like a flame from arsehole to cosmos. His gaze is intense, almost manically attentive and yet calmly and indulgently directed towards the man who stands only a couple of metres in front of him, mumbling his award speech into an occasionally squealing microphone.

What happened then is something of which I have absolutely no recollection. It's as if the story grinds to a halt here, the picture freezes, and the only thing I see, and continue to see, as though it were in front of me right now, is the image of him, Peter Høeg, not the congregation of Great Authors, but Peter Høeg, picked out from its midst as though in spite of it, existing in his own dimension, in another world entirely, that of the Conception itself.

And in that world, from that moment on, I am his shadow, or rather his shadows, the countless shadows of Peter Høeg.

I follow his example, doing everything of which I am unable, living nowhere and everywhere at the same time, on a sofa in the broadcasting corporation's radio documentary department, beneath an overpass north of Marseilles, in the basement of New York's Grand Central Station, in Joseph London's front room, with an unmarried female schoolteacher in a suburb of Prague, with a Jewish glassblower and her Uzbek sister-in-law in their apartment on the "island of poets" in St Petersburg, on the floors of a former ice-cream factory in Hanover and a villa in Maisons-Laffitte. On a daybed in the attic of a public transport director in Risskov, I read *Borderliners* during the course of some nights of despair, a novel I actually *purchase* (albeit with money borrowed from a biscuit tin in the kitchen of a woman who was out). In it I encounter for the first time the author inside the Conception and for a moment I believe that it really is him, until I am told that things are not that simple. I sigh and read on. I read slowly and attentively, almost manically absorbed, as if I were searching for something.

But for what? For Peter Høeg, indeed, but not only for him, which is to say me, and not only for the key to my own life. I am searching for something else, something bigger, a door leading out into another world entirely.

Years pass, I meet the Woman of My Dreams and propose marriage to her, and she accepts, and at the same time *The Woman and the Ape* is published, she buys it for me as a gift and I read it (as if it were my own), yet I'm no longer quite as certain as before. Nevertheless I carry on, getting up in the mornings, performing my exercises, dancing, practising my t'ai chi, doing my sit-ups and press-ups, and so on. Like him, I am still doing my utmost to do everything under the sun, I really am, only now I no longer know why.

Then all of a sudden, one day he is gone. Vanished! Rumours abound, the way rumours do when a phenomenon such as he disappears from one moment to the next after having been at the centre of everything for seven or eight heightened years, appearing everywhere, in all the media, in everyday conversations, in the reading clubs, bookstores and cinemas, even Hollywood. But the *reality* of the matter is that no one knows anything. The truth is that Peter Høeg has disappeared, not only from literature but from the world. At first I am puzzled, then increasingly with each passing day I despair, until at once I realize that this is no tragedy: on the contrary, it is the pinnacle of the Conception, the greatest of all strokes of brilliance: overnight, Peter Høeg went from being everything, everywhere and everyone (at the same time), to being nothing, nowhere and no one, vanished and gone.

And I? I had never been more than his shadow. And now he was gone. I felt I had to follow him and disappear myself. But how? I took the books from my removal boxes in the most distant of my wife's colossal en suite rooms in Frederiksberg and reread the now complete *oeuvre* in the hope of finding the door through which I, in the way of the Messiah's shadow, could proceed behind him into his other world. But the books were as though transformed. What I had thought to be the key to my life and to my redefinition within a completely different world, now seemed merely to be an illusion. Even the *oeuvre*'s tenderest of moments, in which Smilla is reunited with her lover, the electrician, a scene I had read as though it were the primeval love scene, the very image of utopian devotion, revealed itself to be nothing more than deception, a circus trick, something that in essence cannot be done, and yet "He did it!"; the world in reverse: Smilla sticks her clitoris into the slit of the electrician's penis and "fucks" him. *Voilà!* The jingle of cash registers! All over the world, readers rise to their feet and applaud!

It was over. I closed the book and put it back in the removal box with the others. What then? I have no idea. I suppose time passed. Years. I missed him. Not the Conception, not the many lives and certainly not the books. I missed *him*, Peter Høeg the person, whom I had hardly even met, only seen once, many years before. And yet I missed him. I walked along the city lakes and looked across at the school I knew he had attended, Bording Realskole, where *Borderliners* takes place, a fine and uncomplicated red-brick building of three or four storeys. At the very top, on the flat roof, like a mirage, was a little house with a neatly enclosed garden. There it was, on its own, peaceful, as if situated deep inside a wood, among hills or far out upon a plain. I wondered if all the other people around me—the dog owners, the jogging businesswomen and art directors and cinematographers and lawyers and real estate brokers—could see the house too, or if it was only me. I kept wanting to ask, but I feared their replies. In my Conception of Peter Høeg he had moved into that house and was living up there completely on his own. What does a person do when he is no one? He does nothing. He waters the plants, trims the lawn with nail scissors, opens the curtains in the morning and draws them again at night.

And then catastrophe. The 9/11 of this tale. "Where were you on that fateful day?" I was alone in the reading room on the second floor of the library that is housed in the Blågården community centre. I still had my anorak on and was flicking absently through the day's newspapers that lay spread all over the four or perhaps six tables that had been pushed together to form a single surface. Then at one point the front page of *B.T.* emerged from the heap, and on it was the headline: "See where Peter Høeg is hiding". There are certain things in the world one ought never to investigate, inventions and discoveries that ought never to be made, for the sheer sake of humanity. But people don't understand this fact. At least the journalists of the *B.T.* newspaper don't. They had been looking for Peter Høeg, and they had found him. Not in the little house on the roof of the Bording Realskole. Not in a completely different world. They had found him in a modest single-family home in a suburb of Copenhagen. He was divorced, older, and worst of all: still writing. During the past ten years, in which I had believed he had been living the ideal life of no one, he had been working on the same great novel, which sooner or later would be published. There was no picture of him, only of his house. It was a black-and-white raster image on the usual cheap paper, and the photo had been taken from the road. Through a winter or early spring's entanglement of bare branches, garden shrubs and a couple of evergreens of the kind found in cemeteries could be seen a low, whitewashed house and the black edge of its roof. It was an image of dismal grey, everyday life, the world exactly as it is, impossible to imagine any other way.

In the intervening years I had found my own way out of the world, now merely haunting it, a ghost, a shadow of no one. And yet I put down the newspaper and returned outside with a feeling not of despair, but rather of grief, a great and quiet grief.

A few months or years later, the book came out. I tried to hide, not listening to the radio, not reading any newspapers, and when I ventured out into the Netto discount store to buy avocados and carrots, I would avoid looking at the headlines, humming loudly to myself in the checkout line so as not to hear what the people in front of me were talking about. Only after several months, when *The Quiet Girl* suddenly appeared on the display shelf one day at the library, did I pick it up, almost in passing and seemingly quite without thought, and take it home with me to my flat (now, after my divorce, I was living but a pistol shot away from Blågårds Plads). I turned the key and went inside, tossed the book onto the kitchen counter, made some tea, ate a carrot, looked out of the window, and then, as I turned and passed the counter with the steaming mug of tea in my hand, I stopped and opened the book and began to read as I stood. Impossible. I grasped nothing. What

I saw on the pages was at once regular and yet utterly chaotic. I understood the words on their own, of course, or at least most of them, and could even, as though through a dense entanglement of branches, make out a scene, or at least its outline, or perhaps more exactly a structure, and behind that structure another structure, and behind that one another, and so on. If it was a circus trick, then it was of such virtuosity that one could no longer see the artist or the figure he was drawing, the illusion. It was like thousands upon thousands of da Vinci drawings layered on top of each other, so dense and so extremely complex there was nothing to see. It was the opposite of nothing. It was everything. And all too much.

Just the other day—or perhaps this, too, is already several years away in the future—I ran into Peter Høeg, or rather I saw him again, for the second time in my life. It happens like this, out of the dismal grey: I have been visiting my publisher, for like the other Great Authors of Our Nation, I, too, now have a publisher, or rather my publisher has me, though what it wants with me I have absolutely no idea, I am certainly not good business; on the contrary, I am most probably Denmark's leading worst seller, even if, fortunately, no one knows it apart from me, and the publisher, of course, my editor having just informed me after glancing at a screen that my latest book, unlike its predecessors that sold 128 and 329 copies respectively, has now just passed the 600 mark. I go out through the gateway and am walking along Pilestræde; the weather is very windy; the sky, I know nothing about the sky. I am looking down at the cobblestones, they are grey and glistening, slippery-looking in the drizzle. I cross Landemærket and continue on past Aage Jensen's window display to glance

in at the electronic keyboards and drum sets, the cymbals and
hi-hats, the floor toms, the cheap Fender guitars made on
licence in China that you can now get in a "starter pack" along
with a case and a stand and a little amplifier, when suddenly
I sense a slight fluctuation, a dark flutter at the periphery of
my field of vision, and I know he is there. I stop, my heart
suddenly racing, and turn around slowly. He is walking in
my direction, some fifty metres further ahead on the other
side of the street, passing the glass front of the Danish Film
Institute, with the Kongens Have park to his rear. He walks
quickly and with energy, not at any consistent pace, but in
little fits and starts, as though the wind were propelling him
on, nudging him chaotically along the pavement, unnoticed,
it would seem, by everyone but me. He looks at least fifteen
years older, which is not surprising, but nonetheless sad: at
least fifteen years have passed since as a young man with at
least twenty simultaneous lives within me, I saw him emerge
from the congregation of Great Authors, the very hope
of another world. He twirls around the corner and down
Vognmagergade, slight and sinewy, tense, almost quivering,
like a muscle that after forty years of unbroken focus on complete calm and equilibrium has now succumbed to cramp.
He crosses the street and carries on past the windows of the
Egmont Group building, turning his head as he goes, as if
trying, not to look at something in particular, but rather to
at least direct his eyes at something and keep them there for
a moment, however brief. Then abruptly he stops, though
without halting entirely, as yet in some continuing sideways
motion, staring with wild intensity through a seemingly
random windowpane, as though after twenty years someone
has now seated themselves in the high-backed chair behind

the polished mahogany desk of L. Ron Hubbard's office display—but who? L. Ron himself?

And again I see myself reflected in him, the way I did twenty years earlier on the back seat of my parents' car while heading north along the E45 motorway, only this time not as the person or persons I so much wanted to be, but as the one and only no one I have become: divorced, homeless, restlessly roaming, staggering unsettled from one day into the next, with strained and jagged features, and a look in my eyes that is far too intense, desperately searching, focused to the extreme, though without knowing exactly what I am searching for, but surely it can't be L. Ron Hubbard?

It was like a video sequence, not a Hollywood movie, not even a cheap TV documentary, just a black-and-white clip from a surveillance camera, a recording that would certainly be forgotten, consigned to the endless fractal depths of the internet, seen by no one unless someone, me perhaps, by chance happened to notice, like when you're standing in the checkout line in Netto and your eyes absently pass over the shelves of cheap German chocolate, and all of a sudden you see yourself in monochrome on the little monitor to the right of the checkout guy. It lasted less than a minute and concerned nothing, there was no story in it, no Conception, only what remained of one: a man, a human being, twirling around a corner and down a street, then gone.

TRANSLATED BY MARTIN AITKEN

A WORLD APART

ROSA LIKSOM

I

He's over there in the living room. Let's keep the noise down. The computer's still on, and the reading lamp too. I'll quietly switch them both off, the computer at least. I can watch *Emmerdale* on the small telly in the kitchen. Wait here. OK, I switched off the computer but left the lamp on so he doesn't wake up. I've put a blanket over him too. He's lying on his left side. That's good. He's always a bit crabby when he wakes up on his right side. Let's go into the kitchen so he doesn't wake up. Poor thing hasn't slept properly in hours. It's the depression, you see. It started on Monday when he was supposed to be out guiding. Didn't eat his breakfast, though I put it by his bed. I had to leave for the hospital because my shift was starting, so I left him in the bedroom sleeping with his eyes wide open . . . How long will it go on for this time? Last month the depression lasted three days. It might pass quicker this time, seeing as he keeps dozing off like that and sometimes even licks his paws.

II

I decided to have a beautiful summer wedding, the same kind of wedding Jemina had two years ago. She set aside eighteen months for all the wedding preparations. It wasn't enough. Towards the end she was so short of time that she had a nervous breakdown and ended up being admitted to a psychiatric unit. I said there's no way I'm going to fall into the same trap, so I started getting everything ready three years before the big day. A midsummer wedding is a must, otherwise what's the point? And it's got to be at the cathedral, obviously, because that's by far the fanciest scenery going.

When I told my girlfriends they'd better start getting ready for a summer wedding, I got six volunteers straight away: Kelly, Ann, Jenna, Melina, Sara and Tiia. I chose Kelly, Sara and Melina to be my bridesmaids because they're all uglier than me. The show got off to a great start, and I called Daddy in Brussels and he promised to give me ten grand towards the wedding budget, but that's next to nothing. I called Grandad in Madeira, and he was so excited he agreed to give me twelve thousand, because he always wants to go one better than my dad. The rest of the cash came from my mum (though she moaned that she always has to foot the bill for everything), my godmother who is a make-up artist and loves weddings, and my aunt who gave me another five thousand because she thinks my mum—her sister—is stingy and boring as hell. That's already forty grand in my wedding budget—woohoo!

I looked around online for a few weeks, checking out thousands of wedding planners, and eventually employed an American company to design and make all the little stuff, the napkins, the origami, the rosettes . . . Ten thousand went on trinkets for two hundred guests. Then there was the wedding dress. I checked out all of the bridal stores in the city, but everything looked just awful. So me and the girls did three trips to Stockholm before I finally found the right dress in a store in Paris. It was just as cheap as most of the dresses I'd found here, only five thousand. Of course, the shoes, the handbag, gloves, underwear and tights all came separately. We found everything in a store on the Champs Élysées for a total price of six hundred and ninety-nine a head.

Now I had a wedding dress, a ton of knick-knacks and a church. Daddy pulled some strings and helped me book the Halikko manor house for the reception. All this had taken two years. I still had to put together the menu, plan the evening programme and draw up the guest list—then, of course, there were the presents. I sat down with the head chef from the Halikko manor and together we designed the menu. The chef was super-cool right from the word go. We spent five wonderful weekends together getting everything ready.

Two days before Midsummer's, Daddy flew in from Brussels and I showed him everything me and the girls had got together. Daddy was so proud of me he positively sighed. Later that evening, when he was tasting the wines we'd chosen and complimenting me on my choice of vintage, he asked me who the groom was. I was like, what groom? Well, he said, didn't Jemina have some hairy brute standing at the altar saying *I do*? That's right, I gasped, and looked at the girls and asked them what we should do now. Sara suggested I could ask Jasu to be the groom—he's bound to agree, he's an engineer and they've got a weird sense of humour. But I was like, I can't ask Jasu because he's a foot shorter than me. Then I had an idea. I called the chef at Halikko and asked him if he'd join me at the altar and do everything you'd expect a groom to do at a wedding. Why not, he said straight off, but the problem was he was already married. I was like, don't worry, that's just a minor hitch, and so he turned up and from start to finish played the role of the groom with utter professionalism.

III

I'm so fucking ashamed. Last night I passed out on the settee in front of the nine o'clock news and only woke up this morning. Jere had put a blanket over me, like he always does. It feels so shameful to get up after the boys have already left for school. Maija was keeping herself occupied on the PlayStation in a corner of the living room. She didn't even look at me as I dragged myself into the bathroom. I had a loose shit in the loo, went into the kitchen and cracked open a can of lager. Only after I'd stood in front of the fridge and downed the can did I pluck up the courage to call out to Maija. She walked into the kitchen, a sulky scowl on her face, and cast an angry glance at the empty can in my hand. I told her I'd take her to nursery in just a minute. She nodded and went off to get dressed.

I left Maija at the doors of the nursery school around midday. I watched her quickly run inside, went into the corner shop and bought a twelve-pack of lager, a sandwich and a packet of ham reduced to half-price. I walked home and got to work on the twelve-pack, one can at a time. Shame sure fucking stings—a grown woman, a single mother of three, drinking her life away. It's the kids that suffer most, I know that, and that makes me even more ashamed. When I should be putting food on the table for them, I buy lager instead and drink myself stupid.

Even thinking about how I turned out like this makes me feel ashamed. Was it circumstances, society, my parents, was it bad luck, fate, destiny, other people, or was the problem with me? I can't remember my mother or father ever doing anything so terribly wrong that I had to start drinking. I just started. I can't remember how or why. One bottle at a time, I suppose.

I know I'll fall asleep on the living-room settee again before long. Jere will pick up Maija from nursery, I know that. I can rely on him. Then, when I wake up at about seven, I'll go to the corner shop, fetch another twelve-pack and pass out again in front of the nine o'clock news. The boys understand me, they never seem angry with me, and that makes me ashamed too, ashamed that they still love me.

IV

I met Jani in the car park when I reversed into the back of him. As we stood there arguing about his no-claims bonus, our auras collided and he invited me to McDonald's for a bite to eat. We drove off, and that's when everything started. Back then I was still married to Lari and he was with Susse. I've got three boys and a Labrador called Saku, and Jani's got three girls and Lilli the golden retriever. Jani is six foot three, he was into diving and spoke fluent English.

Our relationship got off to a flying start. Jani filed for a divorce and expected me to do the same. Hold on, I said. We'll see about that. As a realist, I wanted to be sure of a few things first. I asked Jani for Susse's phone number. He looked a bit confused and asked why I needed it. I said, I'm not buying a pig in a poke.

I rang Susse and we agreed to meet at the work canteen. As soon as I saw her, I felt like we'd known each other since we were kids. I asked her straight out if she had anything against me. She said she might have had once, but not any more because she can tell I'm a kindred spirit. We agreed to work together. I asked her to list all Jani's good and bad points. There were thirteen good points and only one bad one. He's a total junkie—an endorphin junkie. He can't survive a day without a twenty-mile run. If he can't get out for a run, he turns into a right pain in the backside, Susse explained. Fine, I said, I can deal with that.

After that we talked about the practical side of things. We started with the kids, because divorces have a habit of affecting them the most. We agreed to look after the children together because we had virtually identical ideas about child-rearing. Three boys and three girls make for a perfect match. We shared all Christmas, Easter and half-term holidays. Then it was time to talk about the dogs. Diet, training regimes and agility competitions. We had things wrapped up soon enough. Susse asked if she could keep the house she'd shared with Jani. Sure, I said, Jani can move in with me and Lari can rent himself something cheap out in the suburbs.

As soon as the divorces came through, Jani and I got married. Lari didn't want to move out because he'd become best mates with Jani and they'd started going running together. They were always off somewhere, training for marathons in New York, Berlin, you name it. I began to feel quite lonely because the guys were always away together, so eventually Susse and the kids moved into our place. First, she and I started dating each other, then a few months later Lari and Jani came out of the closet. Now we all live together in one big, wonderful blended family of four adults, six children and two dogs, and everything's going just brilliantly. And we'll soon have a new addition to the family too: Saku and Lilli are expecting sextuplets!

V

First I got the sack, because they were streamlining at work, downsizing, consolidating, cutting back or whatever they called it. I looked for a new job for a couple of years; I even went to three interviews, but it didn't work out. That was my first strike. I was on unemployment benefit, so I wasn't in any trouble at first. The missus worked on a construction site; I sat in the pub all day. I liked the booze, and that was my second strike. Before long the unemployment benefit ran out too and I had to sign on. The missus told me to take a hike, said she wasn't going to work all day just to keep me in drink. I didn't want a fight, so I left. That was my third strike. Once I was homeless, I started drinking even more, living on people's couches. Thank God, I had a car. I parked at the petrol station near Sörnäinen harbour and slept there all summer. Things were fine for a few months, but when autumn came round, it started to rain, and one day when I came back from the pub, the car was gone. I went over to the gypsy camp near the petrol station and asked if they knew anything about it. One of them said a pickup truck had turned up and towed me motor to buggery. I didn't have the cash to reclaim it, and things quickly went from bad to worse. With the help of some hard Russian liquor, I hospitalized myself in the space of eight months. The quack said me pancreas had given up the ghost and I had two options: it's either a coffin or an AA group. Three strikes and you're out, mate. I chose the latter because I figured the AA might buy me some time. I've been clean for two years, three months, nine days and fifty-four minutes now, but right now I'm going to open a bottle of cut brandy and empty it down me gullet.

VI

Sometimes you wake up in the morning, you feel like shit, and you just know it's going to be a bad day, so normally I don't bother getting out of bed at all, I just sleep all day. On days like that, Lauri takes care of Otto. He knows how to open the fridge so that Otto can reach his feeding bottle. When Otto starts whining, Lauri opens the balcony door so that he can crawl outside. I've put a box out there with all the plastic toys that won't go mouldy. He plays with them by himself or with Lauri. Otto already knows to throw the ball where I've hidden pieces of cheese, and Lauri fetches it for him. On bad days I feel like I can't do anything because I've got Otto. I can't concentrate on making the tea, cleaning, listening to music, can't be bothered going on the PlayStation or fiddling with my phone or even watching reality TV. On bad days I just think the flat's a tip, the neighbourhood's a dump, and I'll probably die soon of all the rush and the stress of keeping our little family together, I'm just another fucking loser who can't even be bothered to queue up for my benefits. On bad days I feel like my quality of life is so rough in this shitty world that I might as well stick two fingers up to the lot of it.

When I feel good from the word go, I know it's going to be a good day. I get up, have a shower, wipe Otto's bum and change his nappy, put some food in Lauri's bowl and head

73

out for the queues. First, I walk past the wellness centre, get the bus to Kallio and head for the job centre. While I'm waiting in the queue there, I chat to the other mums about the kids' ear infections and the rotavirus. From there I move on to the social. I tend to keep my head down there, mostly because there are so many junkies around. I don't want anyone to attack me or Otto. The final stop of the day is the food bank. Otto enjoys it there because he gets to see his friends. On good days the volunteers might give me an extra packet of coffee or some washing powder so I can do the laundry. On bad days there's a busload of Russian tourists there too, turning their noses up at the packets of oat flakes because they don't realize how healthy porridge is. Days like that are pretty rare though, thank God. On good days I make a healthy meal, use vegetable oil instead of butter, take Otto to the playground and stand there watching him instead of sitting on the bench. On good days I think I've got nothing to worry about. Everything's going to be fine.

VII

I feel in love with Jore the minute he said he'd give me a lift to the Metro station after work. I'd never met a guy as down-to-earth as that. It wasn't long before I was expecting Jani, and once he was born I was over the moon. Jore wasn't much interested in family life, he preferred to spend all his spare time down the pub, so we split up. I met Fiude when I was on the Metro, coming home shit-faced after a night on the town. When he heard I had a kid with another bloke, he said straight up, it's me or the boy. I thought about it for a couple of minutes and said I could always hand Jani over to the social services. And so Jani was sent off to a foster family in Lempäälä, and me and Fiude had a bundle of fun. We travelled a lot, went to Hamina, Tampere, and once we even got as far as the Canaries. I was as free as a bird and Fiude was really sweet, and before long I was expecting Tina. By the time Tina was born, Fiude had already found himself another bit of skirt on the beach at Hietaniemi and taken a hike. I was pissed off, but thank God, I met Tike. He comforted me, helped me with the transition into my new life, but he got bored before long. We never get a chance to do anything, he said, because everywhere we go the kid's always hanging round. I'd had enough of him moaning all the time, so I handed Tina over to the social services. After that, me and Tike were happy for about two years. After a while, though, I started to feel like I'd had enough of freedom, and I wanted the kids to come back home. I told Tike to sling his hook, and he didn't put up a fight. I went back to the social services and screamed that I wanted my kids back, said I'd top myself if I couldn't have them back home with me. That was the beginning of a crazy legal battle. I fought with the authorities for a full nine months before they agreed to return the kids. When I picked them up, Jani and Tina didn't recognize me. They'd forgotten me, but I hadn't forgotten them. They cried all day long, saying they wanted to go home. Enough of that whingeing, I said, I'm your real mum and this is your home! Eventually the kids got used to me, and sometimes we even had quite a nice time. Then one day, down at the corner shop, Veke looked my way and that was it. Veke liked kids, but he didn't get on with Jani and Tina. I spent a whole week thinking about what to do: do I choose him or the kids? I chose Veke and took the kids back to social services. These two are so damaged I doubt anyone could put up with them, I said, those foster families have turned my lovely, sweet children into right little monsters. I left the children at the social, and me and Veke moved into a flat in the suburbs. We've got loads in common—we've got the same sense of humour and we both like blancmange and double cheeseburgers. Sometimes he threatens to leave me because I'm so fat. I don't believe him. I've got a feeling our love is going to last forever. There's nothing can get in the way of my happiness now.

VIII

For eighteen years, four months and eleven days, I was on a temporary disability living allowance, and it was a really stressful time for me. All you can do is sit at the kitchen table one year at a time, waiting nervously, petrified they'll take your allowance away and you'll have to go back to work. A woman as poorly as me can't go out to work. If I can't even take a tinkle without Jappe helping me into the loo, how the blazes can I go to work? I'm constantly having panic attacks and I've been on mandatory medication for twenty years. And still they only give me disability allowance for a year at a time. Nothing seemed to do the trick—not even when I jumped off the third-floor balcony and landed in a snowdrift. An ambulance picked me up and took me to the hospital, but they wouldn't admit me, though they normally take in all the lunatics. They sent me home and said next time I should try the sixth floor instead.

Last spring I turned sixty-one. As a birthday present, the post brought me a little surprise, and boy, what a real red-letter day it was. The social awarded me a permanent disability pension! It felt like I'd won the lottery. I walked to the toilet by myself, the letter in my hand, and Jappe just sat at the kitchen table staring at me, his jaw almost touching the floor. I pulled on my best clothes and even took the lift downstairs—the last time I used the lift must have been back in the nineties when Nipa was still alive. I strode into the supermarket and filled my shopping bag with food because it felt like the whole world had opened up to me, then I skipped across to the bus stop like some young whippersnapper and took a ride into town. I accidentally left the bag of food on the bus, but at least I still had a bank card in my pocket. The railway station looked so nice that I bought a ticket all the way to Pori. I spent three months dashing from one place to the next, and I can't remember a thing about it. I would probably have carried on like that indefinitely, but one day Jappe turned up and took me home.

Now I'm back sitting at the kitchen table and Jappe has to help me to the loo again. But it doesn't matter. The good thing about this permanent disability pension is that if I get well again, I can jump right back into the jobs market any time I want.

IX

We've been swimming so long I bet you're really hungry. Mummy's brought some grapes. Have some of those. You must be very thirsty. I've got some carrots too. See? The little baby carrots that you like so much. Munch a few carrots first, then have some grapes. Right, T-shirt on, pants on. Mummy's almost dressed already. Let's see which one of us can get our socks on first. Look, here's a banana. Eat that and you'll be able to walk all the way out to the car park. It's such a long way, you can't even see it out of the window. It must be at least fifty metres away. Come on, socks on, please, Mummy's already combed her hair. Have a digestive biscuit—that'll make you grow. Tie your hair back now, Mummy's already got her trousers on. Don't just stand there. Eat your biscuit, trousers on, jumper on, and we'll be just fine. Look, I've brought you a doughnut too, your blood-sugar levels must be low after all that splashing around. Wasn't that fun? Take a bite of your doughnut. Look, give me the biscuit if you're not going to eat it. Sweater on. Chop, chop, Mummy's ready to go. You haven't touched your banana either. Did you eat any of those grapes? Carrots? Goodness me, you hardly eat a thing, you'll waste away. Just think, you're almost three years old and you're still that small. You'll never turn into a big girl if you carry on like that. Do you want to be like Mummy one day? If you do, then you'd better start eating properly. Don't you worry, us girls will be just fine, even though Daddy left us and went off with that bitch. God, I hate her, but we'll be all right though, won't we? If you walk back to the car nicely, there's Coke and popcorn, OK?

X

A stinking salmon carcass had been left lying on the kitchen counter. I chucked it in the bin. I sat down at the kitchen table, but I hadn't quite finished my green tea when the doorbell rang. It was Tuukka, said he fancied a quick shag. I was like, just let me finish my tea, will you? He's like, he hasn't got time to wait around. I took care of him in the hallway.

I nipped into the bathroom, then back into the kitchen; the smell coming from the bin slapped me in the face as I made a fresh pot of tea. I'd just lit a cigarette when my phone rang. It was Tuure. He was sitting in his car outside and needed a blow-job. I was like, come up to the flat, I'm still in my nightie. He's like, no, you come down here. I pulled a dressing gown round my shoulders and took the lift down two floors. Only once the lift had jolted into motion did I remember I'd forgotten the rubbish bag. At least it was warm in the car. Once we were done, I walked up the stairs and popped into the bathroom on my way back to the kitchen. The tea was brewed to perfection and tasted really good, the stink from the rubbish bin notwithstanding. I smoked a Camel and went through to the bedroom. I'd just pulled on a T-shirt when the doorbell rang. There were two blokes standing outside. I was like, what? Can we come in, one of them mumbled. Fuck off, I said and slammed the door in their face. I went back into the bedroom, pulled on my jeans and heard the blokes pushing something through the letterbox. I dashed to the door to look, and there was a piece of paper lying on the mat. I snatched it up and read it: *My name's Mage and that's my mate Samppa. He's a bit of a retard. Can you help him out? He's still a virgin.* I crumpled the piece of paper, threw it in the smelly bin bag. I wiped the counter, and just as I was about to take the whole stinking thing out, my phone rang again. It was Jarkko, said that he was delivering an order to Tikkurila, that he was in the mood, and he'd be at my place in two minutes. I threw the rubbish bag into a corner of the hallway, took care of Jarkko and finally took the whole fucking thing out to the rubbish bin. When I got back to the flat, someone gave the door a sleek knock three times. I couldn't help smiling because there's only one person in the world who knocks like that.

XI

I quickly pull on my clothes, give my teeth a cursory brush and run out to the car. I've got to be at the hospital before nine. I drive through two sets of red lights. I leave the car in the hospital car park, located far away from the main door, and run to the lift. I'm three minutes late. I press the button for the fifth floor; the lift seems to rise so bloody slowly, then finally the doors slide open. He's standing there in a green coat, and he's so livid that there's spittle bubbling at the corner of his mouth, he won't look me in the eye, but keeps his lips tightly shut. We rush into the bathroom the way we always do. I give him the bag and he slaps a five-hundred-euro bill in my hand. He doesn't say anything, but from his trembling hands I can tell that waiting in the operating theatre there's a patient whose skull he's about to bore open. He disappears into the cubicle and locks the door. I step out of the bathroom, head back to the lift and catch my breath. His hands aren't trembling any longer.

XII

So you decided to order a cab in the middle of the night? You're a brave woman; there are all kinds of junkie drivers out at this time of night, and not all of them are nice guys like me. The night shift always brings out the freaks and perverts. Anything could happen. Imagine a situation where

I tell you to undress and spread your old muff on the back seat, so I can get an eyeful of it in this little mirror here. I wouldn't do anything else, I wouldn't touch you, wouldn't say anything, I'd just look. You haven't got the number of my cab because you didn't know how to order by text message, but called the switchboard instead the way people did in, you know, prehistoric times, and besides, by the time we got to the airport, you'd be in such a state of shock that you'd forget to write down my reg number. Just imagine I was some kind of serial-killer cabbie, a real psycho that pulled a gun on you, released the safety catch and pointed the thing at you while I was driving. I wouldn't say anything, I'd just point the gun at you, and once we'd arrived at the airport, I'd slip it back into my pocket. If you went crying to the police, they'd just think you were crazy—which you probably are anyway. All kinds of things can happen when you race around in a taxi to catch a budget flight at this time of night. You're better off flying with a proper airline so you can travel at a decent hour of the day. The predators come out at night, you know that, right? Just think about what happened in Pori. Did you read about that? There was this young cab driver, small and skinny, a guy just like me, spends all night driving around the town centre. Then outside a pub some bitch waves her hand at him, the kind of slag that's slept with at least half the town. *Taxiii*, she squeals. And it really fucks this driver off. He picks her up, turns on to a small lane into the woods and stabs her six hundred and two times with a hunting knife, then drives back to the motorway, washes his hands in a toilet at the petrol station and carries on with his shift until morning. Sure, there was a bit of blood on the steering wheel, but not a single customer noticed it. Was it Terminal 1 or 2?

XIII

There's a really nice clubroom in our house. A while ago, when there were lots of children living in the building, the clubroom was in constant use. Now that the children have moved away, we rent the room to outside groups. Our first tenant was an art club called Picasso. The first week went well enough, but once they started painting, the stench of turpentine came up through the ventilation shaft and it caused a right row. Manninen, who lived on the third floor, made a complaint about the group, as did the old widow on the sixth floor, and I was the one that had to go and tell the art teacher that it was no use, they'd have to go. And so the clubroom was empty for another few years, but when the housing association found itself a bit short of cash, Manninen suggested we rent the room to a group that doesn't make such a stink. I flicked through the classifieds and found a group called Silver Lining. They were funded by the Red Cross, which promised to pay their rent on time. I suggested this to Manninen, who seemed pretty enthusiastic. At first the group was no trouble at all. They were mostly octogenarians who liked to play bingo and talk about CT scans and homoeopathy. But when autumn turned to winter, that's when things started to go south. One day a member of the group had a stroke and we had to call an ambulance. Soon after this little incident the group's volunteer leader died during a meeting of the book club and the body had to be driven away in a hearse. Manninen had had it with all the nonsense and asked me to ring the Red Cross and tell them enough was enough. I made the call, and the clubroom was empty once again.

Our building was about to undergo a substantial balcony renovation and the housing association desperately needed some extra funds. I found an advertisement in the newspaper: the Band of Brothers was looking for a clubroom. I showed Manninen the ad, and Manninen said it seemed promising as the group's name made a nice reference to lost Karelia and the Finnish kindred peoples still living there. I called the number in the ad and arranged a meeting with the group's chairman. He was a patriotic young man—he'd even sewn a Finnish flag on his jacket. We drew up some ground rules, signed a rental agreement, and the man paid six months' rent upfront in cash. All summer Manninen opined about how pleasant it was to discover that there were still some people in Finland with good, upstanding values. And this continued until Christmas. The first setback came on Boxing Day. A young woman had allegedly been raped in the clubroom. Probably her own fault, said Manninen. Then on New Year's Eve a man claimed to be the victim of a grievous assault. An American basketball player had allegedly been knocked unconscious with a taser, dragged into the clubroom and beaten to a pulp. Well, Manninen sighed, relieved—at least he was black, not white. But it was at the beginning of February that things finally came to a head. The case ended up in the headlines: a killer was on the loose and he'd dismembered at least two victims. One of them was Manninen.

XIV

This morning Nazi Mum swallowed the last of Kalle's ADHD tablets and headed off to work, her handbag swinging over her shoulder. By the time he went to school, Kalle was so hyper he punched a hole in the hallway mirror.

I went straight to my aerobics class, and as I was getting changed, I noticed my tub of caffeine pills was missing. Fucking Nazi Mum, I shouted. The instructor ran up and handed me an energy drink to try and calm me down. I thanked her. Over and out.

After school I went to a café with my mates. Gran called and said she'd run out of dementia tablets. Gran, listen, I explained to her at least five times, you haven't run out, Nazi Mum's been nicking them. She's been taking Gran's meds too because they stimulate her brain function. Without all the doping, she'd probably get the sack.

When I got home from basketball training that evening, Nazi Mum was snoring in the armchair in the living room. She'd probably taken a handful of sleeping pills before the news, so she could get a good night's sleep before another tough day at work. I dragged her into the bedroom, covered her with a blanket and opened the ventilation window to give her some fresh air.

XV

I don't need to look him in his eyes or stare at the muscles in his face to see the deep sense of disgust he feels towards my saggy old arse, my alcohol-bloated body, my rotten stinking breath, my stumpy white legs, my puffy ruddy face, my veiny hands, my eyes that have long since lost any lustre. That being said, I've saved him from a Bangkok whorehouse, paid for his flights out here, bought him a pair of fancy white Adidas trainers and an electric shaver. On top of that, I pay for his rent, food and bus tickets; I've sorted him out with gym membership and an English course, lube and insurance and I even wire a few quid a month to his family by the side of a paddy field in the middle of nowhere, so I think it's only reasonable to expect him to do his job properly, though it sometimes makes him retch.

XVI

After a meeting of the housing association, my husband said that he and the other motorists had agreed to cut down one of the trees in the garden. Come September the old rowan will be history because sap drips on to the car bonnets and the little birds feed off its berries and shit all over the paintwork. We've put up with it for thirty years, he said, and enough is enough; the city gardeners can take care of it and it won't cost the housing association a penny.

Without the least hesitation I told my husband I'd file for divorce if anyone touched the rowan. It's only a tree, he scoffed. In the city we live like city people.

September arrived, and one day when I got back from work, the rowan was lying in the back garden, its crimson berries weeping on the grass.

The next morning I marched up to the magistrates and submitted the paperwork for a unilateral divorce. My husband was in the transit lounge at Heathrow Airport waiting for a connecting flight to Singapore when my lawyer contacted him to inform him of the development. Ten minutes after take-off he had a heart attack and died despite attempts at resuscitation.

XVII

If they mutilate my genitals, the Finns will give me those slow, awkward looks. But if they don't, my own people will think I'm weird.

TRANSLATED BY DAVID HACKSTON

THE DARK BLUE WINTER OVERCOAT

JOHAN BARGUM

DEAR MUM,
  You're right, this is a terrible city: noisy, dirty and shabby, and there are piles of rubbish on the pavements which no one seems to care about. The air pollution hangs like a yellowish-grey mist between the skyscrapers. My allergy has already broken out after only a few hours, and I had to put myself to bed in the hotel room with a running nose and streaming eyes. It was icy cold in that room, by the way, because the central heating had gone on strike. There's nothing wrong with my English, as you know, but making myself understood to the lady in reception was impossible to begin with. They're in such a hurry all the time, even when they speak; monosyllabic nasal sounds shoot out of their mouths as if from machine guns. Towards midnight, and out of the blue, there was a knock at my door. I followed your advice and didn't make a move to open it. There was another knock. I lay staring up into the darkness, my heart pounding so that it seemed to echo against my palate. Then I heard the sound of someone putting a key into the lock. The door was pushed open slightly, and then there was an ominous rattling sound, as the safety chain tautened and held fast. I sat bolt upright in bed and turned on the light. I heard a man's husky voice

and a torrent of words outside the door. The only bit I could understand was the "sir" at the end. I grabbed hold of the telephone. "I'm ringing Reception right this minute," I said in a loud voice, hoping to hear hastily retreating footsteps down the corridor. However, the man stayed where he was and the woman in Reception made it clear, in a direct and forthright manner, that the man was a plumber. At least, he was dressed in overalls and had a toolbox in his hand. He was a gigantic black man, who mumbled something incomprehensible to himself, scratched his head, gave the radiator a mighty kick and went on his way.

A few hours later the room was boiling hot, so I hardly got a wink of sleep all night.

At dawn, as the traffic started thundering by, I opened the window and looked out. The people down on the street looked so ridiculously small beneath the towering buildings; dwarfs in a city built for giants.

It all suddenly seemed a little unreal. At the passport desk a forbidding official had asked me what my intentions were in this country. Just suppose I'd explained the situation to him, that I'd told him there had been an envelope lying on the hall floor one morning, with an air ticket and a note from Dad's new wife asking me to come and visit, and at the same time pointing out to me that Dad wasn't able to write personally because he'd turned into a dog? Maybe I should have followed your advice and stayed at home.

There is an almost childlike logic to the layout of this town with its numbered streets at right angles to the avenues. It's effective and unimaginative. It was easy to find where they lived on the map, and I decided to go by bus. This was easier said than done. The bus driver wasn't the slightest bit interested in my dollar bill. He pointed at a glass container beside him, which looked like an old-fashioned money box, then reeled off a long speech I couldn't understand. I shrugged my shoulders and tried to edge back into the bus, but that caused a terrible commotion until a young man took the dollar bill out of my hand and put a yellow token into this "money box". I sat down and tried to look calm and collected; you know how you get stared at at home, well, no one so much as looked in my direction. That's the way things seem to be in this city. Furthermore, when someone happens to glance at you, you still don't have that feeling of having been looked at, rather the feeling of merely having been accidentally caught in someone's gaze.

A few blocks later I noticed I was travelling in the wrong direction: south instead of north. I don't understand how this came about. It really seemed so simple when I looked at the map.

The apartment was huge and elegant. The front door was opened by a fat black woman, who had a cigar in one hand and a vacuum cleaner in the other. So they can afford to have some domestic staff here, I thought, and I told her I had come to meet my father. The cleaning lady nodded and showed me into a well-lit lounge, with a lot of pictures on the walls and a three-piece suite over by the window.

Dad was lying on the sofa in a curious, hunched-up position.

He was much thinner than I remembered, and had lost nearly all his hair.

"Hello Dad," I said.

"Wuff," he replied.

I didn't know what to say at all then.

"So you've gone and turned into a dog?"

"Wuff, wuff," said Dad.

This was embarrassing, especially as the cleaning lady had stayed in the doorway and was watching with interest.

"Do you know where his wife is?" I asked, and the cleaning lady nodded and smiled, and then at once I understood that I had made a stupid mistake and felt myself going very red in the face.

"I'm very sorry."

The woman laughed, loudly and hoarsely. "That doesn't matter at all," she said.

Dad had begun to swing his leg to and fro, his foot moving back and forth like a windscreen wiper in the air.

"Is something wrong?"

"Not at all," said the woman. "He's just wagging his tail."

From now on, whenever I continue a letter to you, Mum, I'm doing so not from my hotel room, but from a room behind the kitchen in Dad's apartment. I haven't ended up here of my own accord; on the contrary, I tried to insist to the very last that I liked it at the hotel. However, it was no use. His new wife put me in the car and drove me to the hotel, settled my bill, packed my things in the suitcase and put both myself and the suitcase back into the car. She had already made up a bed into the bargain, put a potted plant on the windowsill and hung up a clean towel in the bathroom with my name written on a small label sticking above it.

She smokes her cigars continuously, hums to herself and takes charge; it's pointless even to try contradicting her.

Why did you never tell me Dad had got married again to a black woman?

Not that it makes any difference, of course, but it feels a little silly, as if I'd been tricked in some way.

And now about Dad's new wife . . . they've been married for years.

Her name is Melaine. She's an amazing person. Dad's condition doesn't seem to worry her.

"Men get up to everything under the sun," she says, and laughs her hoarse, hearty laugh.

When we eat, she dishes up the food onto Dad's plate, cuts it up into small pieces and puts the plate on the floor alongside my chair. Dad then gets on all fours, picking up the pieces with his mouth. He chews them slowly and meditatively, at the same time looking at me continuously.

It feels odd. He has changed. He seems to have shrunk and funnily enough has something doglike about him. He chews and chews and swallows with difficulty, as if it was painful, and regards me with the melancholy, slightly anxious eyes of an old dog.

In actual fact, it feels damned unpleasant. Furthermore, I can't get him to talk to me.

He never really has done, in actual fact, so I don't know why it's making me so bad-tempered at the moment. I remember when he paid us short visits at home, he always used to spill coffee on our tablecloths; "sorry" was practically all he ever said.

"Dad," I keep saying, "why don't you want to talk to me?"

He hangs his head limply and whimpers pitifully.

"Dogs have their own language," says Melaine and laughs. She has a strange sense of humour.

"Am I supposed to feel sorry for you?" I ask. Dad crawls over to Melaine and rubs himself against her legs; she scratches his chest.

"There, there," she wheedles.

It sickens me.

"You've never given a damn about me," I say angrily. "Why should I feel sorry for you?"

He turns away. His body shakes and twitches all over. Then he crawls up to the toilet door and scratches at it with his hand.

"Good doggy," says Melaine, and lets him in, closing the door after him and laughing again.

She never ceases to amaze me. This morning she appeared at breakfast in a silk skirt and suede jacket, with a white shirt and black bow, and had an elaborate hairstyle with small bows here and there. She looked like a cutting from a fashion magazine.

"I've got to go to work now, sweethearts," she said and sailed out in a cloud of cigar smoke and expensive perfume.

What kind of person is she really?

I don't like this.

Furthermore, she left me alone with Dad. I didn't like that either.

He had sat down at my feet as usual, his head on one side. He looked at me searchingly and attentively, as if he wanted to imprint my face upon his memory.

"What does she do at work?" I asked in an indifferent tone, in order to coax him into beginning a conversation.

But he was silent.

"Dad, say something!"

He looked worried and wagged his foot apologetically.

He was beginning to irritate me.

"What kind of damn stupid idea is it to get me trekking halfway across the world, just so that we can sit here and stare at one another?"

He barked three times as if in protest.

He was beginning to do more than just irritate me.

"Lie down!" I commanded.

He blinked and looked frightened. Then he lay down obediently. I picked up a slice of bread and flung it across the floor.

"Fetch!"

He obeyed. He crawled over to the slice of bread, took it in his mouth, crawled back and placed it at my feet.

This made me furious.

"Lie down!"

He lay down.

"Sit!"

He sat up.

We carried on like this for a while and at an ever-increasing tempo, until he was panting, sweating, and his face began to turn white; this was terrible. I couldn't bear it, I wasn't able to stop and I didn't know how I would be able to resist finally whipping him up into the frenzy of excitement like a dog, so I forced myself to say, "Dad, for heaven's sake."

He crept laboriously over to the sofa, and lay down there, just panting.

"Dad, just what the hell do you want from me anyway?"

He didn't answer. He lay there, wheezing, as if he was thinking of dying.

I spent the rest of the day at a big art gallery nearby, in order to avoid seeing him.

It's true I've never liked looking at paintings, as you know. While I was wondering around amongst all the Madonnas with sheepish faces, I suddenly got the feeling I had done this before with Dad. At the same time, I remembered I'd once had a dark blue winter overcoat with a furry collar. The coat sort of tumbled into my consciousness, as if it had been lurking there for years, just waiting to make itself noticed, and suddenly there it was, with its golden-brown collar, chequered lining, deep pockets and shiny metal buttons, which Dad was trying to do up, but I didn't want him to and began to scream. We were standing on a wide flight of stairs with a lot of large paintings on the walls and it echoed when I screamed, and strange people stared at us.

Did he used to take me along to galleries at some point in the distant past?

By the way, you haven't got any photographs of us, pictures from that time. That seems strange. Have you hidden them away somewhere?

I stopped in front of a painting and stayed there a good while.

It was called *Leda and the Swan*, and portrays a naked woman with her arm around a swan, which is sensuously holding onto her one nipple with its beak. Zeus has disguised himself in one of his tricks. The woman looks lecherously pleased, as if she very well knows who she's fawning upon.

Zeus turned into a swan in order to fulfil his desires.

Had Dad turned into a dog in order to get what he wanted?

Melaine didn't come home until towards midnight. Dad kept out of the way all evening, to my great joy. I opened the door to their bedroom slightly and saw him lying in his basket. (She's put a big round basket in one corner, where he huddles under an old blanket.) I sneaked up to him. He had pulled the blanket over his head. There was no movement at all. What the hell do you do here in town if an old dog goes and dies? I thought, carefully pulling the blanket back over his face, and suddenly I felt something wet rub against my fingers.

He had licked my hand.

And there he lay, smiling like an idiot.

I sat down in the lounge and opened a bottle of gin. I managed to consume a great deal before she returned.

"Greetings from Washington," she said gaily and lit up a fresh cigar from the stub-end of the old one.

"What on earth is this really all about?"

She undid her bow, and unbuttoned her shirt right down to her stomach, loosening her belt, gasped and said, "Is what about?"

"Dad, for heaven's sake. Things can't go on as they are."

"What do you mean?"

"But he's ill, can't you see that?"

She nodded.

"You've got to get hold of a doctor."

She puffed away at her cigar and suddenly burst out laughing. "A vet, you mean?"

She laughed so much, she was on the verge of choking. "Actually, it was a good job he turned into a dog," she said, "and not a seal, for instance, otherwise I should've had to keep him in the bath for the remainder of his days."

She was also beginning to irritate me.

"It's strange that you don't put him on a lead and take him out to the park," I said.

She looked at me in surprise. "Well, I'm damned," she said, "I never thought of that."

The following morning, before I'd had time to get up, she knocked on my door.

"Rise and shine," she called out gaily, "we're going out for a walk."

Dad was on all fours in the hall. She had secured a collar around his neck, and fastened a lead to it. It looked stupid, and seemed like a dream.

I went back into my room and pulled the covers over my head.

After a while, I heard scratching at the door. I hid my head under the pillow. The scratching sound went on and on. Suddenly the pillow was lifted from my face.

"He won't go anywhere without you," said Melaine.

I just stared at her. "You must both be stark, raving mad."

But she just laughed as usual. "You take him down. I'll bring the car around."

An old lady was in the lift, glancing through a newspaper. Dad crawled in on all fours. I kept hold of the leash. Please, I thought, say this is totally insane. However, the old lady didn't take any notice. She glanced at us, without seeing us.

The doorman smiled in a kindly way, as we passed by his desk. "Lovely weather we're having," he said. "Everything OK?"

"Yes, certainly," I replied. "This is just my father who's turned into a dog."

"Oh really," he said. "Have a nice day."

The weather in this city is just as mad. It had suddenly become glorious high summer. People were lying half-naked, sun-bathing on the lawn in Central Park.

"The police will come and take him away," I said.

"They've got other things to do," she replied.

Dad crawled out of the back seat, down on the ground, and put his nose to the wind, sniffing with a contented expression. She took the lead and guided him to an expanse of grass.

I lagged a few paces behind.

A set of fat, bald twins rushed past, each holding a stopwatch.

"What wonderful weather," Melaine called out over her shoulder.

"I don't know you," I muttered, and imagined a group of people gathering around them before long, and at least I wasn't going to be standing there in the middle, looking ridiculous.

But no one took a blind bit of notice. People just glanced at Dad in a preoccupied manner and went on with their walks, as if dads who have turned into dogs are a completely commonplace phenomenon in this crazy city.

A few small children pointed at him and giggled, but that was all.

The only person who took an interest in him was the park keeper.

"Dogs are prohibited on the grass, Madam," he informed us.

"Dear me," said Melaine.

The keeper bent down and scratched Dad behind the ear. "What breed is it?"

"Mongrel."

"Beautiful coat," said the keeper, patting Dad on his thinning fringe. "Has he been castrated?"

"I don't know," said Melaine, "I got him from a lady who didn't want him any more."

"Yes," said the keeper. "Dogs are loyal. It's a different matter when it comes to women."

Melaine nodded.

"Just imagine," said the keeper thoughtfully, "and I thought

I'd seen every possible kind of madness. Madam had better make sure he doesn't foul the grass."

I made off. I can't stand it, Mum. I've got to get away from here.

All day I wandered around this big city where logic seems to exist only on the map. I had dearly wanted to ring you, but all the telephones were either being used or were out of order.

"Can I make a call to Finland?" I asked at a bar, but the bartender looked as though I'd asked for a call to the moon.

There's a permanent shadow down here on the streets. The sky looks its best in the reflections of skyscrapers. I wandered aimlessly on and suddenly noticed I had arrived at the gallery again. Leda looks directly at each person looking at the picture. She has such a remarkable expression on her face; she is so perfectly aware of the person concealing himself in the guise of a swan. She knows what's happening. She understands what he's doing.

Ought I also to understand what Dad's doing?

Towards evening a strange, bluish half-light descends on the streets, while the sky remains bright and clear. This is probably due to the exhaust fumes from the cars for the most part, but it's quite beautiful.

"You've got to rebook my ticket," I said.

"It's a discount ticket," she replied. "It's not possible to rebook it."

"Then you've got to buy me another one."

"That will cost an awful lot of money."

"I expect he can afford it."

She looked at me in amazement. "Your father, you mean? What makes you think that?"

I thought of saying, "Because Mum said so," but restrained myself.

"Look around you," I said instead, "this places reeks of money."

She was silent for a while and looked at the floor. Then she said, "This is my apartment."

"So where has all Dad's money gone?"

She didn't answer. She drew on her cigar and looked at the floor.

This was unpleasant, as if she thought I ought to know the answer to my own question.

"I shall have a ticket by tomorrow," I announced.

She sighed. For once she appeared worried, almost sad.

"He's not going to like this," she said.

"Who cares what a dog thinks?" I replied.

During the night I heard careful, padding footsteps on the landing outside my room. They weren't her footsteps, but lighter and more shuffling.

Someone put a key in the lock. Someone opened the door of the room next to mine.

Someone turned on the light. Someone opened a drawer.

If it isn't a burglar, I thought, then it has to be him.

And he's walking upright.

The dog is walking on its hind legs.

The wall seemed to be made of cardboard. I could hear someone breathing hoarsely and heavily, just like Dad.

Then there was another clicking sound, as if someone had switched off the light, left the room, closed the door, locked it and shuffled away along the landing.

Carefully and stealthily, I got up.

Someone had left the key in the lock.

I didn't get a wink of sleep that night, either.

I have packed my things and in a few hours' time I shall be leaving, so this letter, you see, Mum, will get to you quicker in my own inside pocket than it would if I put it in the post.

I've thought about a lot of things in the night.

There are one or two things I'd like to ask you about.

This, for instance: why did she say she'd got Dad from a lady who didn't want him any more?

That can wait, anyhow. I'll soon be seeing you.

The room alongside mine was a museum. There were photographs on the walls, drawings and letters which had been written on small pieces of paper, all framed; a lock of hair in a box on the writing desk, a toy car, an old school exercise book and some tattered children's books.

All the photographs were of me. They were my drawings, my lock of hair—everything was mine.

I was standing, in person, in a mausoleum dedicated to myself.

There was a small bed by the wall. My dark blue winter coat with its fur collar was on the bed, as if someone had just recently put it there.

It was much smaller than I remembered.

There was an air ticket on the table in the lounge. Dad was lying on the sofa in the same position he'd been in when I'd first gone into the room.

I made one last attempt. I got down on all fours in front of him.

"Look, Dad, I've turned into a dog too!"

He didn't move. He looked at me and was silent.

I got up and put the ticket in my pocket.

He began to blink. He uttered a pitiful whine, as if sobbing. Then he was quiet.

And there wasn't much more to say.

Melaine looked tired.

"I'm sorry it turned out like this," I said.

She didn't answer.

"You've got to take him to a doctor," I continued.

"He's seeing a doctor," she said abruptly.

I opened the rear door of the car, in order to bundle in my suitcase.

"Turning into a dog is just madness," I said.

"Don't say that," she retorted. "That way he managed to see you before he . . ."

She broke off into silence.

The suitcase suddenly felt so heavy, I had to put it down on the pavement.

"Why didn't you tell me about this?"

She looked unhappy. "He forbade me to," she said.

I sat on my suitcase and looked up at the house, and there he was, upright at the window. He waved. He pressed his face against the windowpane, his lips moving as if he were speaking.

Mum dear, this long letter I've been writing during my stay will now have a completely different ending from the one I'd imagined. I'm afraid the post is going to have to take charge of delivery in spite of everything.

I must ask you to ring Hanken and say . . . well, say what you like.

I don't know when I'm coming home. Dad and Melaine say I can live with them as long as I like.

Just say that certain things tend to happen which seem

to throw one's life into turmoil, as it were, like one's dad becoming a dog, for instance.

They're not going to understand a blind bit of it.

Don't ask me for explanations. I don't have any.

Your son.

TRANSLATED BY SARAH POLLARD

WEEKEND IN REYKJAVÍK

KRISTÍN ÓMARSDÓTTIR

B Y THE POND IN REYKJAVÍK stands the National Gallery of Iceland, right next to the Independent Church, which my grandmother built, discreetly tucked away, in a building that once burnt down, the same building where hippies created a civilization once upon a time. On the pond swim hundred-year-old swans; the ducks are younger, and above them web-footed seagulls fly and steal bread from the others. Around the pond rise: a preschool; the town hall; a former theatre; the Downtown School, which was an elementary school that became a high school, but I don't know what the building is used for now; the Girls' School that boys now get to attend; and the house of the man who is considered to be the first magnate of Iceland.

At the National Gallery, they are exhibiting the work of a foreign artist who has lived in Iceland and is a representative of conceptual art. In the small attic, the Gallery exhibits its treasure—*son trésor*—works by artists born in Iceland forty to seventy years ago or thereabouts. In the basement, female artists in their forties exhibit videos of parties they held in a cramped room of an international artists' building in Paris. There the guests played famous and fallen philosophers, movie stars, human rights' apostles and writers. The female artists played animals with movie cameras attached to their heads.

The woman at the reception asks me to take my coat off when I've looked at the exhibitions—12.03 p.m. on a Saturday in the autumn—and show her the sweater I'm wearing. I throw the coat onto the floor, stand tall and show the woman my front and back. She asks whether I sewed the design onto the sweater afterwards, or knitted it in as I went. My sweater displays a picture of an anchor: *here is where I live.* She tells me about her difficulty in knitting a sweater with a picture of a jeep. She shows me her knitting. I'm the knitting woman's escort, I confess, she uses this type of knitting needles too, like you—they're the best needles you can get in Reykjavík, but I don't know anything about the pattern. The woman smiles and looks at my sweater for a few minutes, before opening the door and letting me out into the autumnal air. I walk up the slope, the same slope my mother walked up daily when she was little, but there were throngs of people on the slope back then, my mother told me, whereas now everyone goes by car, and the people appear in the graffiti on the house walls where the embassies' flags fly.

*

The woman who won me at a tombola at my neighbourhood sports club—I waited a whole day, but it was worth the wait, she braided flowers into my hair—opens the door for me, and looks at the clock, then into my eyes. My eyes could be clock dials, the clock dial on the woman's wrist my other eye.

She says: punctual as always.

I say: an escort has to be punctual.

And I storm in, bump into her and whisper in her ear: I drew a flower for you that died.

Then I drew a new flower and it didn't die.

She laughs—this is the Saturday laughter. I laugh a
Saturday laughter too. Her mother steps out of the wall
clock, laughing, and hugs me like a lost son. I am a lost son,
I was a lost son, and I continue being the lost one. Nobody
finds me. An escort and a lost son. The mother of the woman
who bought me at the tombola says goodbye and runs out
with a stocking over her face.

*

Hm.

*

It's good to be an escort and rest in the embrace of a sugary
beetle that plucks the clips from my hair.

*

We take refuge under the living-room table.

I say: I expect the attack will begin at 1.30 p.m.

The woman I accompany says: hardly on a Saturday.

I agree that this would be strange timing. Saturday is not
that kind of day, she adds.

While we wait—for Sunday's or Monday's attack?—we
drink tea from her mother's thermos, have a nap, read the future
Sunday paper, nap, carve little men to sell at the peace bazaar,
nap, carve men for the peace bazaar, talk in whispers, something about the dignity of the teaching profession in Iceland
and my humiliation as an escort. Her mother sends us food that
we accept by tearing a hole in the thin curtain that hides the
other dimension. The woman whom I faithfully accompany
opens the jars with a strong hand. I hold onto the jars with a
weak hand. We eat from the jars. There is also little chance

105

of earthquakes at weekends, I say in a strong, bold voice, such is the effect of food on the voice. Then we have a nap for our digestion. In the evening, we crawl out from the hiding place and sneak out, despite the curfew, and meet very few cats outside—they meow. But the people do their time sitting inside, do their time sitting inside, do their time sitting inside and eating out of jars. The stars don't penetrate the smoke over the city: it doesn't smell of powder though, not yet; and the Northern Lights dancers haven't yet snapped their skates to their ankles.

*

In an unmarked art gallery a four-person group, myself among them and the woman I accompany, eavesdrop on the most cramped lavatory in the city of Reykjavík: two young men lay eggs that contain night-protein, or Tindersticks, as some call it; the hens speak a foreign language. We who sit on this side of the partition don't know the language. They wash their hands and laugh—that's an international language—squeeze out of the bathroom and say goodbye to us with joy and gratitude for free use of a toilet, and leave. We go into the bathroom and examine it all over. The seat is up, what does that mean? The fairy-tale princess drags us out with a fairy-tale rope: the story is about a rich man who lived in a villa and decided to eat her; to gobble the fairy-tale princess up, he'd boiled water in a person-size pot, taken her in his arms to throw her into the pot when an old woman came running in with a flyswatter and saved our fairy-tale princess.

I once drew that flyswatter, I say, in a drawing that I gave my cousin who died.

We hang our heads, think about death and the Statue of Liberty for a minute.

*

We step into the yellow, pink and silver woods. Some kids had sprayed the woods, put glitter on the bark and shimmer on the leaves; it gladdens eyes that pretend to be clock dials every half hour: tick-tock, tick-tock. The ground is feathery soft. Soft as moss. We sense, feel, the movement of the Earth around itself. I say something. You say something. But we don't talk about the conditions and dignity of preschool teachers, but about something else, and it's forgotten as soon as the words forsake us. Your dress has taken on another colour, and my clothes glisten like fish-skin, a moment before I turn into one, and swim through the woods in search of you.

*

Yes, now I remember what you said because fish remember everything:

You told me about a patient, a girl who sang in a two-person room on the hospital floor where they send people with gastro and infectious diseases. The girl woke up in the morning singing and fell asleep at night singing. But she also napped several times a day so she didn't sing non-stop all day. She sang for the woman who fed her, and used the rests to swallow the gruel. Patients wanted to die in bed beside her, but were not granted their wish. It's not possible to arrange death in advance, you said, before I turned into the fish who seeks its mermaid, the one who will hold onto the fish in her arms a while before eating him. I want you to eat me, says the fish to the mermaid. I want you to eat me.

*

Speaking of hospitals, it says in the loudspeaker system of the shimmering woods, and isn't that the fairy-tale princess's gravelly radio voice? Yes, I just think it is, her voice branches out between the trees:

At the end of the working day, people head down to the hospital grounds with their children. The patients come out into the lobby escorted by orderlies, say hello to people, say hello to their fans and go for an energetic walk around the garden, on crutches, in a wheelchair, unsupported, with a drip on a stand, some with new nappies, and give the children who come up with their parents money for lollipops and chocolate sultanas; good to make it easier for the families. The fathers nod their heads and mumble: thank you. The mothers smile nicely. The patients bow: my pleasure, it's more blessed to give than to receive, this is a sweet kid you've raised, this is a sweet piggy bank whose hair you've done so prettily and put ribbons in, thanks, thanks, it's our pleasure, it's more blessed to give than to receive.

The dry nappies rustle like dried-up leaves this autumn when nappies thus dropped dramatically in price. The show manager announced that despite the show running at a loss, nappies would be on sale. That alleviated the seriousness of the show considerably, to season it with delicate wit: cheap nappies. This trifle of joint funds shouldn't harm anyone. The joke may be at the expense of those who will never stop wearing nappies. This counsel will also encourage people to have children, so that the future actors-to-be will continue to be born in the country, said the show manager and then bowed.

Says the fairy-tale princess in the loudspeaker system of the shimmering woods and laughs beautifully. That's what princesses who adventures follow do. Her laughter follows us on the way home: two women who the stray cats shield, with elongated shadows and elongated caterwauling, so the guards don't notice our journey under the quivering street lights.

*

I follow my friend and crawl again under the living-room table. I don't find my nightdress: it's made of letters and my eyes are without numbers. We dress ourselves in the bags. 23.32. It's safer to wait here than elsewhere. Under the table there is shelter from the fireworks. May I have a piece of paper, I ask; she hands me a piece of paper. May I have a pen, I ask; she hands me a pen. What is the escort going to write, asks the voice on the radio that rests on top of the table. I: a letter to parents-to-be who can't afford IVF treatment.

With these instructions I will potter about until Monday morning, when the curfew ends:

Instructions for parents-to-be
who can't afford
IVF treatment.

A)

Pay close attention every day to keeping your belly, bottom, hips and genital area warm. Don't show too much skin during the winter months. At issue is the area from the navel down to the loins, front and back. This applies both to the girl and the boy.

Importance of this element: 5*

B)

Beware of cold floors.
   Importance of this element: 5*

C)

Before the couple starts making love, the boy can massage the girl, her hips, lower back, bottom, belly and groin. Then he can massage his own groin. Then the love-making may begin.
   Importance of this element: 3*

D)

Before the couple starts making love, it's good to dance barefoot, even though the floor is cold—in the living room—to three or four lively songs and cheek-to-cheek songs, and laugh a little.
   Importance of this element: 3*

E)

Go into a cowshed, sit for half an hour in the warm or tepid grass, and breathe in deeply the smell of sheep and cows.
   Importance of this element: ?

F)

Don't let your hands get cold throughout the day.
   Importance of this element: 3*

G)

Decorate each other's hair and head with flowers.
    Importance of this element: ?
    Have fun.

*

Life doesn't end. I was a building that stood by the pond in Reykjavík: one day I stood up, walked away and left behind a grave in the landscape. I was an escort whose services people bought at the sports clubs' tombolas; one day I fell off the shelf. I was a frightened animal that lived under a table. One day the table walked out of the living room and out of the house, down the street, nobody knows where to. I was the rain that fell down the roof and washed your windows, washed your eyes, washed the windows, washed the eyes. I was the decoration in your hair and you decorated my hair with flowers. Now the farmer shears my hair, the flowers fall down last and land on top of the pile of wool. Perhaps you'll knit a sweater from me.

I was a lost son who was found, and got lost again. I was the nail polish on your fingers: the knife of night will scrape that off.

*

A theatre critic on the radio that rests on top of the table says: the director didn't manage to communicate the sorrow and oppression to the audience.

I ask the table leg: do you know the couple sorrow and oppression? Do they suit each other? Will the relationship last? Will they conceive a child? What is the child of sorrow and oppression called?

111

The table leg: the one who oppresses has the sorrow, the oppressed have the hunger.

I feed the table leg leftovers from the jars.

*

Finally: this is not a theatre, this is a *former* theatre, and the show is a danger to me. The poet who sleeps under the vertical shafts of sunlight on a bench in another country far from here says with dignity dressed in black: I am never afraid.

*

Two female artists inside an apartment where the floor is made from the blocks of chocolate that are only available in the most liberal of countries—the escort women's delivery service sent me here—tie me to a chair, blindfold me and gag me. They carry the chair between them down the highfalutin stairs and into the frosty night.

Is this a throne of woven arms?

Am I part of a performance?

Judging by the Sunday chimes of the Independent Church, they are travelling with me south along Brook Street, in the direction of the pond—I also know the direction because I know the Brook Street wind, the temperature and the toxic, biting mildness. The women set up my throne out on the ice. I listen to the women skate around me on the ice; on the frozen pond, the swans warble, I also hear:

The children squealing at the preschool, yelling, shouting. I hear the theatre ghosts writhe and complain about the constriction and hip pain. I hear the hippies dance in their burning Funville. The magnate milks a cow, a din in the udders, inside his gazebo behind the National Gallery, where the woman in the lobby knits a jeep onto a sweater that is too small and tight. The milk spurts into a can. The ghosts writhe in old and new roles. Hamlet runs away from Ophelia, her face rime-white. Nuns sweep the floors at the Downtown School. I have to go over there and look for the green crown I once lost. Where is the fancy chocolate from the floor in that house? And the breadcrumbs for the swans and ducks?

TRANSLATED BY JANE APPLETON

THE DOGS OF THESSALONIKI

KJELL ASKILDSEN

W E DRANK MORNING COFFEE in the garden. We hardly
spoke. Beate got up and put the cups on the tray. We
should probably take the chairs up onto the veranda, she
said. Why? I said. It looks like rain, she said. Rain? I said,
there's not a cloud in the sky. There's a nip in the air, she
said, don't you think? No, I said. Maybe I'm mistaken, she
said. She walked up the steps onto the veranda and into the
living room. I sat there for another quarter of an hour, and
then carried one of the chairs up to the veranda. I stood a
while looking at the woods on the other side of the fence,
but there was nothing to see. I could hear the sound of Beate
humming coming from the open door. She must have heard
the weather forecast of course, I thought. I went back down
into the garden and walked round to the front of the house,
over to the mailbox beside the black wrought-iron gate. It was
empty. I closed the gate, which for some reason or another
had been open; then I noticed someone had thrown up just
outside it. I became annoyed. I attached the garden hose to
the tap by the cellar door and turned the water on full, and
then dragged the hose after me over to the gate. The jet of
water hit at slightly the wrong angle, and some of the vomit
spattered into the garden, the rest spread out over the tarmac.

There were no drains nearby, so all I succeeded in doing was moving the yellowish substance four or five metres away from the gate. But even so, it was a relief to get a bit of distance from the filthy mess.

When I'd turned off the tap and coiled up the hose, I didn't know what to do. I went up to the veranda and sat down. After a few minutes I heard Beate begin to hum again; it sounded as though she was thinking about something she liked thinking about, she probably thought I couldn't hear her. I coughed, and it went quiet. She came out and said: I didn't know you were sitting here. She had put on make-up. Are you going somewhere? I said. No, she said. I turned my face towards the garden and said: Some idiot's thrown up just outside the gate. Oh? she said. A proper mess, I said. She didn't reply. I stood up. Do you have a cigarette? she asked. I gave her one and a light. Thanks, she said. I walked down from the veranda and sat at the garden table. Beate stood on the veranda, smoking. She threw the half-finished cigarette down onto the gravel at the bottom of the steps. What's the point of that? I said. It'll burn up, she said. She went into the living room. I stared at the thin band of smoke rising almost straight up from the cigarette: I didn't want it to burn up. After a little while I stood up, I felt unsettled. I walked down to the gate in the wooden fence, crossed the narrow patch of meadow and went into the woods. I stopped just inside the edge of the woods and sat down on a stump, almost concealed behind some scrub. Beate came out onto the veranda. She looked towards where I was sitting and called my name. She can't see me, I thought. She walked down into the garden and around the house. She walked back up onto the veranda again. Once again she looked towards where I was sitting.

She couldn't possibly see me, I thought. She turned and went into the living room.

When we were sitting at the dinner table, Beate said: There he is again. Who? I said. The man, she said, at the edge of the woods, just by the big . . . no, now he's gone again. I got up and went over to the window. Where? I said. By the big pine tree, she said. Are you sure it's the same man? I said. I think so, she said. There's nobody there now, I said. No, he's gone, she said. I went back to the table. I said: Surely you couldn't possibly make out if it was the same man from that distance. Beate didn't reply right away, then she said: I would have recognized you. That's different, I said. You know me. We ate in silence for a while. Then she said: By the way, why didn't you answer me when I called you? Called me? I said. I saw you, she said. Then why did you walk all the way around the house? I said. So you wouldn't realize I'd seen you, she said. I didn't think you had seen me, I said. Why didn't you answer? she said. It wasn't really necessary to answer when I didn't think you'd seen me, I said. After all, I could have been somewhere else entirely. If you hadn't seen me, and if you hadn't pretended as if you hadn't seen me, then this wouldn't have been a problem. Dear, she said, it really isn't a problem.

We didn't say anything else for a while. Beate kept turning her head and looking out of the window. I said: It didn't rain. No, she said, it's holding off. I put down my knife and fork, leaned back in the chair and said: You know, sometimes you annoy me. Oh, she said. You can never admit that you're wrong, I said. But of course I can, she said. I'm often wrong. Everybody is. Absolutely everybody. I just looked at her, and I could see that she knew she'd gone too far. She stood up. She took hold of the gravy boat and the empty vegetable dish and went into the kitchen. She didn't come back in. I stood up too. I put on my jacket, then stood for a while, listening, but it was completely quiet. I went out into the garden, round to the front of the house and out onto the road. I walked east, away from town. I was annoyed. The villa gardens on both sides of the road lay empty, and I didn't hear any sounds other than the steady drone from the motorway. I left the houses behind me and walked out onto the large level stretch of ground running right the way to the fjord.

I got to the fjord close to a little outdoor café and I sat down at a table right by the water. I bought a glass of beer and lit a cigarette. I was hot, but didn't remove my jacket as I presumed I had patches of sweat under the arms of my shirt. I was sitting with all the customers in the café behind me; I had the fjord and the distant wooded hillsides in front of me. The murmur of hushed conversation and the gentle gurgle of the water between the rocks by the shore put me in a drowsy, absent-minded state. My thoughts pursued seemingly illogical courses, which were not unpleasant; on the contrary, I had an extraordinary feeling of well-being, which made it all the more incomprehensible that, without any noticeable transition, I became gripped by a feeling of anxious abandonment. There was something complete about both the angst and the sense of being abandoned that, in a way, suspended time, but it probably didn't take more than a few seconds before my senses steered me back to the there and then.

I walked home the same way I had come, across the stretch of flat ground. The sun was nearing the mountains in the west; a haze lingered over the town, and there wasn't the slightest nip in the air. I noticed I was reluctant to go home, and suddenly I thought, and it was a distinct thought: If only she were dead.

But I continued on home. I walked through the gate and around the side of the house. Beate was sitting at the garden table; her older brother was sitting opposite her. I went over to them; I felt completely relaxed. We exchanged a few insignificant words. Beate didn't ask where I had been, and neither of them encouraged me to join them, something that, with a plausible excuse, I would have declined anyway.

I went up to the bedroom, hung up my jacket and took off my shirt. Beate's side of the double bed wasn't made. There was an ashtray on the nightstand with two butts in it, and beside the ashtray lay an open book, face down. I closed the book; I brought the ashtray into the bathroom and flushed the butts down the toilet. Then I undressed and turned on the shower, but the water was only lukewarm, almost cold, and my shower turned out to be quite different from and a good deal shorter than what I'd imagined.

While I stood by the open bedroom window getting dressed, I heard Beate laugh. I quickly finished and went down into the laundry room in the basement; I could observe her through the window there without being seen. She was sitting back in the chair, with her dress hiked far up on her parted thighs and her hands clasped behind her neck, making the thin material of the dress tight across her breasts. There was something indecent about the posture that excited me, and my excitement was only heightened by the fact she was sitting like that in full view of a man, albeit her brother.

I stood looking at her for a while; she wasn't sitting more than seven or eight metres away from me, but because of the perennials in the flower bed right outside the basement window,

I was sure that she wouldn't notice me. I tried to make out what they were saying, but they spoke in low tones, conspicuously low tones, I thought. Then she stood up, as did her brother, and I hurried up the basement stairs and into the kitchen. I turned on the cold water tap and fetched a glass, but she didn't come in, so I turned off the tap and put the glass back.

When I'd calmed down, I went into the living room and sat down to leaf through an engineering periodical. The sun had gone down, but it wasn't necessary to turn the lights on yet. I leafed back and forth through the pages. The veranda door was open. I lit a cigarette. I heard the distant sound of an aeroplane, otherwise it was completely quiet. I grew restless again, and I got to my feet and went out into the garden. There was nobody there. The gate in the wooden fence was ajar. I walked over and closed it. I thought: She's probably looking at me from behind the scrub. I walked back to the garden table, moved one of the chairs slightly so that the back of it faced the woods, and sat down. I convinced myself that I wouldn't have noticed it if there had been someone standing in the laundry room, looking at me. I smoked two cigarettes. It was beginning to get dark, but the air was still and mild, almost warm. A pale crescent moon lay over the hill to the east, and the time was a little after ten o'clock. I smoked another cigarette. Then I heard a faint creak from the gate, but I didn't turn around. She sat down and placed a little bouquet of wild flowers on the garden table. What a lovely evening, she said. Yes, I said. Do you have a cigarette? she asked. I gave her one and a light. Then, in that eager, childlike voice I've always found hard to resist, she said: I'll fetch a bottle of wine, shall I?—and before I'd decided what answer to give, she stood up, took hold of the bouquet and hurried across the lawn and up the steps of the veranda. I thought: Now she's going to act as if nothing has happened. Then I thought: Then again, nothing has happened. Nothing she knows about. And when she came with the wine, two glasses and even a blue check tablecloth, I was almost completely calm. She had switched the light on above the veranda door, and I turned my chair so I was sitting facing the woods. Beate filled the glasses, and we drank. Mmm, she said, lovely. The woods lay like a black silhouette against the pale blue sky. It's so quiet, she said. Yes, I said. I held out the cigarette pack to her, but she didn't want one. I took one myself. Look at the new moon, she said. Yes, I said. It's so thin, she said. I sipped my wine. In the Mediterranean it's on its side, she said. I didn't reply. Do you remember the dogs in Thessaloniki that got stuck together after they'd mated, she said. In Kavala, I said. All the old men outside the café shouting and screaming, she said, and the dogs howling and struggling to get free from one another. And when we got out of the town, there was a thin new moon like that on its side, and we wanted each other, do you remember? Yes, I said. Beate poured more wine into the glasses. Then we sat in silence, for a while, for quite a while. Her words had made me uneasy, and the subsequent silence only heightened my unease. I searched for something to say, something diversionary and everyday. Beate got to her feet. She came around the garden table and stopped behind me. I grew afraid, I thought: Now she's going to do something to me. And when I felt her hands on my neck, I gave a start, and jumped forward in the chair. At almost the very same moment I realized what I had done and without turning around, I said: You scared me. She didn't answer. I leaned back in the chair. I could hear her breathing. Then she left.

Finally I stood up to go inside. It had grown completely dark. I had drunk up the wine and thought up what I was going to say—it had taken some time. I brought the glasses and the empty bottle but, after having thought about it, left the blue check tablecloth where it was. The living room was empty. I went into the kitchen and placed the bottle and the glasses beside the sink. It was a little past eleven o'clock. I locked the veranda door and switched off the lights, and then I walked upstairs to the bedroom. The bedside light was on. Beate was lying with her face turned away and was asleep, or pretending to be. My duvet was pulled back, and on the sheet lay the cane I'd used after my accident the year we'd got married. I picked it up and was about to put it under the bed, but then changed my mind. I stood with it in my hand while staring at the curve of her hips under the thin summer duvet and was almost overcome by sudden desire. Then I hurried out and went down to the living room. I had brought the walking stick with me, and without quite knowing why, I brought it down hard across my thigh, and broke it in two. My leg smarted from the blow, and I calmed down. I went into the study and switched on the light above the drawing board. Then I turned it off and lay down on the couch, pulled the blanket over me and closed my eyes. I could picture Beate clearly. I opened my eyes, but I could still see her.

I woke a few times during the night, and I got up early. I went into the living room to remove the cane; I didn't want Beate to see that I'd broken it. She was sitting on the sofa. She looked at me. Good morning, she said. I nodded. She continued to look at me. Have we fallen out? she said. No, I said. She kept her gaze fixed on me, but I couldn't manage to read it. I sat down to get away from it. You misunderstood,

I said, I didn't notice you getting up, I was lost in my own thoughts, and when I suddenly felt your hands on my neck, I mean I see how it could make you . . . but I didn't know you were standing there. She didn't say anything. I looked at her, met the same inscrutable gaze. You have to believe me, I said. She looked away. Yes, she said, I do, don't I.

TRANSLATED BY SEÁN KINSELLA

ICE

(extract from the novel)

ULLA-LENA LUNDBERG

S HE CAME TO FINLAND on foot across the ice, through
the forests, tied to the underside of a freight car, in a sub-
marine that surfaced for one short moment by the outermost
skerries where a smuggler's speedboat waited. She jumped
into the Carelian forests by parachute. She changed clothes
with a Finnish military attaché and rode to Finland first-class
on his diplomatic passport. Once over the border, cars with
dimmed headlamps waited on secret forest tracks. Signals
were flashed. Finally—Papa! General Gyllen, without whom
there would have been no hope.

Well and good. The more versions the better. How it
actually happened, no one will ever be told. Except for Papa,
the names of the people intentionally or unintentionally
involved will never be revealed. The fact itself is momentous
enough—in 1939, Irina Gyllen was the only known case of a
former Finnish citizen managing to flee to Finland from the
Soviet Union. If any other human being is ever going to do
it again, it is of the utmost importance that no one ever finds
out how it all took place.

Irina Gyllen sleeps alone. If she has to spend a night
among other people on a boat, she doesn't sleep. When she
goes to bed, she takes a pill. Which makes her hard to wake
up when she has to deliver a baby. The Örlanders know

this, it is one of her peculiarities, along with the fact that her medical licence is Russian, so she cannot practise in Finland until she has taken the necessary Finnish examinations. In the Soviet Union, she was a gynaecologist. In Finland, she took a course in midwifery and has now taken this job on the Örland Islands while she studies for her Finnish medical certification.

The Örlands are safe. Mama and Papa have spent their vacations there and know that the locals have boats that can get to Sweden in any weather. They also know that no stranger can slink in unseen. Persons that Irina Gyllen has reason to fear never come ashore without the islanders reporting on their every movement. For much of the year no one comes at all.

It is quiet. You can hear your own heart, your breathing, your digestion. All in good condition, though she's already into her second life. She lost a lot on the other side; she hardly looks like a woman any more. Tall and angular without any visible softness. A sharply sculptured face, feet that have walked and walked, hands that have worked and worked.

Her body has smoothed over the fact that she has given birth, but people on the Örlands know that Irina Gyllen has left a child behind. A son.

When she wakes up, she takes a pill. Her hand is then steady, her mind adequately dulled, her memory manageable. It is then she works, writes and keeps her records. She lives in the Hindrikses' little cottage while the community builds a Health Care Centre with the help of a Swedish donation. The people are good—friendly and considerate—but they make no attempt to treat her as one of them. They call her doctor, although she assures them she is not one, and they do not gossip about her in the village. It is only much later that she realizes the reason they don't is that their silence implies that they know things which can't be told.

The Hindrikses are good people—happy, talkative, lively. Being always greeted with friendly smiles, always getting an analysis of the weather before she goes out, being praised for having the sense to dress warmly, eating her meals with the family and not forgetting to thank them for the food—all of it helps to keep other things at a distance. There is nothing to see on the surface. Or is her closed expression striking evidence of unnatural self-control?

Of what, exactly? Of the terrible desire to live that forces people to sacrifice everything. As a doctor, you have no illusions. Early on, you notice the hope in dying patients, see how they take note of the slightest sign of improvement, refuse to admit that it's only a matter of days. The will to live is stronger than any pain or affliction—even medical students make that sober observation. It adjusts to any reality if it means that life can be augmented by one small measure. Just a few more moments, during which salvation may appear.

In theory, Irina Gyllen had understood the situation precisely. In practice, the feeling ambushed her and knocked her senseless. All she could think about was saving her own life. They took her husband first. For the boy's sake, she did what they had agreed on. Repudiated him, filed for divorce. Continued to work, because the regime always needs doctors; doctors are not something they could afford to discard. Except he was a doctor too. Yes, but surrounded by informers and jealous men. As if she wasn't. Born in Russia, father a Finnish general.

Working isn't enough. Even the best disappear. There is no way out except Finland. Even that exit is closed because she has given up her citizenship. But Papa has connections, contacts, and she can still be in contact with Papa through the Finnish legation. Which in recent years she has not dared to visit. But there are employees whom, with her heart in her throat, she can run into on the street.

Papa Gyllen is also a former officer in the Imperial Russian army. The reason she will be arrested, that she should already have been taken, even before her husband. Will he be pressed to inform on her? Just a matter of time. No.

You live out your final days, you prolong them—if you can hold out, one more day, a week, then something may save you. You think only about saving yourself, everyone else can be sacrificed. It's why people become informers. The only reason Irina Gyllen doesn't become an informer is that she doesn't want to draw attention to herself.

In order to save yourself, you can also abandon a child. You don't even take him to your husband's parents and entrust him to their care. You just run over to the neighbours, whom you hardly know, and ask if he might stay with them for an hour while you run to the hospital. In his pocket, he has a slip of paper, fastened with a safety pin, with the address of his paternal grandparents. It's like pushing him out onto the Nile in a basket of reeds. Maybe he'll be sent to his grandparents, themselves deeply compromised, perhaps about to be arrested. Maybe he'll be put in an orphanage where his identity will be erased. Maybe they can be reunited quite soon. Through the Red Cross, now that the war is over.

He was eight, understood a great deal. Had stopped asking about Papa, knew that was best. Don't think about what he's going through now. Above all, don't think about what he's thinking and feeling. Think instead about how adaptable children are, how they manage to adjust to every new situation. Remember how they're able to find pleasure even in small, irrelevant things. Don't forget for a moment that they can so easily grow attached to new people, that they forget. Don't forget that they forget.

Don't think about the fact that seven years have passed, half his life. That he is now a difficult teenager, nearly an adult. All further contact impossible, grandparents unreachable, evacuated during the war, gone. Broken diplomatic relations during the war made all efforts impossible. But now that there's peace, there's hope. The Red Cross, new personnel at the legation, sooner than you might think.

Yes. But Papa Gyllen is old, retired, so too are his contacts. The new people look at them with suspicion. You have to hurry slowly, arm yourself with patience. If the boy made it through the war, he'll make it now, in peacetime. Become an independent person. Do what he likes. May not want to have anything to do with her. Entirely understandable. But there must be some way to find out where he is.

But what if he is not? A helpless child dying alone in an epidemic hospital, frozen, starving, not even thinking "Mama". Then she takes a pill. It's quiet on the island, everyone is friendly, the women giving birth are brave and capable, she likes her work. It was a piece of luck that someone told her about this job. Nice that Mama and Papa, who've grown so old during the war, like it so much out here and rent a place every summer. Everything has worked out much better than she might have feared.

She saved her own skin. An odd expression. It makes her think of skin and bones, which is all she is—tall and gaunt and stiff. Her skin and her bones are the crutches that keep

127

her going, and it's going well, it's all going very well. The main thing is that you have something to keep you busy. Of course, she gets called out as a doctor sometimes, though she's always careful to point out that she has no medical licence and no right to treat patients or make decisions that should only be taken by a licensed physician. Yes, yes, they say, we know, but, Doctor, if you would just please come, it's impossible to get to the hospital in Åbo. Well, all right, she supposes she can come and have a look, maybe give some advice, a bit of help, as long as it's understood that it's unofficial, the way old women through the ages have helped those who sought them out.

That's an argument they understand. Yes! That's the way it's always been. The previous midwife, who'd never been to medical school, was a thousand times better than the nearest doctor! Suddenly she's swamped with effusive stories about the previous midwife's miraculous cures. And she herself? She does indeed answer their calls, and soon the stories about her own deeds begin to make the rounds. They are seldom difficult things—cuts and wounds that need stitches, broken bones that need to be set and splinted, simple remedies for pneumonia and catarrh, medicines for pain. She sends thrombosis to the mainland, and when she finds cancer, she persuades them to take the boat to Åbo. They have an operation, come home and eventually die. Good practical experience for Irina Gyllen, who plans to be a general practitioner. She gets daily practice in diagnostics, and the stories they tell in the villages confirm that she is always right.

She treats a relatively rugged population, sheltered from epidemics by the islands' winter isolation, surprisingly well nourished during the war years thanks to their healthy diet

of Baltic herring, their mental state robust. When she sometimes commends them for eating sensibly and not coddling
themselves, they are as pleased as punch.

But they cannot understand why she has such a strong
Russian accent and often has trouble finding the right Swedish
words, although General Gyllen speaks fluent Finland Swedish
and even her Russian-born mother manages well enough. Why
does Russian cling to her speech although she wants to forget
it? Why can't she find her way back to the language that was
her father's native tongue? Why does she have such a frightful
accent, even though she spoke Swedish as a child? Why do
the Russian words come more quickly than the Swedish ones,
even though she lives in a completely Swedish environment?
As soon as she opens her mouth, Russian jumps to her lips
and renders her monosyllabic and abrupt.

Of course, people speculate. For example, that maybe she's
not Irina Gyllen at all but a completely different Russian, a
famous spy smuggled into the country perhaps, or a defector,
a female scientist that Russian agents are looking for, a person
whose head is full of Russian state secrets! Someone who's
taken Irina Gyllen's identity, with General Gyllen and his wife
standing surety. Because does she really resemble them? No,
not a bit. Papa Gyllen is a head shorter and stout, Mother
Gyllen is taller and thinner, but not like her in any other way.
There is definitely *something* fishy, because "Irina Gyllen" speaks
Swedish like a Russian.

Undeniably. But whoever she is, she has a good name
on the islands, and whoever she is, the Bolsheviks have been
outsmarted and taken it in the chops. Which is excellent and
makes people proud and protective. Not that she can't take
care of herself, if it comes to that.

Yes, she can and does take care of herself, and she works hard at being normal, although it doesn't come naturally. Out here you're supposed to be full of fun and jokes, and that's the hardest part for her. The loss of her sense of humour is perhaps the most striking evidence of everything she has left behind. Large parts of her are missing as she moves among the people and tries to generate interest in the local chatter, at the moment all about the newly arrived pastor and his wife. Eyewitnesses have seen him at the Co-op and shaken hands, and the coastguard has seen her on Church Isle—a woman with get-up-and-go. They also mention that there is a one-year-old among the household goods and give her a meaningful look, warning her in good time that she may have another expectant mother to attend to. Now every last one of them will be going to church on Sunday to hear him and have a look at her. There will be several boats going from the village, and Dr Gyllen is heartily welcome to ride along!

A difficult point, this. She who's been saved from the god-less Soviet Union is supposed to throw herself into the arms of the Church. Of course, she's thankful to be in a country with freedom of religion. And if she really was a stranger who'd taken on Irina Gyllen's identity, she would be a devout member of the congregation. But Irina Gyllen doesn't believe in God. On the contrary, she sees what has happened to Russia as proof that a benign Divine power does not exist. Truth to tell, the very young Irina Gyllen was a freethinker even before the Revolution, and what has happened since has not given her any reason to reconsider her views.

Religion is an opium of the people. The Örlanders go to church. Irina Gyllen takes a pill. Opium is what all of us need. So in essence, perhaps, she's a friend of the church.

130

Here, where she lives very visibly among the people, she will stand out less if she occasionally goes to church on the major holidays or, like now, when the new priest is going to be closely examined right down to his buttonholes. She's going to have a lot to do with him, for the pastor is usually the chairman of the Public Health Association. And the priest's little daughter will be coming to have her regular check-ups with her mother. So why not, yes, of course, she'll go. There will be a lot of people, and she likes that better than when the pews are nearly empty and everyone looks around at her to see if she sings along and reads the general confession and how she reacts to passages that they imagine will be painful to her.

"Yes, thank you," she says. "I think if you have room in the boat, I'll come."

Her Russian accent thickens whenever she's conflicted. That doesn't escape them, but they look at her sunnily and say there's always room for the doctor, and she's heartily welcome to ride along.

TRANSLATED BY THOMAS TEAL

"DON'T KILL ME, I BEG YOU. THIS IS MY TREE"

HASSAN BLASIM

H E WOKE UP AND, before the last vestiges of the night-mare faded, made up his mind. He'd take him out to the forest and finish the matter off. Fifteen years ago, before he'd shot him, he'd heard him say, "Don't kill me, I beg you. This is my tree." Those words had stayed with him all that time and would maybe stay with him forever.

Karima made breakfast for him. She had a black scarf on her head and eyes as still as a tree by night in spring. Absent-mindedly, the Tiger slowly drank water from his glass. He took his time setting the glass down on the table and then stared at it.

"Now the water's inside me," he said, "and you're empty, you fucking empty glass!"

The Tiger spoke to everything around him in this way, as if he were acting in a play. These conversations took place inter-nally. No one else heard them—or else the Tiger couldn't have kept his job as a bus driver, his source of income and the way he helped himself forget. The Tiger would often glare at the television screen and, regardless of what was on, give it a piece of his mind: "You whore, selling and buying your mother's arse!"

Karima would go and sit in the living room with her fingers on the buttons of the remote control, switching channels as if she were playing a nonsensical tune on it. She settled on an Iraqi station: an announcer in garish make-up smiled as she introduced a traditional Iraqi song about maternal devotion. Karima shed a tear at the first *Ah* from the well-known rustic singer. The Tiger walked past and, without turning towards her, went into his room. He opened the wardrobe and put on his bus-driver's uniform. From the shelf he pulled out a pistol wrapped in a piece of cloth and tucked it under his belt. He left without even saying goodbye to Karima, his wife and companion of twenty-four years. Many years ago he had given up looking into those eyes, which had enchanted him and wrenched his soul in his youth. In those days, the Tiger's claws dripped with blood from the brutal water wars, and Karima's radiant eyes suggested deep reserves of love.

The Tiger worked the night shift, but today he left home early. His eyes were severe, as if he were on a serious mission. He went into the Hemingway café, ordered a coffee and sat down at the fruit machine. He played and won. He lost and played again. In the end he lost forty euros. He threw a contemptuous glance at the fruit machine and left the café. It had started to snow heavily. The Tiger gazed at the snow.

"You know if you were in your right mind, you wouldn't shit in the bowl you eat from," he told it—in just the kind of tone you'd expect of a kid from a neighbourhood run by pill poppers and brutal police. The Tiger called it the "Cowards' District"; he'd had the energy and callousness to commit any crime he wanted to without falling into the hands of the police. That's why they had awarded the crown of "Tiger" to young Said Radwan. They gave him the title and cheered him off to the water wars.

The Tiger headed to the public library and spent some time there before work. He seethed with anger as he looked for a new crime novel, and addressed the row of books on the shelf. "I know you've jumped out at me from nowhere, but I know how to fix you up good and proper, you fat, rotten bastard. You lousy novel," he said.

He pulled a novel from the shelf and sat down to read.

His passion for crime stories had begun when he started living in Finland. That was before he joined the bus-driving course. The Tiger felt an overwhelming desire to write, but he didn't dare, and deep down inside he still thought it impossible to turn the images of horror in his mind into words. Sometimes he would spit out the names of the writers on the covers of the books in one of his inner dialogues: "You geniuses, sisters of whores, authors of blood and violence everywhere in the Cowards' District, in the water wars and on paper. My God, curse the father of the world you live in."

The Tiger left the library to smoke a cigarette outside. He watched the snow falling but didn't talk to it. He went back to the reading room, set sail with the crime novel and drowned in it. The time soon passed. The Tiger's skin suddenly shivered and he looked at his watch. He put the crime novel back in its place, borrowed another one and left.

The Tiger's fingers gripped the steering wheel tight as he drove the number 55 bus through Helsinki's icy streets. A stream of images and memories ran like a trail of ants through his blood, down from his head and ended up, crowded and swarming, in the tips of his fingers. He looked at his face in the rear-view mirror. His skin was as dark as rye bread, flecked with a sparse white beard. Who would have thought the Tiger would ever become so frail and wizened?

The bus halted at a stop close to the Opera House. He turned to the building and gave it a sigh: "Sing, sing. Farid al-Atrash used to sing, and say that life was beautiful if only we could understand it. Well, you can lick my arse."

The Tiger looked for his quarry, the fat man, in the mirror above his head. No sign of him among the passengers. The fat man hadn't appeared for more than two days. But he's bound to turn up at the last stop, the Tiger thought to himself as he fingered the pistol in his belt. He closed the bus doors and stepped on the gas, cutting a path though the continuing blizzard.

It was more than a month ago now since this new passenger had started riding the bus: a fat man with Iraqi features. The Tiger had never managed to work out how he got on the bus. Passengers were supposed to board through the front door, but the fat man didn't. The Tiger kept his eyes on his mirror—a constant vigil for the fat man sneaking on via the rear doors—which was a strain on his nerves. The fat man was like a ghost: he would appear on the bus and then disappear, until eventually they came face to face and the strange man revealed his identity.

Apart from the fat man appearing on his bus, the Tiger's life went on at the same depressing rhythm, as he struggled with his family and himself. For the last three years his son Mustafa, who was now twenty, hadn't been in touch with him or his mother. The kid had rebelled early against the Tiger's cruel treatment, and now sold marijuana and lived in a small flat with his Russian girlfriend.

His wife Karima—"the woman with the stunning eyes", as those around her used to call her in the old days—was lost in her own world, mentally and physically detached from her husband. The Tiger felt she was punishing him for the years of bitterness she'd spent with him. Karima spoke for hours on Skype with her brothers in Baghdad, sharing their joys and their sorrows. She would laugh and cry on Skype, yearning for the past and bemoaning her luck. There was nothing left of Karima, the young cheerful English teacher: with the old Finnish woman next door, her only friend, she'd go through photographs from when she was an elegant young woman with stunning eyes. When the old woman died, Karima's pictures died too, because there were no longer eyes to grieve over the shadows of the past with her.

The Tiger showed no interest in Karima's isolation, because he too had turned in on himself, focusing on his bus, and his conversations and the fruit machine. His only remaining consolation after work was to meet up with a hard-drinking Moroccan friend in some bar. His friend would always talk about the difference between Finnish and French women, or between Spanish and Arab women. He knew the stories of all the regulars in the bar and gave each one a nickname. When the Moroccan had his own business to attend to, the Tiger would sit in front of the fruit machine and throw away his money.

As far as the Tiger was concerned, it was obvious from the start that the strange man was targeting him with his appearances and disappearances on the bus, even before he managed to confront him about it. On that occasion the fat man was sitting in the back seats. The Tiger went up to him and told him in Finnish that this was the last stop. The fat man smiled and stared at the Tiger's face.

Switching to Arabic, the Tiger asked him, "Are you Iraqi?"

The fat man took some chewing gum out of his pocket and began to chew as he answered: "Don't kill me, I beg you. This is my tree."

The words struck a powerful chord in the Tiger's mind. He stepped back a few paces, then took one confused step forward towards the man. They were the same words he'd heard years ago in the pomegranate orchard.

"What is it you want?" the Tiger asked.

"Nothing," the fat man replied.

The Tiger had a good look at the man's face.

"Did you used to work with the water gangs?" he asked.

"No, but you killed me."

"I killed you! But you're not dead!"

"How are you so sure I'm not dead?"

His wife Karima didn't know what kind of work he'd been doing in those years. He'd excused his absences by saying he had to travel to other cities to buy and sell used cars. When the police got on his trail, the Tiger and his family fled to Iran, and from there to Turkey, where he applied to the United Nations for refugee status after forging some documents and claiming that he was an opponent of the dictatorial regime then in power. Finally, through the United Nations, he reached Finland.

That night, the night of the pomegranate orchard, the Tiger was driving the car, accompanied by another killer. The mission was to go to a posh house in the pomegranate orchards on the outskirts of Baghdad. The owner of the house was a boss in a gang that controlled a small river that flowed in from a neighbouring country. The gang owned special tankers for carrying water, which they would sell in

137

areas hit by drought. The government had lost control, over-whelmed by problems: rebels, groups of religious extremists and then the drought, which disrupted a bureaucracy that was already corrupt. The government started bartering oil for water from neighbouring countries. Most of the gangs that had been dealing in arms and counterfeit banknotes expanded their operations and started trading water. Some of them controlled wells and began to impose taxes on the farmers. The mission of the Tiger and his companion was clear: to eliminate everyone in the posh house in the pomegranate orchards. There was intense rivalry between the gangs to win control of the water market. The Tiger and his companion crept through the fence into the grounds of the posh house. They burst into the building, where there were five men sitting at a table, eating and talking. The Tiger and his companion killed everyone in the room. Then he rushed into the kitchen while his companion started looking for some documents in another room. The Tiger found a servant girl cowering in the corner of the kitchen. At the far side of the room, there was an open window. He realized that someone else had been in the kitchen and had escaped. He caught sight of the man's shadow heading deep into the orchards. The Tiger killed the servant girl, jumped out of the window and started running after the man who had escaped. The Tiger was soon out of breath; he couldn't see the man, but could hear him stepping on dry twigs somewhere. There wasn't much time. After running some distance further in the pitch black, the Tiger pulled back some branches and found a man kneeling close to the base of a pomegranate tree. The Tiger couldn't make out the man's features. He heard him saying that it was his tree and begging him not to kill him. The Tiger aimed his pistol and fired several shots.

The Tiger gave a bus ticket to a drunk, turning his face away because the man's clothes smelled so rank. He looked for the fat man, but couldn't see him. He spat out one of his rants at the road in front of him: "Roads . . . roads . . . all the roads we have walked, when the world is done for. Where are you, fatty? Where are you? Do you think the Tiger's frightened? A tiger who's seen all the roads, afraid of a sheep!"

He hadn't prepared a specific plan for getting rid of the fat man. All he'd decided was that he'd bury him and rid himself of the ghost of his shitty past forever. Once, when the fat man spoke to him, he'd made a strange request: that the Tiger take him for a drive around a forest by night—it didn't matter which particular forest. At first, the Tiger tried to ignore this man's weird and foolish words, but his appearances and disappearances so unnerved the Tiger that he asked his Moroccan friend to get him the pistol.

The Tiger drove the bus back and forth along his route. His shift was due to finish at two o'clock in the morning. The fat man appeared, just before midnight, at the bus stop close to the public swimming pool. The Tiger kept a close watch on him, in case this ghost disappeared again.

The last passengers got off at the final stop. When the fat man tried to alight, the Tiger closed all the doors and moved off quickly, changing course. The fat man laughed and asked, "What are you doing, man?"

The bus's absence would soon be discovered. It was a stupid, reckless act by an ageing tiger; there was only an hour before the bus had to be back in the depot. But the Tiger was in another world. His anger blinded him and paralysed his thinking.

From the back of the bus, the fat man shouted out in derision: "Are you going to kidnap a dead man? Well, if we're going to the forest, then fine."

The Tiger didn't really answer, just threw him one of his rants. "Dead, alive, it's all the same. I'm dead and alive. You're alive and dead. So what? Do you think you're a scarecrow and I'm a crow? It's amazing, these questions of the dead and the living. They don't repent and they never learn . . . Today I'm going to teach you!"

The bus crossed the main road towards the dirt track that led to the forest. The man moved up and sat close to the Tiger. He rambled on about various subjects—the past, coincidence, water, war and peace. The fat man said that over the past years he'd not only been interested in looking for the Tiger but also in piecing together the events that led to his murder. He said he'd often spoken to others about his death. The fat man put a cigarette in his mouth but didn't light it. Then he took it out of his lips and started to tell the Tiger his story:

"That night I was driving my old Volkswagen, with a little pomegranate tree in the back of the car. The branches were sticking out of the window and the cool night breeze was refreshing. My only daughter had leukaemia and we'd been taking her from one hospital to another. But her condition was deteriorating as time passed. I tried getting blessings from holy men, and when I despaired of them, I went to fortune-tellers and magicians. An old woman well known for her psychic powers told me to plant a pomegranate tree in an orchard where pomegranates already grow, and that I should do this at night, without telling anyone. 'Give life its fruit so that it will give you its fruits,' the old woman said.

"'And why a pomegranate?' I asked her.

"'Every one of us is also something else—a pomegranate, a flower or some other living thing. He who knows how to move between himself and his other lives will have the doors of serenity and well-being opened for him,' the old woman answered.

"'Excuse me, but why can't it be an orange tree or a grape vine?' I asked her.

"'Oranges cure nightmares and grapes are for treating grief, whereas the pomegranate is the pure blood of your daughter,' the old woman said, and then asked me to leave.

"I would have liked to ask her some more questions, but the psychic said that too many questions undermined the power of mystery. I didn't understand what she meant. I was thinking about the requirement that I plant the tree by night and in secret. I was desperate, and willing to do anything that might improve the health of the flower of my life, my only daughter.

"I drove there by night. I parked the car and took out the pomegranate tree and a spade. I cut the barbed wire and went deep into the orchard. I chose a suitable place. While I was digging, I heard gunshots. I didn't pay much attention because the farmers in those parts used rifles every now and then. It might have been a wedding. I was kneeling next to the tree and levelling the soil when you suddenly appeared between the trees and aimed your pistol at me. It was pitch black. But you opened fire and killed me. Why?"

The Tiger didn't believe the fat man's story. That night, he'd chased and killed a member of the water gangs. Yes, it was true that the wretch had begged for mercy and said something about his tree. But the Tiger hadn't seen his face in the dark, so why should he believe it was the fat man? Confused, the Tiger summoned up his courage once more. He had only one thing in mind: getting rid of this ghost of the past that had risen up from underground. The Tiger held his tongue for the rest of the journey.

Inside the forest he stopped the bus, waved his pistol in the fat man's face and forced him out. He was inclined to stick the barrel in the fat man's back there and then, but he was frightened of doing so. Could he really shoot a ghost?

The fat man made fun of him. "You've already killed me, man," he said. "What are you doing?" Then he made a run for it.

The Tiger opened fire, but the fat man didn't fall. He was running like an athletic young man. The Tiger chased him between the trees and in the darkness a shiver ran across his skin and he felt that he was back in the pomegranate orchard that night, as if the fat man, the bus, the snow, his son and Finland were just a waking dream in his head, as if he were still there, a strong Tiger, hunting down his victims in the vicious water wars, without hesitation.

Through the open window the Tiger caught sight of a shadow in the orchard. He fired a bullet into the head of the girl in the kitchen. Then he jumped through the window and ran after the shadow of the man who had escaped. He heard the sound of footsteps breaking dry twigs. Then he caught sight of another man sitting, levelling the soil around a pomegranate tree. He ran past him and continued to chase the man who had escaped.

The forest came to an end and opened out onto the frozen lake. The Tiger kept chasing him over the icy surface. Finally the man who had escaped came to a halt. The Tiger came up to him, aiming his pistol at the man's face. The man from the water gang quickly raised his hand and pointed his own pistol in the Tiger's face, and shots rang out.

Blood flowed across the icy surface of the lake.

TRANSLATED BY JONATHAN WRIGHT

ZOMBIELAND

(extracts from the novel)

SØRINE STEENHOLDT

MOTHER IS JUST A WORD

IT IS UNCOMFORTABLE to stand so close. They must live simple lives, these people, who are here to send my mother off on her final journey. I start to feel angry. I can see that the man standing next to me has not bothered to shower. He still has bed-head. I can see that he has sleep in his eyes, yellowish gunk stuck in the corners because he hasn't washed his face yet. The woman on the other side of me has at least tried to do something with herself. Her hair has been washed and tied up tightly into a ponytail. She coughs, and I see her teeth, which haven't been brushed for many years. She smells of smoke, and her fingernails are brownish-yellow. Standing next to her is a man, who I'm sure is wearing his best jacket. It's too nice to wear just any day. It's too big for him, though, and it makes him look comical in a sad way in contrast to his threadbare, washed-out jeans with holes in the knees. He pulls a small bottle of schnapps out of his inside pocket and takes a drink.

I'm being choked by my Greenlandic national costume as well by my thoughts. The heavy beaded collar is making my brow sweat, the dark thoughts are making me claustrophobic. I can't bear the beads any longer.

When I unpacked them this morning, I admired their colours and felt the immense love I have for my country. *My* country. The clear colours, distinct colours. These colours are not transparent, not half colours. My country is painted with the colours of love, painted with warm colours.

Since I put them on, the heavy weight has made me feel that all my country does is weigh down on me, that my people weigh down on me. I feel like taking a gulp from the man's bottle. I want to live like them. To fall. To give up. To live without the weight of the world, just existing and being there. I want to seem as if I'm OK. I want to rely on people to take over. I want to be able to count on other people to deal with all of it. I am fascinated by the people who have given up, but continue to live. I could let myself fall down with them. Leave here with them, go drink with them, forget about the future and live by the bottle. Stop working, stop having an opinion about myself, stop paying the rent, stop having a place to live. I could just spend the nights wherever. I could just drink and be happy. How easy life would be: to be the living dead.

There isn't a single man in a white anorak here. I get angry. Not one single man wearing an anorak! If just one man had an anorak on, I would feel better about the future. But now the men's anoraks swill around instead inside of them, so they need to wear jackets that are far too big for them with inside pockets filled with more floating anoraks. They are no longer men; they are empty containers with floating insides.

It is one of those days again. I am a little girl, and I go to bed. My mother stays up. She sits alone in the kitchen and drinks. I can hear her getting ready to go out around eleven, as I expect her to, despite it being a weekday. I close my eyes and try to fall asleep, but I can't because I keep listening to her, even though I don't want to. I hear every single movement she makes. I can hear by her walk how drunk she is. How many bottles she has drunk. And I hear by the way she fumbles putting her glass down how hard she is trying to keep her head clear. I can hear by the way she talks to herself that she is in a good mood. I can even work out how the night will go. Many years, many nights of practising, have made me capable of predicting whether I will be able to sleep peacefully through the night or if I need to spend it constantly sleeping with one eye open. She needs to hurry now if she is going to make it to the bar, even if she does, perhaps, have a couple of bottles left still.

I hear them come in on Saturday night, and there are a lot of them. Sounds of laughter, of jokes and of people trying too hard to laugh at them, reach me through the wall. I feel calmer knowing they are happy, even though I won't get any sleep as long as they are here. They move into the living room and start drinking, and I can hear that they have kept their shoes on. It will be me who will have to clean up after them in the morning. The music is turned on and turned up high, and they talk, and yell and laugh. I cover my ears with my pillow, but it doesn't help. My mother is talking louder and louder as she gets more and more drunk. She gets this hoarse voice that doesn't sound like her own. I hate that voice more than anything else in the world. It's a voice that changes when it has taken a swig of what it likes. A voice that becomes friendly. A voice that sounds like the voice of fearlessness. A voice wearing a mask.

Even her greeting has changed. *Hi.* I have listened to that voice all too often.

I start to nod off, because I am so sleepy, and when, a little while later, I wake up again, I can hear that there are fewer people in the living room, and that they are calmer now. I can't hear my mother; perhaps she has passed out somewhere. I can hear two Danish men. One of them is about to leave, and the other one will follow. Once the first one has gone, the second man goes over to my mother and tries to wake her. He calls to her softly. I know very well what he wants. When he can't wake her, he goes over to the door. I prick up my ears and listen to every step he takes. He continues moving towards the door, but just as I allow myself to relax, I hear him creeping even more quietly back towards the living room. I lie down in my bed and pretend to be sleeping heavily. I can hear him approaching my room. A thousand thoughts seem to whirl around me. I know very well what could happen. Somehow, I have to prevent it. He moves into my room, and I can hear him quietly placing his jacket and his large rubber boots on the floor so as not to wake me. But it is not until he walks slowly over to me and starts taking off his damn belt that it truly dawns on me what he wants. I open my eyes, lift up my head and stare directly into his eyes. "*Shhh* . . . calm down," he says quietly, as he puts his hand out and moves closer. I sit halfway up and shake my head. I am angry, terrified. But I know it won't help to act like that. It is not enough. It takes all my courage to say something: "I'll scream." He steps closer, and I repeat: "I'll scream!"

When, many years later, I look back on that night—and so many others like it—I wonder over the scale of the courage and the strength of the will I possessed. Thin and fragile; an easy prey for the horny, drunken men in my mother's life. But no. I could not accept a fate of being a rape victim. I knew that my womanhood, my life, my future would be ruined completely by such an act. I would not let that happen to me. If it happened, I would never be able to forgive myself. When I grew up, I would give up and become an alcoholic. My life would be over in a split second. I could scream, I could fight against it, I could bite, I could kick, and I would do anything to protect myself. No one was ever going to break me.

I can see that the Danish man understands what I mean, what I'm saying. I can see that he understands that I'm ready to do whatever it takes to fight back. He starts moving backwards as he repeats, "OK . . . OK . . ." He picks up his jacket and his rubber boots and walks out of my room. Shortly after, I hear him going out of the front door. As soon as he has gone, I hurry over to the front door to lock it, checking in all the rooms on my way back to see that there is no one in them. I want to know if I can sleep safe and sound for the rest of the night.

Sometimes, when my mother was drunk, she would call for me, so she could tell me things. She would cry, sometimes, while she was telling me them, and you could see in her eyes that she had slipped back into her memories. Her father had worshipped his four sons. They were destined to be fishermen like himself. His only daughter was a thorn in his side. She was good for nothing. He took to hunting her around the house with a knife, but fortunately many years of fishing had worn out his body and made him slow. He would yell at her. Tell her that she shouldn't go to school, because it was her brothers that would earn the money, so she ought to be making food for them, washing their clothes and making sure they came home to a clean house. My mother stopped going to school.

Several times I have been woken in the middle of the night because I was being choked by smoke. The smoke would be large and greyish and would have gathered into a bank of fog that grew larger and heavier, until it sank from the ceiling to the floor. I would wake with a shock, without knowing what awaited me out there, how it would look, how much damage there would be, and the adrenalin would start pumping around my body. Luckily what had usually happened was that my mother had passed out cold while she was making food, and I would awake just before the food burned to a charred, black crisp.

One night I awake at dawn to the smell of fire. My throat stings. I get up and walk out of my room, but I can barely see anything for the smoke. When I come into the living room, I get a glimpse through the smoke of my mother's legs on the floor. She has passed out again. I go directly into the kitchen, over to the oven. As I get closer, I can see that she has put some food in the oven and then fallen asleep, and that the legs of meat have burnt away to nothing. I go to set the oven door ajar and turn off the oven, when a thought hits me . . . I could leave the oven on. I could leave the oven on and walk away. But where would I go? I could go to my grandmother's, but then she would ask why I was over there in the middle of the night. When she discovered that there had been a fire over at our house, wouldn't she then ask me what had been going on when I left, and how would I answer?

As I stand and think about whether I should leave the oven on, a mass of memories pop up. I decide to turn it off. If I let her die, I would end her suffering, and I have no wish to help her. Let her suffer. Let her battle her own shitty life. When she can no longer handle it, when she finally gives up, then she can end her life herself. I will not help her.

*

As I stand here and say my last goodbyes to you, it is hard to keep my thoughts in the present. I think about everything you have done to me and everything you never did for me. *Mother* is just a word.

EXTRACTION NO. I

Without a sound, she takes out her gear and tries to open the driver's door. Her face clenched, she looks around her, ever on guard. She gets the door open, gets in and closes it quietly. She tries to start the engine. Successful, she immediately turns the heater on high and lets the warmth hit her hands which cover her mouth. Quietly and carefully she lets the car roll. When the house has disappeared from sight, she hits the accelerator. The heat begins to spread slowly throughout her body and a tense smile appears on her otherwise expressionless face. She laughs forcefully, but it is false and hollow. She turns on the radio and, screaming to the blasting music, she drives way too fast out towards the airport.

She drives as if intoxicated. She owns the asphalt. With yet another forced laugh, she aims directly at the street light, before straightening up the car right at the last moment. Over and over she plays "chicken" with the street light. Her eyes grow moist, but she dries them as if it doesn't matter. On a long straight stretch, she floors it. With a firm grip on the steering wheel, she lifts her body up towards the windscreen and screams, then slumps back into her seat. The tears run freely down her cheeks, and she lets go of the steering wheel to dry them away.

ZOMBIE

You would see Louisa out walking in town with her mother. Like a wounded animal, following its owner, always with its head bowed, always compliant. She walked with small, hurried steps, shifting her weight between each foot. Stopping when her mother stopped; walking when she went onwards. Pulling on the sleeves of her coat, she scanned the ground intensely, but without really looking. There was no longer any Louisa left in Louisa. When people greeted her, she would laugh like a small child. But the laughter was toneless, not a child's. A cold, empty laughter. The laugh of a crazy woman.

I remember clearly one day, when my mother picked me up from school. I wasn't very old. When we went outside, I couldn't zip up my coat. The zip on my coat began to taunt me: it wouldn't work as it should do. Scared of making my mother mad, I tried frantically to zip up my coat. The more I tried, the harder it got. She had already gone a few feet when she turned around and saw that I had not followed her. When she got back to me, she grabbed hold of my coat by the chest, lifted me up and began to shake me. Stupid, useless, kid. It was during a break-time in front of a load of kids who were out playing. She shook me so hard that my coat was ripped to

151

shreds along the zipper, and the down began to fall out over the playground like fake snowflakes. I cried: not because of the pain, but out of shame.

I have always known my mother's rage. Her recurring break-downs. The number of pills she took rose and fell like the tide. There were periods when she would be drained of energy and strength. Her mother had apparently suffered from this too. I didn't know what this immense exhaustion was. I couldn't understand it, but I bore witness to it every single day. I was just a child.

It was me alone who took care of the household chores. My mother never cooked, she never did the washing up, she didn't do laundry, she never took care of anything, including me. She could spend an entire day on the sofa. She must have been really tired. In the beginning I would refuse when she asked me to do something. I thought I could say no, thought I had a choice. I quickly learnt that I was wrong. Her wish became my command.

I met a man. He was quite a lot older than I was, but that didn't matter, because I loved him. Fari was a nice man, he had an education, a steady job at a fish-processing plant, and that made me feel safe and secure. I really felt like I had met the man who I would spend the rest of my life with. When we moved into our own home, we started a new family. We had three children, one after another, and I was going to be a good mother. My children would not have to go through what I had endured.

At times—and I am so grateful for being able to see this—I find myself being too hard on the children. When this happens,

I always make sure to apologize to them, to look them deep in the eyes and promise them that I will pay more attention to my behaviour in the future and be better at controlling my temper. I don't know why I sometimes act like this towards my own children. I can never really put my finger on what it is that makes me do this.

I hurry home as soon as I get off work. It's become a habit for me to hurry, even if there is nothing in particular I have to do. I have a husband now, we have our own home, but still I can't seem to shake off old habits. Perhaps I ought to do some cleaning before I go and pick up the kids.

When I step in through the door, I am surprised to see my husband's work overalls and large rubber boots in the hallway, but also glad to know that he is home already. I dash into the kitchen. It's empty. Then I hear a sound from the bedroom. As I get closer, I'm met by voices and other sounds. I open the door and my "Hello" is replaced by a scream. Like a punch in the face I see my husband . . . with my mother. Her nakedness has infiltrated his. They are like a patchwork quilt; legs locked around each other, his hands all over her back, even on her flabby, wrinkled buttocks. Pearls of sweat dot her bare neck. Despite her long hair covering his face completely, I still know that it's him. The scar over his knee glows white and mocking up at me.

I scream and try to get my mother out. Point towards the door. I am no longer the master of my own body or my conscious thoughts. Both of them are busy getting dressed. I become immersed in the nightmare, I feel only disgust. Neither of them attempts to apologize. They just want to get out. Fari takes a long time to put on his sweater, but my mother has

153

disappeared. With an imploring look on his face, a "Let me explain", he reaches out for my arms. With my entire body I ask him to go to hell.

As soon as the front door has slammed shut, my body starts to shake wildly and feel weak, and I fall down to the floor and break down in painful tears. I sob so fiercely that I can barely catch my breath. In the hope of waking from this nightmare, I scream my lungs out—I don't give a shit if the neighbours can hear me. I could somehow have expected this from my mother, but from my husband? Never. I would never have imagined that he could do this to me. I hit myself and imagine that it is Fari, that shit, who I'm hitting. I want to beat him until I'm not angry any more. Right in the gut. Or the head. I can almost feel his nose as it crunches under my fist, and the warmth from the blood as it streams down his face. I reach for a cushion, press my face into it and scream as hard as I can as the tears keep running.

Some days have passed, but I am still exhausted from the rage I'm feeling. I take care of the kids alone, I will not fail them. I'm not that kind of mother. I am not ready yet to see Fari. Fuck Fari. When I get off work, I pick up my two eldest from preschool and the youngest from daycare and head home. They are whining and impatient. I decide to make their tea early so I can get them into bed as soon as I can. They are fighting in the living room. I hear a little bump, someone's fallen, two of them are shrieking. I ask them to say sorry to each other, to come to an agreement. I am patient. Gentle. A good mother. They turn on the TV.

As I stand there making the dinner, I start to miss Fari. God, this is gross! The bastard! Why in hell should I have to take care of our children—I could just as well drink myself to pieces! Making me miss him. Failing me. Making me lonely. Shitty, shitty love! Why me?! Everything is shattered. I know that *she* did it on purpose, out of jealousy. She's jealous, because I am happy and have built myself a good life. So she tries to destroy it. That's why. The injustice of it all hits me hard in the gut. The sound from the TV becomes a faint hum, which merges with the yells of the kids. Constant squabbles. Strife, violence and jealousy. *Why do you have to decide . . . Ow, let go, that hurts . . . Mummyyyy . . . Stop . . .* Crying, my youngest child walks in and nags me to be picked up, as she pulls persistently at my trouser leg. I grab hold of her neck and knock her head into the table. Everything is quiet.

I'm sitting on the floor when I regain consciousness. Everything around me has been painted red. My two eldest children are crying and calling for me, bringing me back to life. Once I have come around, I start searching manically for my mobile phone. I find it and dial 999. I need an ambulance right away, my daughter is not breathing.

I look at her through eyes that are not my own. Her lifeless body, swaddled in a blanket of blood. Feelings race through me. Restlessness. Shock. Repulsion. I feel only one thing and everything at the same time, as a dream. My whole body is shaking. My legs feel drained, so I remain on the floor next to her bloody body. I don't know whether I am crying. The sounds around me return, and the crying of the two eldest children finally reaches me. I get up, take them into the living room, try to calm them, to soothe them. I hold them tight, and while I sit with them in my arms, our cries become one.

The paramedics get here. I can see on their faces that it is already too late. We drive to the hospital in the ambulance.

With a child under each arm, I try to keep calm. Tears run down my cheeks. *Don't take them from me. They are mine. Don't take them from me. Calm down, Louisa. You're still in shock. Don't take my children away from me . . .*

The police show up in the waiting room. They have come for me. Fari has apparently been contacted, because he shows up too. He takes the children and goes into another room, and I am left alone with the police. They start on their rain of questions, questions which I answer as best I can. I tell them everything I can remember.

The doctor also asks me questions. How much anger do I feel towards Fari? How great is my hatred towards my mother? Am I capable of harm? Do I want to harm other people? My children? I don't want to hurt anyone. I could never dream of hurting anyone. *Louisa, it is the 19th of May, the time is 5.55 p.m., and you are under arrest for the crime of murder. You have the right . . .* I cry.

With a firm grip around both my arms, they lead me out of the room, and as we walk down the hall, I see my mother in the waiting room. I am suddenly filled with anger, consumed with the thought of why in the hell she should be here. I lose control, I scream. *You shit mother! You are a shitty mother! It's you that is the shitty mother!* I yell it over and over again as the police lead me out of the hospital. They toss me into the car and we drive to the holding cell.

The days pass. I don't know exactly how many. I am quite sure that I am the talk of the town. I haven't spoken to anyone I know since I came in here, no one at all. And that's fine with me, I have no wish to see or to speak to anyone. I will, however, have to speak to the doctor some day soon. I find it hard to fall asleep with my constant stream of thoughts, and when I finally do, I always awaken with the feeling of having slept for eternity. It doesn't help much that the days are long and full of light. Unlike my soul.

I am admitted onto the hospital's psychiatric ward—the secure one—and referred to a shrink. I miss my children. A lot. To escape my constant stream of thoughts, I have started walking. Up and down the hallways like a stray mutt looking for an owner. I count my steps. A doctor walks past. His smell, the smell of men, hits my nostrils, and I think immediately of Fari. If he could see me now, he would think it would be best to put me down like the dog I am. That I deserved it. Even though all of this is his fault! *Stop using scent! What the hell do you get out of it?! You are a bastard, an abuser of women! You shit!* I am immediately surrounded by hospital personnel. They take me back to my room and strap me to the bed. I'm still screaming. *Louisa, calm down. Bastard! Never come here again! You mean nothing to me!* My broken voice carries itself down the hall. Like the whine of a wounded animal.

After having been on the ward for days, examined closely under the psychiatrist's magnifying glass, I receive my diagnosis: nervous breakdown. The psychiatrist suspects that this is a *result of inherited patterns of behaviour* . . . As soon as I hear this, it feels as if my muscles finally relax. Resignation. When I look at myself in the mirror, a stranger looks back at me. I no longer see myself.

I resume my walks up and down the halls, but these are led now by the conversations I have with the voices, which have taken up residence in my head. Without having consulted with me first, my body has started to walk differently. The steps are shorter, and when I stop and stand still, my feet fight restlessly to carry the weight of my body. I am no longer in control of my body. I am convinced that I share my body with someone else. Another me. The voices in my head never agree: one voice says that I am here because I killed my daughter, while another says that it is the doctors who are out to kill *me*. That I have been filled with lies and manipulated into believing that I have killed. I don't know what I should believe.

I am placed before the District Court. It decides that, due to my psychological state, I should neither serve time nor be punished in any other way. *Can this really be true? Can I really come home?* My reactions are slow. *My mother . . . My mother . . . My mother . . .* The sentence sits waiting in my throat without wanting to come out. It is my mother's fault. She is to blame. But my mouth will not obey.

There are conditions for my verdict. Conditions for the freedom I have been sentenced with. My children are taken from me, and complete custody given to Fari. I am classified as incapable of taking care of myself, as someone you have to be careful with, someone who could be a danger to her surroundings. It is further concluded that the best option for me would be to be placed in the care of my mother. To my horror, she has offered to be my guardian. *My mother . . .* I stutter. The judge looks at me calmly, smiling faintly. *Yes, yes . . . you can go home to your mother . . .*

EXTRACTION NO. 2

I hide away in my thoughts. It would be best if I just ended it all here. I can't get over the urge to take my own life. I begin looking in the cupboard, I want to be free from the pain of the mind. Now. I can't, the pain, my body simply cannot handle it. I open the cupboard, where we keep all the little things, and find a cord that would work. I take it out without hesitating.

In my restless state I can no longer control my thoughts. My pain, my grief is too consuming, it has swallowed me whole. I go into my room and tie the cord securely to the door handle. With my back against the door, I lower myself slowly down into a squatting position. I carefully wind the cord around my neck. I try to work out how long it should be. Deliberately, I make it a little shorter and then, finally, I tie it firmly around my neck.

I am calm when I let go. I cannot think clearly. The only thing left is the pain. It will be gone soon. In a little while there will be nothing left. The cord is tight around my neck, and my arse is almost touching the ground. I hang there, noticing how the pain and the grief are gradually leaving my body. Sounds become muted. They are coming from far away now. My heart is pumping blood rapidly around my body in a vain attempt to save something which cannot be saved. My pulse increases as too much blood gathers in my brain. My vision starts to flicker and fill with white noise. It is too late to regret this. My whole body aches with doubt now, but everything goes black. It is too late.

DUST

They say that she need not do anything, because she is an only child. From morning until night her parents wait on her every need. They cut up her dinner for her. Zip up her jacket when she is getting dressed. Tie her shoelaces when she puts on her shoes. She is the beloved only child, the favourite child, Arsugaq. She is picked up in a car when school is out. She must not walk, no, because she risks being run over or being kidnapped by some drunkard. As soon as she comes home, it's ". . . don't run around like that, you might hurt yourself. Sit down and relax and play with your iPad . . ." Between the piles of dusty toys she sits all day with her iPad, sneezing.

Mum is always saying how Arsugaq is the second tallest in her class. She acts like she is concerned about her height, although really she's proud. But when she talks about her daughter, she omits to mention how Arsugaq cries when she doesn't win in a competition. Because Mum knows that she has not raised her right. She dismisses it with comments like ". . . she's just so stubborn!", but Arsugaq, the little doll, finds it hard to understand what Mum tells her. She only knows that she mustn't make her angry.

One day Mum and Dad come home in a particularly good mood. "We've got something for you," they say with smiles of anticipation. Arsugaq looks at the package on the table. It's a large package. "Go on, you can open it," they say. She opens her gift; it's a puppy. Dad places it down on the floor and turns it, so that it starts to move around on the floor. Mum claps her hands together and laughs. But Arsugaq doesn't find it funny. The hard puppy with the fake fur stops moving. She picks it up, examines it carefully and then tosses it in with all the other toys covered in dust. She has always wanted a dog. A dog to walk her to school. A dog that would wait outside for her all day. A dog that would be overjoyed when she came home. A dog that she could sleep with in her room filled with toys. A dog that could keep her company in her loneliness in the midst of all the dust.

Her classmates are on their way to the after-school club, while Arsugaq is getting picked up in the car, as always. She runs over to the car; today she has something to be pleased about. She gets in the back and takes a gift out of her school backpack, which she hands to her mum.

"I'll open it at home," says Mum, smiling into the rear-view mirror. When they get home, Arsugaq reminds Mum about opening her gift. "Oh, yes!" she says. It's a trivet, which Arsugaq has made in school from a cork plate covered with orange fabric, on which coloured needles have been glued to each other to form circles. Mum is pleased and thanks her, kisses her on the cheek and places the present in the cupboard. Arsugaq is sad because she used so many of her needlework classes on making this for Mum, simply for her to shut it away like that. She knows that the cupboard is used for storing all of the junk that never gets used. Arsugaq had hoped that Mum would like it because it was so colourful. At home, everything is white.

As Arsugaq's birthday approaches, Mum gives her enough invitations for two classes. Arsugaq would prefer to celebrate it with just Mum and Dad, not together with a load of other children. But what can Arsugaq do when Mum has already made up her mind? "Mum decides!" is what Mum would say. As she stands by the school's entrance and waits to be picked up, two girls walk past. Wrapped around each other, they walk arm in arm, the one girl's hips moving in time with the other's. Arsugaq studies them. How do they do that, she wonders. *Perhaps I'll get to try this with someone on my birthday.*

Once they have sung the birthday song, they eat the cake. "You must sit very still while you eat the cake. Try not to spill anything!" says Arsugaq's mum in a strict voice. After they have eaten their cake, they wash their hands carefully before they start playing games. "Me, me . . .!" There are children everywhere, fighting over who gets to go first. They all want to win. They are arranged in a line for the competition to start. The miniature winners run around all over the house being smug. Arsugaq can't stand it any longer. They are so obsessed with the competition that they have forgotten the birthday child. Arsugaq begins to cry, ". . . it's mine!" She doesn't understand. Why isn't she the one who gets to decide what games they should play? She runs up to her room and throws herself down on her pile of toys, noting the dust that falls slowly around her. *No one wants to be friends with me. They think I'm weird. They hate me.* In the evening, Mum comes up and comforts her. She reads aloud to her from the Bible, before they pray together to God.

Arsugaq sits alone in school. "That's *her*, the one who had a birthday party and it was *her* mum who yelled when someone dropped some cake on the floor . . ." some of the girls whisper, as they walk past, giving Arsugaq a contemptuous look.

Arsugaq is slim and slender. She gets called the abandoned child. When she answers a teacher's question, she looks as if she is ashamed. When you see her walking from a distance, she looks like someone who is afraid of taking a wrong step. She appears very cautious. Her huge school backpack makes her tiny body appear even smaller. A child you have to walk around in big circles, because she is so fragile. And she knows how much it irritates Mum when she tries to make herself smaller, to hunch herself up, to go unnoticed. "For God's sake, don't stand like that, straighten your back!" Mum tells her off, only to enquire tenderly moments after: ". . . what kind of sweeties would you like tonight? Because you must feel like something sweet, right?"

Mum and Dad disagree about the bills. Which bill is most important? What should we buy first? What do we need the most? Arsugaq can't understand why they would fight about things like that. When they eat dinner, Mum doesn't really feel like answering when she asks her about something. Why does Mum get like this sometimes? And when she asks Dad, he doesn't say anything. The next day, Mum comes home buzzing with energy. She has lots of bags. She has bought a thick warm coat for Arsugaq because it will soon be autumn. "I don't want one in black!" says Arsugaq. "Everyone has one like this. It was very expensive, you should be pleased. We'll have to starve ourselves for the rest of the month!" answers Mum. "Yes, but," says Arsugaq sulkily, "I just wanted one suitable for a princess."

One day Arsugaq is upset when she comes home from school. "Arsugaq, what is it? Tell me instead of behaving like that!" says Mum. At teatime Arsugaq is still upset, and Mum says to Dad, ". . . go on, pick her up and get her to cry, she just wants to have a good cry!" Arsugaq's dad holds her firmly as he sits watching television. Arsugaq struggles, she wants to get away. She cries louder and louder and gets all sweaty from being held by Dad. Finally she screams, fighting against him. "Let go of me!" she shouts. "Do you feel better?" asks Arsugaq's mum every now and then as she cooks the tea. Once tea is done, Arsugaq doesn't want to eat, so Mum orders her up to her room. "Go up and play with your dolls. You'll be a mum, when you're older! Why don't you play with your dolls when you have so many?" As Arsugaq throws herself down onto the floor between all the toys, she notices the dust that falls slowly around her.

In the morning Arsugaq doesn't answer when Mum calls for her. Mum goes into Arsugaq's room and gets a shock. Arsugaq has cut the hair off her dolls, removed their legs, arms and heads. Her bed is filled with dolls' hair. Their legs, arms and heads are spread out everywhere. She has taken Mum's make-up and painted the dolls' faces. Mum is stunned with fear. Arsugaq, who is sitting in the middle of the floor, turns now to face Mum. She has cut off her own hair and made up her face just like the dolls'. Big red lips run across her face, and the excessive eyeshadow makes her eyes look like cold, dark stones. She looks up unaffected at Mum, whose scream now fills the room and filters out through the windows into the pale pink morning.

The dust falls slowly around them.

TRANSLATED BY JANE GRAHAM

AVOCADO

GUÐBERGUR BERGSSON

S HE HAD POPPED OUT to the shops to buy an avocado
for dinner. It was Christmas Eve and fortunately they
were open until noon. She had forgotten the latest gastronomic
fads yesterday and wanted to be like other arty people. Avocado
had become a must among those who had been educated
abroad. She no longer worked in their midst, but had studied
overseas and maintained the fads, out of respect for herself
if for no one else. Avocados were easy to find in shops and
she had read that they were healthy and good for the skin
and old people's bowel movements. On this occasion she only
needed one. It was just the two of them now; the sons were
gone and ate with their own families. She had trouble walking,
even though it was a short distance, but she set off to buy the
avocado and other small sundries. It took some time to find
a suitably ripe avocado. Most of them were hard. She grabbed
them in her right palm, squeezed them and felt a tinge of
satisfaction. A memory from her student years in London
fluttered into her mind when she had met a black man in a
park who leaned her against a tree and guided her hand into
him to let her feel the weight of something similar in her
palm. The memory lingered a moment. She stopped squeezing
and calculated how long it would take for the avocado to
soften if she wrapped a newspaper around it and placed it
on the kitchen radiator. Finally she found a ripe one, but

perhaps not ripe enough for the evening. She bought it and bit her knuckles for having left everything to the last minute. When she got home she enveloped the avocado in paper and laid it on the radiator. It made no difference because nothing tasted of anything any more, vegetables or fruit. Life had lost its flavour too, not least the arts. Then she began to wait for her son. He was going to fetch the old artificial Christmas tree in the attic for her; she couldn't get up there any longer. Her husband had never troubled himself to help her with Christmas preparations, which he found idiotic. She agreed, but the custom had persisted since her childhood and while the kids were small, so she could do nothing else but uphold it, despite her husband's opinions and her own. Which was why the artificial tree was needed. Her son arrived and gave her two strips of Danish Kringle, one with chocolate, the other with cream. He showed no favouritism for either of his parents and knew that his father didn't want cream and his mother didn't want chocolate. The only gratitude he got was a reprimand from his mother who told him he shouldn't have bothered to bring them; she still had the leftovers from last year's Danish pastries in the freezer. The son said he did it out of habit, but didn't keep up the tradition in his own home—the kids wanted something else. He fetched the Christmas tree and ran his hands over it until the branches sprang out. Then he screwed the tree into its plywood stand and hung the last ball from his childhood on a branch. The others were broken; only one was left on which he had stuck white cotton to resemble Christmas snow. Once he had done that, he was about to leave but his mother asked him to wait and to sprinkle the oatmeal from the pan along the pavement for the birds. He promised he would and said it was lucky he hadn't brought along his daughter, who had been a know-it-all from the day she could speak. Now she knew that oatmeal could wreak havoc on birds' stomachs, causing blockages and making them die of constipation in the bushes. "But still, we've always given them oatmeal," said his mother and asked about her granddaughter whom she called her ewe and her grandson whom she called pet lamb because they had been so fond of Grandad and Granny when they were toddlers but never showed their faces now. Pet lamb was developing his ambitions as a film-maker and the ewe wanted to be an actress. Granny knew she would become one. She was also a know-it-all in her own way. Knowledge and know-how ran in the family because actors knew how to tackle every role in the theatre of life and on the stage. "I, a veteran actress, the daughter of an actor, should have given the ewe my support to help her fulfil her aspirations," she said. The son then added that his daughter felt she had limited chances of getting into theatre and said the same about singing or writing books. "The arts are a very closed circle," he said. "It all runs in family dynasties and cliques; the children of actors become actors or something in the theatre, the children of singers singers—even if they're tone-deaf they get some job in music." "Wasn't I a famous actress?" his mother asked. "And your father a lighting designer. That should stand your daughter in good stead." The son didn't listen and continued, saying that it would be no better if it occurred to his daughter to become a writer. "Every author has grandfathers or grand-mothers who have been writing for generations," he said excitedly. "Artistic talent is innate, but the drawback is that talent deteriorates as arrogance grows with the sense of being entitled to praise!" the father called out from the sofa in the

167

living room. "Now Dad is pitching in!" said the son. "Don't listen to him," said the mother. "If you hadn't given up acting, you could have got my daughter on the stage," said the son. "You trained in London, which was regarded as a big deal in your day." The mother didn't answer, while the son carried on, saying that when artistic events got poor reviews, it was regarded as harassment and gender-based violence, especially if there were actresses involved. "Stop it!" the mother ordered, but the son wouldn't stop. "My daughter says critics work from a preconceived mindset and write their reviews accordingly . . ." "Stop it!" the mother ordered. The son didn't stop but continued: "Now everything is supposed to focus on crises. Middle-aged men working out their issues and women being raped on top of vibrating washing machines in front of their children." The mother shook her head. She pretended to be well acquainted with matters that weren't new and yet were always unfamiliar and said: "Maybe I should have continued, but I wanted to be a woman and have you. In my day women were expected to accept the female virtues of motherhood. That was the only true role. I didn't listen to your father. He wanted me to continue on the stage and to carry on himself as a lighting designer." "You've never listened to me except to indulge me, because physically you're lustful, but you don't have the same lust for art. It's vital to be seen to have a burning desire for that!" the man yelled from the living room. He had moved from the sofa into the recliner and was fiddling with the settings. "Still, I got a gold medal in the school in London in a class with Sylvia Stone. She became famous on the stage but got no prizes at school to begin with because of her slurred diction. Then it became fashionable, even in the role of Desdemona. But despite her fame, Sylvia ended up working

168

in a pub and drank herself to hell. They wrote a book about her. What about me? Won a gold medal like a model student, awarded by a foreign board, and then came home to become nothing." "Isn't it the same story everywhere?" said the son. "That's what the world's like. All records have been broken. Even in sports. Then what? Things have to be turned on their head—they hold Olympics for the disabled, allow actors who can't act to act and allow the tone-deaf to sing with crappy whining voices." "I can't be bothered to listen to this, heard it all before," said the mother. "Stop quarrelling with your mother!" the father called out and asked his son to explain the controls for the chair to him, it was all so complicated. "Just countless buttons, no results." The son went over and pressed the chair so abruptly that his father's legs were almost catapulted over the back of it. "Are you trying to kill me?" the father asked. "This is the posture I was in when I was adjusting the lights in the theatre." "I'm off," said the son and added: "Mum, should I buy a piece of jewellery for my wife from Gulli?" "He's long dead," said the mother. "Your dad often went to him to take a look. He occasionally gave me trinkets." "I mean his son, who's also called Gulli." "Goldsmithery obviously runs in the family then," said the mother. The son wanted to add that Gulli junior was known as Gulli Blow-job but kept his mouth shut. On the way out he felt an urge to say "blow-job" to himself, and it occurred to him to pop into Gulli's workshop if there was no one in the store. He felt he deserved a blow-job from Gulli; to ease his conscience towards his wife, he would buy her a ring at a Christmas discount. Gulli and he had met on a dating site and corresponded before gaining each other's trust. The members of the dating site remained anonymous, but he was cautious and didn't fancy stumbling on his brother or father or cousin in quickie-land. Gulli said that such things happened, but not to worry, it would go no further; everyone is complicit in what is not a crime, unless people believe that sin lies between one's legs and that nature and pleasure are punishable offences. "No one in the shop suspects anything is going on in the workshop," said Gulli at their first encounter, telling him not to be so scared of himself; this was a pleasure not a crime. "Don't go giving your wife a present after every golden moment with me. She might start to suspect something. Gifts often give rise to suspicion rather than joy. Then you'll be crying in a crisis, not me. I fearlessly blow my way through life with a wife and kids." It was dark by the time the son left his parents. In the lift he met a man who always seemed to be there whenever he came for a visit. As he stepped outside, he saw his mother at the kitchen table by the window. She didn't look like a former actress, but rather a librarian with grey hair that dangled over her cheeks. Thinking about it, he felt she had never been a real mother, but had just played the role in the theatre of marriage. It triggered a vacuous feeling in him and he decided to shake it off with Gulli, after which he was bound to be in a lighter mood when he met his wife and children. He had paused below the window; his mother seemed to sense his presence, although she could barely see in the dark. She waved. Then she started to carry things to the living-room table, while her husband tried out the controls again. He had managed to master the recliner by the time the food was ready and moved to the table unaided. The starter was avocado. The woman had sliced it in two and de-stoned it. They sat opposite each other in the glowing red candlelight. The man was about to dig into the avocado, but

gave up and said: "I can't handle your food. This is inedible."
"Yes," the woman agreed. "No point in talking about it."
"What, then?" he answered, irritated, pushing his plate away.
"Could it be true what they're saying on the news, that Christ
is having a sex change to move with the times and being
turned into a woman in the New Space at the National
Theatre?" she answered.

TRANSLATED BY BRIAN FITZGIBBON

SOME PEOPLE
RUN IN SHORTS

SÓLRÚN MICHELSEN

A RUNNER ASKED ME ONE MORNING on my way to work, "Hey, you. Can you tell me what time it is?"

I replied, "Ten to."

"To what?" he asked.

I stared at him briefly. "To eight," and added an "*of course*" under my breath.

Had it been any other time of day, I might not have found it so self-evident. But at eight? When everyone was rushing to get to work on time?

"OK. Thank you. I know neither day nor hour."

He shook his head and carried on running.

I went on my way, more than a little confused. Questions tumbled around my brain like bumblebees.

"It's also Wednesday, 18 October. Anything else you'd like to know?"

I toiled away my eight hours and, truth be told, had forgotten all about the incident when I passed the pitch again and spotted the guy still running.

"Hey, you. Can you tell me what time it is?"

"Ten past five," I replied.

"Morning or evening?"

I found myself staring at him again. "Evening," I said curtly.

"Thank you. Must run."

He ran on. I noticed a track on the pitch where he had been circling all day.

I headed home, but thought a lot about the man. Actually, to be honest, I couldn't get him out of my mind.

For how long had he been running, seeing as he didn't know what day, let alone time, it was? Had he been running for so long that he had completely lost his wits? Or was he a foreigner? Was he perhaps one of these roaming aliens who had taken human form? Perhaps he was lost. Who knows? Wound up in Gundadalur when he was supposed to take part in some intergalactic marathon. Programmed wrong.

I had always wanted to travel in time like that. But I would want to decide for myself where to go and who to visit.

Later that evening I went for a walk. I hadn't planned on walking that way, but without realizing I had taken the same route as in the morning. The closer I got to the pitch, the more I regretted my choice of route. I didn't feel like walking past it, so I just peeked around the corner of the spectators' shelter to find out whether he might actually still be running.

Sure enough, after a while I saw a shadow passing by down on the track.

What should I do?

Call the police or something? The man was wearing himself down. If he couldn't stop himself, I had to help him. But I was reluctant to get involved in this strange affair. The shadow passed me again on its endless orbit. I slipped home.

I went to bed, but couldn't sleep. My thoughts were running in circles. Chasing after that guy. Following him around the track. I tried to guess where he might be now: on the north or east side. Then it occurred to me, and all thoughts stopped in their tracks, he was running the wrong way. Everyone who usually worked out there ran with the sun. Was *that* why he couldn't find his way out again? Perhaps there was some way for me to break his orbit.

I sat up and switched on the bedside lamp. I could put down a plank or two across the track to ease him out, without him fully realizing it. Maybe I should do something now, immediately. This was urgent. I thought I remembered seeing two suitable planks in the garage.

I jumped out of bed, quickly put on a pair of jeans and tucked in the large singlet I slept in. Then I rushed down the stairs and pulled the brown leather jacket off the coat hanger. I had a disturbing feeling that this was extremely urgent. As if it had something to do with me. As if it was a matter of life or death.

It was pitch black outside. The lamp post in front of my house was dark.

I fumbled my way towards the garage door, only to remember that we now used a remote. No pulling. I fumbled back in again for the remote. That did the trick. The door rolled up under the ceiling. It was so noisy in the silent night that it made me nervous. At night, when it is quiet, you have to listen. Hear everything that is going on. It is the only salvation.

The light came on automatically. And there they were. I pushed aside a few old pots of paint with brushes sticking straight up without support, and grabbed an old newspaper to brush the cobwebs off the planks. The planks were so long that they sagged in the middle when I lifted them. I hesitated very briefly, and then headed for the football pitch.

Of course, I had no way of knowing whether the man was still running, but, if he was, I had to try.

I have always been both night-blind and afraid of the dark, so this was no easy task. I hoped I wouldn't come across anyone on my way. They might think the planks were a ladder.

I hurried until I neared the pitch. Then I walked more cautiously. But suddenly I ran into a fence—actually, I ran the planks into a fence and dropped them. I felt the burn of splinters piercing my palms. Cursing, I felt my way to the opening. Then down the stairs, along the barrier and over to where I knew there was a hole. I pushed the planks through and listened, stock-still. The quiet seethed in the darkness. Suddenly I heard something. I did. It was so dark there. I heard the breathing before I heard the footsteps of someone running past, panting. I felt the hairs rising on my nape.

The runner stumbled over the planks, groaned, got back on his feet and carried on running. I flinched in sympathy, but thought I had to give it another shot. Some time passed. Then I heard panting approaching again and once again he stumbled over the boards and fell on his face. He whimpered so pitifully that I immediately pulled back the planks and took them home. I threw them into the garage and closed the door with the remote. Getting any sleep tonight was out of the question, so I made coffee and sat down to mull things over. I was in two minds about the whole thing. In the end I was so exhausted that I fell asleep draped over the table. A crick in my neck woke me up, but my first thought wasn't the pain or that I was late for work now.

I prayed that he had stopped that nonsense.

I rushed to work, passed the pitch; the man was running all the same. My stomach tied in knots.

"Stop it. Stop it!" I yelled silently. He looked up and I felt a jolt when our eyes met. This time he didn't ask what time it was, he just gave me a pleading look. My eyes welled up. I had never felt more helpless.

I went to work, but couldn't focus. My thoughts were spinning. I usually had every situation under control, but now it was all a mess. I couldn't focus enough to sit still. I paced the floor.

Finally, work was over. I couldn't remember a longer day. Usually, they were over before I knew it. There was only one thing on my mind: getting down to the pitch as quickly as possible.

I had a fierce battle with myself, but finally pulled myself together, turned around and walked up towards the bank. There was an art exhibition I had been meaning to see for a while.

Most of the images portrayed the same thing: the dim outline of a man and a door opening to darkness. One differed. It was just a door, which was closed.

The images unsettled me.

I couldn't resist any longer, I ran down to the pitch. The weather had been nice in the morning, but now it was windy with sleet. I was soon drenched, but there was nothing for it. My legs were shaking when I finally came to a halt, panting.

My heart sank to the bottom. His gait had changed. He was dragging himself along like an old man.

I built up my courage and approached the barrier.

"Please stop that!" I implored him, when he passed by.

"I can't. Don't know how to," he gasped and his blue eyes were brimming with tears.

I gripped the barrier so hard that my knuckles went white.

The next time he passed, I heard him say: "Some men run in shorts, although they own trousers."

It sounded apologetic, as though he knew that he was inconveniencing me.

I went home, dragging my feet along with me.

I fixed myself something to eat, but felt like I was chewing paper.

"Stop it, woman. Stop it!" I shouted and startled myself.

I lay down in bed and fell asleep. When I woke up, it was pitch black.

I checked my watch. Two thirty. I had slept enough. I got up, wrapped a blanket around myself, took a CD and put it on. I leaned back in my chair, closed my eyes and tried to enjoy the music, but was interrupted by beats, which weren't supposed to be there. My heart was pounding in my chest and blood was boiling in my ears. Thump. Thump. I listened: that wasn't just my heart. There was also a knocking at the door.

Who the hell could that be, disturbing people in the middle of the night? I ignored the knocking, but whoever it was, it was not someone easily discouraged. It sounded as though someone was pounding on the door with both fists. I flicked on the light and stood up. I could make out a shape through the pane in the front door. I didn't like this one bit. I wanted one of those peepholes. I wrapped the blanket tighter around me.

When I unlocked the door, there he was.

I felt immensely relieved, and took a deep breath. He finally stopped. I gave him a tender look and sighed.

He looked exhausted. His face ashen, dark circles under his eyes and drenched in sweat. He was trembling. He had worn out his shoes and his toes were sticking out. I suddenly realized that he was running on the spot. He could barely lift his feet, but he was running. Behind him snow had started to fall.

He tried to say something, but couldn't speak. Then he cleared his throat a few times.

"Can you lend me your thoughts, so I can escape this?" he asked hoarsely with pleading eyes.

"Yes. If that's all it takes, then, by all means, do take my thoughts."

He stopped dead, thanked me and left, and I have to admit that since then I haven't had a single thought.

But I have taken up running.

TRANSLATED BY MARITA THOMSEN

1974

FRODE GRYTTEN

IN THE SUMMER OF 1974, my mother fell in love with a man named Lars Paalgaard. On Midsummer Night's Eve he showed up at our cabin in a white, open Ford T-Bird. He took us on a drive along the coast, over the bridges and out towards the ocean. My brother and I sat in the back seat, staring at this man who had unexpectedly come into our lives. He was dressed in a black suit and white shirt. Around his neck he wore a string tie with a silver heart. He smoked Winston cigarettes and sang along to the music on the car radio. Mother explained that Lars Paalgaard loved convertibles; he almost always drove with the top down, never mind the wind and weather. She said he wanted to see the sky above him, feel the hot or cold air, inhale the scent of the ocean. Or the smell of shit, Paalgaard added, turning halfway around towards us. I love the smell of shit, he said.

We drove out into a landscape I couldn't remember ever having been in before. We whizzed up hills and alongside meadows, past small holdings that sprawled into inlets and coves. There were new houses here and there with gardens and lawns that hadn't yet been sown. A sweet aroma rose from the car seat, so different from our Opel. This car didn't even have a seat in the back, it was more like a couch. Now and then mother pushed her sunglasses up on her head—she wanted to show the driver that she was watching him. Her

179

blonde hair fluttered in the wind; she tried to get it under control with a blue shawl. She no longer looked like our mother. I could hear the noise of the tyres and feel the warmth of the evening air against my face. My little brother sat with his mouth open, like he was singing along too. I asked him to shut up, he looked like a retard.

After driving for half an hour, Lars Paalgaard slowed down and pulled over on the roadside. There were several cars parked along the road and a man wearing white shorts waved the T-Bird into place. On the gravel pitch down by the shore, I could see merry-go-rounds and a Ferris wheel. I heard shouts and laughter. It wasn't until we came closer that we discovered how jam-packed it was. People bustled back and forth, ran around aimlessly or stood in groups and in lines. Children walked around holding balloons and candyfloss in their fists. Fathers tried to fish up prizes with small metal clamps. Some tried their luck on the wheel of fortune, others shot air rifles or threw balls at cans. Shouts came from the merry-go-rounds, and over by the roller coaster there was a sign that read: Do you dare?

You have to take some chances in life, Lars Paalgaard said and tickled my mother's ribs flirtatiously. Not in a million years, she said and pulled free. She took her wallet out of her handbag. Why don't we meet back at the car in an hour? she asked and gave me a five-dollar bill. I accepted it and didn't know whether to thank her or give the bill back. My parents had never given me so much money before. I want to ride the bumper cars, my little brother said and stuck to me like glue. Fredrik was six years younger than me. He'd been born prematurely and that was probably why my mother had made him her favourite; she'd told me that she'd been sure she would lose him. The summer weeks we were at the cabin, Fredrik always latched onto me. He trotted behind me, always had to know where I was. He was teased by the older boys because he was tiny and thin. I boxed and was a loudmouth, nobody dared mess with me. At the fair the roles were switched: I trotted after Fredrik, I let him do whatever he wanted. A lot of girls made eyes at me and giggled, but I didn't have the strength to think of anything except whether my father knew about this deal with Lars Paalgaard. I refused to believe it. Father was at home in Odda working and the plan was that he would come join us next weekend.

When we walked back up the gravel road an hour later, Lars Paalgaard and my mother were leaning against the T-Bird. He looked relaxed, had his hands in his pockets and a smoke in his mouth. She waved a huge teddy bear at us. Just before we reached the top, I noticed Paalgaard checking his fly. He tugged at the zip and laughed with my mother while he whispered something into her ear. She leaned against him, giggling in a way that seemed wrong to me. At that moment I understood that I was not in any sense out of danger. I could be hurt or injured in a way that would be fatal, not just because of my own actions, but also because of the bad decisions of others.

Mother asked if we'd had a good time and if we'd spent the five dollars. I didn't answer. Fredrik said that we'd gone on the Kamikaze, where we'd been shot 20 metres up into the air before it dropped us down again. We got into the car without saying anything else. The last of the evening sun tinted the T-Bird pink. Paalgaard stepped on the gas and the car pitched into the twilight. I turned around and looked back at the fair where the blinking lights were now just start-ing to appear. At different places along the highway, out on headlands and down on beaches, people had lit bonfires. The T-Bird slid mightily away. It bore no resemblance to any cars I'd ridden in previously. The wind was hot against my face, even at 70–80 kilometres an hour. It was around eleven by the time we turned into the road to the cabin. People were still outside, nobody wanted to go to bed and maybe miss the most beautiful night of the summer. The sound of the usual gang rose up into the night like a yellow wave. They sat smoking outside the cabins; they were playing football over on the grass; but most of them had gathered around a bonfire down by the fjord. On the days before Midsummer Night's Eve, we'd gathered up branches and kindling left by the loggers, we'd even got hold of an old rowing boat. We were outsiders, but always had to have the biggest bonfire in the village.

Every summer my father drove us to Skånevik, and then we stayed there until a couple of weeks before school started. It was the smelting works that owned the cabins and the employees could use them for free. They were called sports cabins, though I never understood why, there was nothing sports-like about them. The cabin we always stayed in was made of logs and painted red. It was located at the top of the hill that started by the highway and sloped down towards the pebble beach. During the summer weeks the entire area was filled with the dynamite-kids whose fathers were union-ized under Chapter 5 of the Norwegian Chemical Workers Union. Everybody knew everybody else and it was like a part of Odda had been moved a few miles further south, to a place that smelled better, looked better, and where it stayed light until much later in the evening. We dived and jumped off the dock by the store. We went fishing and played ball all day long. We boys chased the local girls, the ones who didn't know us already and were still curious about who we were. The girls from Odda who were here on vacation with us had long since understood we were trash.

The mothers usually stayed throughout the summer, while the fathers drove back and forth, showing up when they had a long weekend or vacation. At this time I had begun to understand that not all the fathers, not even my own father, were necessarily all that interested in making a beeline for Skånevik. Home alone, they could drink at the general store, sleep late, be free of nagging and scolding, kids and the wife. For my own part, that spring I'd started sleeping with the daughter of the director of the works, and I just longed for home. She was two years older than me and there were all kinds of rumours about her in Odda. She had called me one afternoon to invite me up. I'd no idea she even knew who I was, but I didn't give the rumours in circulation a second thought. I had a shower and took the path leading to the villa at Toppen.

Even so, I didn't dare touch her or do anything at all until the next time she called and I wandered up the same path. Then she put my hand on her right breast; it was buried beneath a layer of sweater, blouse and singlet. She didn't say anything that afternoon, just led me up to a bedroom on the second floor. She didn't stop me or barter with me—I can't go along with this or that—the way other girls carried on. Afterwards, she said I had to hurry and leave before her mother came home and found us. I gathered up my clothes and shot a glance at her before I went out into the hallway. She lay half-naked with her panties on her thigh. She was slender with light brown hair pulled back into a ponytail. She had thick lips and her eyes were almost closed. Downstairs I stood looking out of a window with a view over Odda.

Every time I went up to the house to sleep with her, I justified it by deciding it was her fault. She was the one who'd called me. She was the one who wanted this. But I couldn't stop. I wanted to hear her breathing when she was transformed from being someone everyone saw to someone I imagined only I was allowed to see. I wanted to hold her and be with her and do all this even though I didn't know what it was. She was so different, she was a place beyond shame or sin, her desire was without inhibition. Don't stop, she said to me. Don't come yet, she said. Don't do it like that, she said. Do it like this instead, she said and showed me. In the evenings I stood in the room I shared with Fredrik. I looked up at the lights that were on in the villa at Toppen. I stood there and waited for her to call.

If you'd walked past our cabin a summer night in 1974, I'm sure you would have wanted to be with these people, have a beer with them, and you would have talked bullshit with them and sung songs around the fire together. You would have wished that your mother was as beautiful as my mother. You would have stood there and thought that now everything was perfect, this had to last forever.

On the night we climbed out of the T-Bird, Lars Paalgaard shook my hand and thanked me for the trip. I'm glad to have met you finally, he said, then repeated the same thing when he shook Fredrik's hand. I remember I thought he was a kind of gentleman: he shook our hands as if he wanted us to understand that he really meant it. After we watched the tail lights of the car disappear between the trees, I went straight up to the cabin. My mother called after me, asking if I didn't want something to eat, a hot dog or a steak. Fredrik came running after me too, but I wanted to be alone.

Inside the cabin it seemed as if nothing was standing still. Everything was spinning around, I didn't know whether I should lie down or stay seated upright. I couldn't remember ever having been so angry before. I took out all my cassettes to choose one in particular that would drown out the sounds of laughter and jabbering from outside, but the tape got tangled up in the player, and I ended up on my feet trying to fix the cassette until finally I pulled out the tape and threw all of it on the floor. After a while my mother came. She knocked on her own front door, as if she were unsure about how I would react. She said that Marita had asked about me, she was down by the bonfire. Are you going down to see her? my mother asked. I didn't answer. Don't you want to go down with Marita? she asked. No, I said finally. Are you all right? my mother said. No, I said. Have I done something wrong? she asked.

I walked right past her and out of the cabin. I started walking down the steep hill that lay like a natural amphitheatre facing the shore. Fredrik came up beside me, but I shoved him in the shoulder. He stumbled and ended up lying on the grass. He shouted my name. I'd decided to tell Marita that I was screwing the director's daughter. Keeping my mouth shut would be the same as cheating on her, I had decided. I hadn't said anything earlier this summer; I thought that it was none of her business because we weren't going out together. We just hung out every summer—she worked over there in the store and that was where I'd seen her the first time. Everyone assumed that we were going out, or at least that one day we would be a couple.

She was sitting a little way away from the others when I got down there. I sat down without saying hi. Where've you been? Marita asked. At the fair, I said. She sat with her hands folded around her knees. There was something in her eyes that made me think she already knew, that she had seen through me this entire first week. I couldn't take her gaze and looked away. Over by the bonfire I caught a glimpse of shadows moving beside the flames, potatoes in tinfoil and beer bottles being passed from hand to hand. I heard glasses clinking against glasses, and people shouting "cheers". Some bratty kids came running up behind us and teasing, they howled: *Sweethearts, sweethearts*. What's wrong? Marita asked. Nothing, I said, everything's fine. I hardly recognize you, she said. Me neither, I said. We sat in silence. A guy over by the bonfire had pulled out a guitar and was singing. Everyone sang along. Do you want to go for a walk? Marita asked. I stood up with a soft sensation of amazement in my body.

When we had come a little bit away from the bonfire, Marita took my hand. She looked back, towards the light from the cabins and the buildings that made up the tiny hub of the cove. I could smell a faint scent from her skin and felt her hair tickling my face. She pushed up against me. Her mouth searched for my own. I stroked her on the back, looking at her bum. She took me into the woods, held my hand and pulled me towards her. She turned around quickly. I saw her pale face between the dark pine trees. She pulled her dress down off her shoulders, so I could caress her breasts. I laid her down on the ground and lifted up her dress. I heard her crying as I came carefully inside her.

After we'd slept together, I thought that she was every-thing I'd ever wanted, and now I'd lost her. She must have known this too when she brought me here. This wasn't the way to do it. This was a way to end it. We lay there on the moss in the densely wooded forest. She kissed my cheek, I stroked her throat, but there was a definite feeling that was spreading through my body and which penetrated all of me, pumping out into my hands and fingers, into my tongue, making my skin prickle.

In the morning I could see from the cabin window that many people had slept outside. They were lying on lawn chairs and on a green couch that somebody had dragged outside. The smell of grilled meat still hung over the place when I sat down on the steps. The morning sun hit everything they'd abandoned the night before: bottles, glasses, plates, plastic bags. The seagulls squabbled over the leftovers in the meadow between the cabins. Sometimes I would get up early, run through the dewy grass and push the rowing boat that belonged to the smelting works out into the fjord. I loved pan-fried coley for breakfast. This morning I went inside again to pick up and read a newspaper, but ended up sitting there, turning the pages without knowing what I'd read.

Mother came down from the second floor dressed in a bathrobe. Aren't you going fishing today? she asked. No, I said. Why not? I answered that I didn't feel like it. Mother went to make coffee, but from the corner of my eye I could see that she was watching me. She stood expectantly, holding the bag of coffee in one hand and the measuring spoon in the other. I could hear her breathing. I didn't move, I waited for her to turn around and continue. When she'd made the coffee, she came over and stood in front of me. Sometimes you have to do things that are wrong just to feel like you're alive, she said.

She said it in a way that made me think that this was something she had practised saying, as if she'd lain awake and figured out exactly this sentence, because she knew she had to come up with some kind of defence. I didn't say anything. I didn't want to give her anything back. It's not what you think, she said. I still didn't answer. She sat down at the kitchen table and lit a cigarette. It's not what you think, she repeated a bit more faintly. And how do you think I think it is? I asked.

She said that Lars Paalgaard worked in the oil industry. He had money, he could help her start up the beauty parlour she'd dreamed of. She wanted to work in her profession. With a beauty parlour, she could make her own money. Completely by chance Paalgaard had dropped by the clothes shop where she worked. He had driven through Odda and had pulled up outside Prêt-à-Porter to buy lingerie, a gift for the woman he'd been seeing at the time. She said that she liked the guy, he was the type who made things happen around him—he got other people moving. She smiled. That is a bit his style, isn't it?

What do you think? my mother asked. Isn't it a good idea? What's that? I asked. The beauty parlour, she said. Sure, I said, without really having thought about it. But I understood her: my mother was beautiful and slim, with a sense of humour; she was always the centre of attention at parties, her laughter was infectious. When Mother danced, or simply walked across the floor, the needle on the record player at home skipped. She wanted something more. She wanted everything all at once. She had met my father in Bergen, she had cut his hair a couple of times, and later he had asked her out. Finally he'd convinced her to come with him to Odda. She hadn't wanted to move, she thought it would be lonely living at the end of a fjord. At that time, though, she must have been in love; she must have thought this was a normal life. That was before she acquired this aura that beautiful people often have, as if they bear a grudge against everything around them because the world has failed to keep the promise beautiful people think it has made them. This was before my father's rage, before he started drinking seriously. It was before he started destroying different rooms at home. Always late, always drunk. He used to limit the damage to one room at a time, so that when we woke up in the morning, before our parents had got up and had the chance to clean up, we could see where his anger had found its particular expression in the course of the night.

You think that I'm getting carried away with this, don't you? my mother asked. I don't know what you're doing, I replied. She stood up and walked over to the window with a view of the fjord. She said that she was going to give me some advice. Nobody will really help you in this life, she said. People just help themselves, she said. You get help only if you have a common goal with someone. And that is the closest you will come to happiness. She went over to the kitchen with her coffee cup, then she came back and caressed me through my hair. Why do you think men do stupid things? my mother asked. She said that men either messed up for their own sake or else they did terrible things because of women. Often they do both at the same time. But what do you know about this? she said. How can you know, you're fifteen, you haven't done anything at all yet.

My little brother came down while we were standing there; he was still half asleep. He walked straight over to our mother, who hugged him and sat him on her lap. She asked if he'd slept all right. Fredrik had been awake when I came up to the room last night. It was hot and stuffy and he was lying on top of the quilt wearing only his pants. How much do you think that car costs? he'd asked me. Don't you understand? I'd said to him. She's fucking him, you know? Fredrik hadn't said anything. A little later I'd heard him crying in the semi-darkness. Mother rocked Fredrik on her lap and kissed him on the head. When is Dad coming? he asked. Next Friday, mother answered. She waited a bit, then she added: But it's not certain that he's coming. Why not? Fredrik asked. We'll see, mother said.

Lars Paalgaard showed up again in the T-Bird that same evening. This time he was wearing a pale suit and sunglasses on his nose. We were playing football in the meadow when I saw him come driving up. Mother went up to greet him. Fredrik wanted to follow her. He asked if I thought we could go for a drive in the T-Bird today too. I held him back. Don't, I said. Fredrik looked at me, then he pulled free; he was irritated and disappointed. Don't, I said again when I saw he was on his way up the hill. Paalgaard and my mother were laughing between themselves. He stroked her neck and she let him do it. I didn't understand why they were so careless: they were broadcasting what they were up to, showing it off so any old idiot would have to get it. I didn't understand why my mother wanted to risk so much; she behaved as if nothing meant anything any longer, or as if losing everything could be satisfying in its own right. She was willing to give up everything because she wanted something else so intensely.

A good hour later they came out of the cabin, and Mother introduced Lars Paalgaard to the others who were outside barbecuing. Everyone tried to behave normally, but they'd seen what they'd seen and the usual chatter fell silent and the atmosphere grew confused. Nobody really knew what to say, or how to stand or look or move. We were about to start eating pork chops and potato salad when I heard the sound of a motorcycle coming down towards the cabins. My mother heard it too; she spun around suddenly. I peeked over at Lars Paalgaard. He got up out of the folding chair he was sitting in. He looked up towards the motorcycle and then over at Mother. She laid her hand on one of his arms.

The motorcyclist parked beside the T-Bird. I recognized the body type and the vehicle, but prayed to God that it wasn't him. I prayed that it was anyone else but my own father who was standing there and slowly pulling off his gloves and helmet. Fredrik was already on his way up the hill; he received a hug and was lifted up high in the air. Then the two of them came walking down the path, hand in hand. Somebody handed my father a bottle of beer as soon as he came down to us. His co-workers made a toast and welcomed him, greeting him in a way that was both heartfelt and anxious. Later I understood that it must have been one or more of these co-workers who'd called and told him. They'd probably thought this had gone too far. Now he was here and nobody had any idea of what was going to happen. My father went over to my mother, kissed her on the cheek and put his arm around her waist. Mother didn't say anything. Then he greeted Lars Paalgaard politely. They both said their names and then Father said: What a

nice day. What did you do? He nodded towards the food that
was prepared. He said that he'd come home to dinner on the
table, he said that he felt like a king. He lifted his bottle and
smiled. Well, cheers then! The fathers raised their bottles in
reply and drank. The mothers threw themselves with relief
into the job of serving.

While we were eating, the men discussed the World Cup
match between the GDR and West Germany. Everyone loved
Jürgen Sparwasser, the way the centre forward got around
the defence and drilled the ball up into the top of the net.
Most of them believed it proved Communism was completely
superior to Capitalism. I stared at Lars Paalgaard while I was
eating. He didn't say anything. Either he had no clue about
football or his mind was far, far away. After we'd eaten—I
ate quickly and ravenously—my father turned towards Lars
Paalgaard: The two of us should have a talk. What do you
think? Paalgaard turned to Mother questioningly, but she
just looked down into the drink she held in her lap. Are you
coming? my father said to Paalgaard. He'd got to his feet. The
two of them walked up towards the road: a tall man in a pale
suit and a stocky guy in T-shirt and flared jeans.

They stood there up by the T-Bird, almost in the same way
Paalgaard and my mother had been standing on the shore
the night before. After a little while the two of them got in
and sat in their respective seats. It didn't seem like they were
talking. To me, it looked as if they were just sitting there, staring
straight ahead through the windscreen. Lars Paalgaard had
both of his hands on the steering wheel. My father had lit a
cigarette. It was comical, it was as if they were just playing
that they were driving at full speed down the highway. If
somebody had taken a picture of them from a distance, it

would have looked like an idyllic image of two men taking a drive through a beautiful summer landscape.

Mother had risen to her feet now and was standing with her back to the others; she smoked and stared almost demonstratively out towards the fjord. The neighbour family's dog ran around with a ball in its mouth and tried to get people to play, but everyone was watching those two up in the T-Bird. I saw people rolling their eyes and some of them whispering among themselves. After a couple of minutes, Paalgaard twisted the key in the ignition and the car began rolling slowly out onto the gravel road. Somebody sighed; my mother turned around. She called Paalgaard's name, but the car didn't stop. She started walking up the hill, at first quickly, then more slowly. She shook her head and crossed her arms over her chest as if warding off a fit of the shivers. The car drove through the aggregation of cabins and disappeared between the pine trees. That was the last time I saw Lars Paalgaard alive and, had I known it then, I would have said something to him. I don't know what, but I would have said something or other.

Father came back around 12.30 that night. I was sitting by the window in the cabin, waiting for him.

Fredrik had gone to bed. My mother said I should get away from the window, but she didn't have any kind of sensible reply when I asked her why. You should do it because I tell you to, she said. I couldn't see anything unusual about my father when he came walking up under the street lights and cut across the way up towards the cabin. As he approached, he was met by a co-worker, a dark-haired guy they called Elvis, but I don't know why. He neither looked like Elvis nor could he sing like Elvis.

Elvis offered my father a long drink and a pack of cigarettes. They spoke to one another. Without warning, my
father ploughed the glass into Elvis's face. When the guy lifted
his hands to protect himself, my father grabbed his hair and
smashed his face against his knee in one swift movement. He
repeated this movement several times with great force, until
the guy collapsed on the grass. I don't really know whether
I heard any sounds, but later I imagined that on that night I
heard Elvis's face crack.

My mother started yelling and screaming. She chased me
into bed. You go upstairs, she said and pointed towards the
second floor. You go now! I did as she said. I didn't want to
be confronted with my father when he was so furious, I knew
what he was capable of. I lay in bed listening, trying to put
together what was happening from the sounds. I heard voices
that got mixed up in one another, loud and excited, but I was
unable to distinguish one from the other or make any sense
out of them. The view from the tiny window on the second
floor faced the grove, away from what was happening out
front. I stared over at Fredrik and wondered whether I should
wake him. This clearly involved him too, but he was sleeping
calmly and I thought it was best to let him sleep in peace.

Ten minutes later I heard a car outside, more voices, arguing
and shouting. There was a revving of a car engine and then
silence. I must have fallen asleep, because the sound of loud
voices arguing down in the living room yanked me awake.
I heard my mother say that she was a grown woman. Why
can't you behave like a grown man? she asked. I heard a man
sobbing. At first I thought there had to be a third person down
there, someone who was with my mother and father, and that
it was the third person who was crying. But I tiptoed over to

the door, opened it a crack and looked down. I couldn't see my mother. My father was hiding his face in his hands and when he took his hands away, I saw that he was crying. I had never heard or seen my father cry before. I crept back into bed and put the pillow over my head.

The next morning my father was sitting out on the steps reading the newspaper. He was smoking. I saw that they were Winston cigarettes and I wondered if they were Lars Paalgaard's. My father whistled while he read, as if everything was fine. Good morning, he said. Did you get any sleep? Yes, I said. I went to get a glass of water. I sat on a rock with my back to the cabin. Jesus, my father said and started reading out loud from the newspaper. It was an article about an American politician who'd been caught red-handed with two prostitutes in his car. People want to have a whole lot of things for nothing, my father said, have you thought about that? I'd never thought about that, so I didn't reply. Without looking up, my father said that people cheated on their taxes, people stole and made promises and lied and tricked each other. He said there was a clear line between right and wrong in this life, and that I must never decide to study law, because the job of lawyers was to mess with that line. I had to promise him that I would never study law. As if I had ever even considered it.

I didn't understand what he was babbling about and I felt restless. I didn't know what it was then, but I do now. Something was taking shape inside of me, in my own life, something that was going to explode inside of me when the time was right. Where is Mum? I asked. She drove off at five this morning, my father answered. Why were you crying? I asked. When? he asked. Last night, why were you crying? Grown-ups cry sometimes, he said, it's OK. He finally looked over at me. Don't be disappointed about what your parents do, he said and waited for me to answer. Do you love your father? he asked. He said my name twice. Yes, I said. Do you think I will take good care of you? he asked. Yes, I do, I said. I will take good care of you, he said.

I read somewhere that 1974 was the year with the greatest number of working-class people in the world. After 1974 the percentage of people working in industry started going down. In 1974 Odda had its historical moment—when social democracy reached its peak, all visions were within reach, the working class had civilized capitalism, and the welfare society was as close to reaching fruition as it ever would be. After that, things didn't run on their own steam any longer, and a few years later the world changed direction with Margaret Thatcher and Ronald Reagan. Even Jürgen Sparwasser defected to the West when he retired in 1988. He had been promised a car, a house and heaps of money for his goal against West Germany. He got nothing.

In the year 1974 my father started attacking his own family. In 1974 I waited for phone calls from a crazy girl who I knew was going to drop me the minute she got tired of me. But that's how it is, that's how you lose a city, and it's only afterwards that you can write the story. When you're in the middle of it, you think everything will stay the same, everything will remain the way it is, just a little bit different.

Then you're standing there one day on the empty street when you've come home after having been away for a long time, and you meet people you don't know, or people you don't recognize. The grey factory buildings and the grey mountains are the same as they have always been. But everything has changed and the workers don't walk through the gate to punch the clock any more. That's how it happens: first your best friend moves, then you move, then they shut down the smelting works, then there's a whole gang of men nobody needs, and then the radio stations don't play the records you like any longer. Then they ship the entrails of the factory to Poland, China and Argentina, and then they start arguing about what's going to happen to the shells of the buildings that have started falling down. The benches are empty, there's no longer water in the fountain outside city hall, and the neon lights on the cinema have stopped working.

There used to be something here, something beautiful and disturbing all at once, and it seemed important, a sparkling future that perhaps nobody fully believed in, but which was ingrained in you—this is your city, this is your time, this is what you are. And look now: I can't even remember everybody's names. That's why I decided to create this little booklet with a list of all the people who used to be at the cabins in Skånevik for those weeks of the summer every year. I have written short biographies of people, made copies of photographs of them and tried to piece together what has happened to everyone.

After that summer I was sure that I would never go up to the director's residence again. We weren't going to sleep together any more. It was best to avoid one another or not speak to one another ever again. But I longed for her, I dreamed about her, how she took my hand and stuck it in between her legs. How she took my foot and put it between her thighs and then started moving on top of me until she came. How she shoved my head down towards her crotch and whispered for me to show her what she had taught me. My parents were like children that summer, consumed with trying to find one another anew. My mother had come crawling back and asked for forgiveness. They spoke in soft, secretive voices and I tried to interpret everything they said, but pretty soon they were yelling at one another again, loudly and without consideration. They had disappointed one another too much; neither of them managed to live up to what they had been when they'd first fallen in love. I wanted to get away, I wanted to be free. I slipped up the path to the director's residence every time she called. As soon as I was inside, she fumbled with my belt, then she pulled off my trousers. I wondered whether there was a name for this. And if it didn't have a name, was there a way out of it?

This was the worst thing I could know about myself—that I was just like her, that we were two of a kind. I wanted to get out of there; I wanted to stay. I gave in to her hard hands every single time. Afterwards I lay with her back against my stomach, like an accident victim. We lay in the dirty afternoon light and I saw that her skin was young and smooth, without wrinkles, free of all the scars that were waiting somewhere in the years to come. I wanted her to start talking, for her to explain to me what had happened. Or that one day she would cry or crack, say that she wanted to be with me or at least that she needed me. I lay as close to her as I could. On some afternoons I could hear her breathing change and I realized she'd fallen asleep. Their house was so different from ours. They had, for example, a pool table and a huge fireplace in the living room. On the stairs and on the second floor, there were bookshelves filled with novels and reference books. The rooms were dark and solid. The dead stared down at me from up on the walls, oil-painted ancestors who'd perhaps been real bastards when they were alive, for all I knew. The carpet was thick and soft; walking on it was like walking across a lawn. I thought that one day I would live in a house like this, a house as huge and as expensive. At the time I didn't have any idea just how badly all this was going to end.

TRANSLATED BY DIANE OATLEY

MAY YOUR UNION
BE BLESSED

CARL JÓHAN JENSEN

T HE HEAD-TEACHER'S WIFE, Mrs Rybert-Hermansen, was quite unlike her husband. A tall, angular woman five years his senior, sometimes prone to kindness but mostly brusque and bossy, she spoke Danish when she spoke at all, and allowed no one to address her in Faroese with impunity, although she rarely cared to make a fuss.

She was the daughter of a stern postmaster, Jens Erich Rybert. He had become known across the land for having fought at the battle of Dybbøl in the 1865 Dano-Prussian war, when an explosion had left him with a limp. His dark disposition could sometimes transform him through fits of demonic rage.

In Tórshavn his thin, high-pitched voice earned him the nickname "Bleater". Having completed his military service, Rybert, who was from a well-bred but not equally well-to-do family, studied economics and law in Copenhagen, but delayed taking his final examinations.

He came to the Faroes one spring in the early 1870s to work at the Governor's office as a temporary replacement, but ended up staying on.

For the first few months he rented lodgings together with the surgeon Paul Fobian in the house at Bakka owned by the shopkeeper Knút Hermansen.

As fate would have it, there were two housemaids working for the newly married shopkeeper. The housemaids took turns tending to the lodgers in the house at Bakka—one day to clean for them, the next day to prepare their dinner.

One of these housemaids was called Thalia, originally from Elduvík.

Her age was uncertain.

Thalia was more plain than beautiful. She was short with narrow shoulders, a small, full bosom and a dark complexion with black slanted eyes, a flat nose and a wide mouth.

She had, however, one particular attribute that distinguished her, more than any external feature, from other women. She was possessed of an internal, almost supernatural power to command any man's desire with the same cool glow of innocence and oblivion as the moon commands the tides.

But Thalia was a gentle soul.

She considered her power a sin for which she must atone every day.

But she accepted whomever it drew to her.

She satisfied, soothed and satiated, all with the same humble diligence.

Soon after taking up employment with Knút Hermansen she had been given a room of her own in an annex which had originally been used for storage. The entrance was from an alley at the back of the house.

The shopkeeper would certainly not allow himself to be diverted by any special powers. He kept an accurate account of everything he saw, heard or thought. He was a prudent man with a strong sense of honour. After the household had retired for the evening, it was his habit to keep an ear on all the goings-on in the annex.

And sometimes also an eye.

A row of old deck boards formed a wall separating Thalia's room from a passageway that followed the length of the house from the shop to the annex. There was a knothole in one of the boards that was situated at a height particularly convenient for peeping, when the small mirror covering it was pushed aside.

Not infrequently, the shopkeeper had trouble sleeping. Despite her young age, his wife Gisela could snore like a bull. Thus any movement in the alleyway would easily compel him from the marital bed, and he would eventually find himself standing in front of the little mirror.

It would also happen that if he thought he heard rustling in the bed on the other side of the boards, he would poke his finger under the mirror so that chance provided him with a vision of how—when least expected—unaccountable impulses could get the better of reason and sense.

Each time this vision was equally clear.

Thalia knelt by the side of the bed, unbuttoned the front of her nightdress and performed carnal sacrament on whatever frustrated soul had sought her out, with a firm hand and an air of compassionate wonder.

Each time the procedure was the same.

But the men were as different as they were endowed.

Knút Hermansen stood gaping, pressing and panting against the boards, his heart aflame and his eyes watering with guilt-ridden pleasure.

The knowledge that providence gave the shopkeeper through the knothole was credited in his accounts alongside his other earnings.

One mild Sunday night around the feast of St Lawrence,

this chapter of his book-keeping, however, came to a quick and dreadful end.

The causes were twofold.

The first was a watchful eye, and the second the point of a lancet, which reduced his sight by half.

The watchful eye belonged to the undergraduate in economics and law. The lancet came from the desk drawer of Paul Fobian.

Word got around. For several weeks Knút Hermansen was in agony, even though physician Smertz, seeing the state his patient was in, had been quick to remove the eye from the socket.

The incident had no immediate consequence other than that, on the following morning, Rybert moved from his rented lodgings into a half-constructed house at Ryggi, owned by the provincial authorities.

A week later, on a Tuesday, Thalia left the shopkeeper's annex and moved in at Ryggi.

Shortly before Christmas she and the young Dane married.

For many years relations between Knút Hermansen and Jens Erich Rybert were strained, to say the least.

It was nevertheless a comfort to the shopkeeper that even with his semi-vision, he couldn't help noticing that Thalia continued to perform her sacraments, despite her marital status. Neither her power nor her will to atone for her inherent sin showed any sign of abating.

That Rybert's mood darkened as the years passed, and his devilish rages became ever more frequent, was no less of a comfort.

Then came the children.

First Rybert's daughter.

Then the shopkeeper's son, Mats Kristian Hermansen.

Miss Rybert was unlike both her parents in appearance, but as she grew up, it came to light that in certain undeniable ways she was clearly her mother's daughter.

Finally, her father decided the only recourse was to send her away to Denmark.

This settled the score for Knút Hermansen, who felt no shame about his own offspring.

For a long time nothing much happened.

But then Rybert was appointed as postmaster.[*]

Hermansen was shocked, but adjusted to this development sooner than might have been expected.

Madam Thalia had taken to the bottle in her later years. Rybert's advancement in professional standing was outweighed by his wife's deteriorating reputation, as she became ever more brazen in her shamelessness.

---

[*] Postmaster J.L. Rybert came to the Faroes, as the author says, to take up a temporary position at the Governor's office. This was in 1879, the same year that Jens Davidsen retired. H.C. St Finsen was Governor at the time.

The author is correct in stating that Rybert studied law, but he did not study economics, and he had recently taken the first part of his exams when he came here. He was supposed to fill in a clerical position until the autumn, when he had a passage reserved back to Denmark on the state-owned steamer *Diana*. But he ended up staying on at the Governor's office until 1901, when he was appointed as postmaster.

There are no sources to confirm that Rybert fought in the war in 1865, and this would hardly have been possible, as he was twenty-five when he came to the Faroes and could not have been more than eleven years old in 1865. He was said to have an effeminate demeanour and always dressed as if he was on his way to a social festivity. He was also known to be long-winded, short-tempered and high-handed. The people of Tórshavn called him "Queen Arsehole".

Rybert married, as the author says, and his wife was quite rightly from Elduvík, but her name was not Thalia and she never worked for Knút Hermansen, nor was she a slattern as Thalia is depicted in the story. Rybert's wife was Marin Kristina Frederiksen. She was the seventh daughter of the farmer Fríðrik á Flatumørk, who died in 1889. She did keep house for Rybert for many years but they were both well advanced in age when they married, which was, according to the church records for South Streymoy, in the summer of 1917, and therefore they had no children together.

And when one morning word had it in the shop that the postmaster's wife had let the missionary and quack Brond pull out all her teeth, the shopkeeper decided that the time had now come to settle the accounts for good. The knothole, the lancet and his missing eye were written off forever.

The shopkeeper and the postmaster took to greeting each other in the street. Sometimes they could even be seen attending the same funerals.

Years passed.

Jens Erich Rybert became ill. Having managed to recover from a stroke, he suddenly died.

One Good Friday morning as he sat in the church loft listening to the vicar recounting the works for which rewards are reckoned not by grace, but by debt, the postmaster felt a sharp, stabbing pain in his side and chest and left the church earlier than was his wont. He arrived home to find his wife on her knees on the parlour floor in front of the sofa, dressed only in her undergarments, with bodice unbuttoned. The devil took hold of Rybert. As he kicked and thrashed Thalia in a blind rage, his wife cringing and grovelling around on the floor in search of her dentures, he suddenly clutched his chest with both hands, jerked his head to the right, then to the left, and with ashen face and upturned eyes fell dead onto the sofa, his head landing in the lap of a tender, downy-cheeked young man who had not had the presence of mind to pull up his trousers.

The young man was Mats Kristian Hermansen.

A year later, embittered, the shopkeeper settled his own mortal accounts and soon afterwards the shop was shut up for good.

The following year, in the autumn, Miss Rybert returned

home, spirited and voluble, despite her waning youth. She moved in with her mother at Ryggi.

By this time, though, Thalia was entering her second childhood. Before long, darkness and dementia had engulfed her so firmly that her power was finally extinguished.

Nothing now prevented Miss Rybert and Mats Kristian from forming a union, which they did nine years later, shortly after he took his teacher's diploma.

It began one uneasy day in June.

Flies were buzzing.

The sun beat down and everything was still, trembling.

Then a sudden breeze picked up.

In the parlour of the shopkeeper's house, an infusion of smells swirled in the air. The tang of wood shavings, varnish and ethanol that lingered after Gisela, Mats Kristian's mother, had been borne out earlier that day, mixed with a whiff of mould, eau de Cologne and sweat. Into this concoction the scent of angelica wafted in on the breeze from the garden.

Miss Rybert stood with her back to the parlour door, her eyes half closed, head tilted, and nostrils blazing.

Her arms around Mats Kristian's neck.

He kissed her throat hungrily.

My dove, my Shulamite, he muttered, fumbling with her clothes, aroused and ardent. It was, however, with an inkling of the misery and regret which would become his steadfast companions that he finally managed to grope his way to her Zion's gate.

Thick, coarse hair grazed his fingertips.*

---

* The reader should be extremely careful not to take anything the author says about the head teacher too seriously. It is at best unreliable and at worst malicious fantasy.

First, his name was Kristin, not Mats Kristian. He took his diploma at the Faroese Teacher's College in 1915. That same year he married Elisabeth Magdalene Huber. She was the daughter of the postal assistant J.M. Huber, who came to the Faroes in 1909, and not postmaster Rybert, as the author maintains. This assistant Huber was said to have been a small, frail man easily given to chills. The people of Tórshavn called him "Draughty".

Kristin Hermansen was a temperate man, scrupulous and efficient in his work, see *Føroysk Lærarafólk* (Bókadeild Føroya Lærarafelag, 1995, p. 57). After qualifying as a teacher, he was appointed to a position in Tvøroyri where he became head teacher in 1921. In 1933 he returned to Tórshavn and worked at the Intermediary School until he retired in 1965.

Kristin Hermansen began early on to make a name for himself in the cultural life of the Faroes. While he was in Tvøroyri, he founded the Tvøroyri Theatrical Society and was its chairman until he moved back north. During his years in Tvøroyri, he also published a collection of poems, *Yrkingar* (1923), and produced the weekly paper *Tímin*.

Above all else he was known for the provocative articles he published about Charles Darwin and evolutionary theory in the journal *Varðin* (see no. 2, pp. 29–31; no. 5, pp. 53–5; and no. 9, pp. 81–3). He left behind various unpublished short stories and plays, and also tried his hand as a translator. Among this work was a translation of *The Pelican* by August Strindberg, which the Tvøroyri Theatrical Society staged in the winter of 1925 and *Tímin* published the same year.

In the literary history *Úr bókmentasøgu okkara*, published by Varðin in 1935 (p. 151), the late Professor Christian Matras briefly discusses Hermansen's translations, but has not a single word to say about his poems, plays or articles. Of his translation of *The Pelican*, Christian Matras says that while bearing the marks of a rare enthusiasm, the divergence between interest and competence is unfortunately often very great. The translator is no great stylist, writes the Professor, and his translation never manages to capture the vitality and intensity that gives Strindberg's text its brilliance.

Today, few would deny that Kristin Hermansen is one of the foremost Faroese literary figures of the last century (see also the article by Steinfinnur Miðgerð in the weekend supplement to *Dimmalætting*, 23 September 1997).

Kristin Hermansen was, as the author mentions, also involved in politics. He was a candidate for the Unionist Party in Tvøroyri in the 1920s and later for the socialists in Tórshavn. That was in the 1930s. He was never elected. He did take up a seat in parliament for one term, however, when D.N. Jacobsen became a government minister after the 1953 election. Kristin Hermansen died in 1975, aged ninety-seven years old.

TRANSLATED BY KATE SANDERSON

SAN FRANCISCO

NIVIAQ KORNELIUSSEN

"**G**o!" I discover to my horror that she has decided to do just that after I have told her to for the fourth time. I regret rebuffing her even more when she sticks her arm into the sleeve of her pale-blue Peak Performance jacket and gets ready to leave the flat. Consumed by self-loathing, I tell myself to go over and embrace her, apologize and beg her to stay, but my body refuses to obey. I glower at her while she puts on her jacket and her shoes, drops the cigarette packet into her handbag and heads for the door. I really don't want her to go. I want her close to me again and I want to tell her that I love her, over and over. But all I can do is watch her sad face as she leaves because I'm unable to move or utter a single sound. Get it together, you moron! I know that I'm in the wrong, it was my fault that we started arguing, and that it was stupid, ugly me who provoked, offended and hurt her after a crap day that left me bursting with suppressed anger. Now I look at her adorable, wistful eyes and my remorse is so great that the ocean seems but a drop by comparison. My shame leaves me silent and immobile, but still overdosing on madness. Why can't I just admit that I was wrong? I look at her beautiful face when she gives me a placating look just as she is about to leave.

"I'm sorry," she says.

I'm sorely tempted to show her how contrite I am, but why, why is she apologizing? Why does she take on the blame? Once more I'm overcome with rage and I glare mercilessly at her with my ridiculous face. I watch her go.

"I love you," I whisper and the door shuts.

I jerk violently and then I rush to the door, taking big strides, and I lock it so ostentatiously that my beloved must be able to hear it. I hope desperately that it will make her so angry that she will come back and bang on the door, but I realize that she has given up when I hear her fetch her bicycle and her presence starts to fade. I run to the window to look for her, but she is already too distant to hear my frantic knocking on the windowpane. She is far away, gone, and I am left alone with myself. A dreadful loneliness starts to grow inside me. Serves you right, go on, feel sorry for yourself, be lonely, stop whingeing, you got exactly what you wanted, she has left, she is gone. Fia, you bloody idiot, it's your own fault that she left you. I bang my heavy head against the wall to punish myself for my impatience and stupidity. Darling. Beloved, I'm sorry. Come back, beloved, and I will prove to you that my love for you knows no limits. Beloved, give me another chance; believe me when I say that you're more important to me than I am. Please understand that I didn't mean what I said. Come back and kiss me again, cry in my arms, scold me and give me the chance to comfort you. I will die unless you return.

The feeling crawls from my heart to my lungs and then up my throat before it explodes out of my mouth. My body grows limp and I start to wail, my face distorts, and the snot runs. I don't care if the people above or below can hear me because there's no way I can control myself. I throw my heavy body on the bed and sob into her scented pillow which is drenched by the time I fall asleep.

Sara, my beloved Sara, come back.

I wake up thinking that a mouse is trying to escape from my hand, but realize that my mobile is vibrating. Last night's dreadful events hit me full force. Then a feeling of joy grows inside me: my beloved is calling because she wants to come back to me.

"My darling, I'm sorry. Come back to me. I love you. Sara, I love you, I love you so so much."

I don't bother with hello because I'm so busy telling her all the things I should have said before she left, so that she will understand. I'm still half asleep and I can't make out what she is saying. There has to be something wrong with my brain since her voice sounds so different. It is unrecognizable.

"We're calling you because we can't find anyone else to contact, and we can see that you've called Sara's mobile. Do you know Sara?"

Perhaps she is still pissed off with me. Perhaps she is trying to wind me up and maybe she is not yet ready to forgive me.

"Sara, darling. I'm sorry."

I'm not angry with her at all because I can still remember the horrible and crazy stuff I said to her. Sweetheart.

"Fia? You're Fia, aren't you?"

Slowly it dawns on me that the person I'm talking to is not Sara.

"Come on, pass the phone to Sara. Or tell her that I love her. Yes, tell her that I love her and that I want her to come home. Tell that I'm not upset and that it's my fault and mine alone that we argued last night. Would you? Please would you

tell her? I can understand if she doesn't want to talk to me.
Tell her that I understand. No, tell her that I love her more
than anything in the whole world."

The woman I'm talking to, who must be one of Sara's
friends, heaves a deep sigh. She might be about to pass the
mobile to Sara or tell her what I have just said.

"Ubgofsjfuofbwjnfjsbfjn sfjfou ofbosjkfbsobegjb ojefbkjbfjbf
cnjfeojfbjbfdjgfnaoe," the woman replies—and when I fail to
understand her, I ask her to say it again.

"Rkfkgjbdkfjb kekhjbg efkjekgjuuenaljefkjebgaebug."

"WHAT?"

I'm in agony, all my muscles tense up, and for some inex-
plicable reason, my heart starts to pound. I don't want to
listen to her gobbledygook any more. I feel dizzy and I want
to throw up. The words align inside my head and take shape.

"She has been knocked down by a car and I'm afraid that
she's dead."

The idiot woman's words start repeating inside my head:
knocked down. Dead. Knocked down. Dead. Knocked down.
Dead. And all I can think of is San Francisco, SF . . .

Prussic's song "Qarasat neri10ppoq, imaaru10lerpoq vakaler-
poq" from my childhood returns. I wonder why that silly song
is going around my head and when I can't come up with an
explanation, I just blame it on my messed-up brain.

Right . . . If I ignore my madness, then I think that I'm OK.
I'm not sad. I'm not happy. I feel nothing. I don't know if I'm
alive or dead. I only realize that I have arrived in Denmark
when I hear young, angst Danish teens talk: "It's fucking sick,
that's what it is. Bitch nicked my iPhone, and she can't even

be bothered to admit it! I mean, what the fuck! Stupid slag, but she won't get away with it if that's what she thinks! Bitch!" It is like being on a bus full of teenagers in Nuuk on a Friday night. They remind me of Nuummiuts who talk just like that when they mess with each other, mixing Greenlandic and Danish and shit, but end up sounding like a bunch of fucking morons. "Shit, whorersuaq niaqulaaruloorpaat! Kalassuaq, utaqqilaar unatagaaruluussaatit! Arnapalaaq!" The Danish teenage slang takes me back to a period I can't bear to think about, and it pains me so much so that I can no longer control myself. As they are in front of me and are still mouthing off, I run to catch up with them. I slap the boy with the big mouth on the back of his head, snatch his baseball cap and position myself right in front of him. I fling out my arms as wide as I can, shove my face up close to his and start screaming so loudly that the sinews in my neck stand out.

"Shut the fuck up! Learn to talk properly! I've had it up to here with you bloody kids!"

I turn my back on them and start to walk away, but then I spin around and erupt in one last roar.

"AARGH!"

I hurl the boy's cap at him and stumble along, away from them. What the hell? What just happened? What do I think I'm doing? When I turn around to apologize, they are already gone; they have probably fled. Fancy me being in Denmark. I don't even remember being on the plane.

There are people everywhere. Unknown women, men, children and elderly people block my path; I lean against a building to calm myself down because I feel like I'm suffocating. Behind all the people rushing about like ants, I spot a large, flashing sign: "Welcome to New York!" I experience a sense of urgency when I realize that I'm in America, and I join the ants to get to the exit. It is evening. The atmosphere is strange. Exhaust fumes from cars fill my nostrils and almost stop me from breathing. I look at the giant, luminous skyscrapers towering against the sky. I feel dizzy; I look down and I see a long line of yellow cabs. I walk up to the one at the front and a dark, heavy-set driver gets out. New York, USA. I wonder if I brought luggage. I can't remember if I checked in a suitcase or if I remembered to pick it up. When I see the driver put a large rucksack inside the cab, I realize that I did bring it. Well, that's all right . . .

"Where to?" the driver asks me with a smile.

"Midtown," I say to him.

I get out of the cab when we appear to reach the city centre. Even though the city is fabulous and amazing, I can't help staring at something dreadful that has caught my attention. I drag my heavy rucksack across the wide street and towards the thing I cannot help but look at. I reach it and see a poor man with a long beard sitting by a pedestrian crossing. His hair is grey and his face swollen from a red rash. Embarrassed, he looks humbly up at me and cautiously extends his begging hand. I find him bizarre in the extreme and I squat down and look straight into his eyes. I'm struck by a stench so sour that I almost throw up. Sweaty armpits, urine, shit, bad breath, mould, rotten fish. His gaze shifts from me; he bows his head and withdraws his begging hand. I cup his cheeks in my hands to raise his head and I smile at him. He frowns at me, trying to work out if I'm making fun of him. As I don't fancy lugging around my rucksack, which might be crammed full of clothes, and because I need to get the scent of fabric conditioner which I recognize from somewhere out of my brain, I offer it to the abandoned wretch. The homeless man is stunned and hugs the rucksack. I feel so sorry for him that I almost kiss him, but his acidic stench makes me nauseous, so instead I get up and leave. My body is lighter now that I'm no longer carrying anything. The scent of freshly laundered clothes has finally disappeared. I want to escape the bright and busy streets so I slip in between two big buildings. It is twilight and silent. I walk past two large rubbish containers, spot an illuminated sign and go inside what I presume is a bar. A couple of elderly men are drinking beer. I order a large draught beer from a vile-looking bartender and sit down, well away from them. New York. I wonder where I'll go next. What will I do? Why am I here?

I realize that I have finished my beer. As I still can't feel it in my blood, I get up to order another. I return to my table and find a young woman, who wasn't there before, sitting right next to my chair. I look at her in surprise as she turns to me, but when she doesn't react, I sit down next to her so that my body brushes hers and I start drinking my beer. We sit in silence for a long time, drinking greedily. We don't look or talk, but she is so close to me that I can hear her breathing. I place my almost empty glass on the table. She puts down hers, she has drained it completely. We sit quietly, doing nothing, making no sounds, making no movements. Suddenly she takes my empty beer glass and drinks the remaining foam and licks clean the rim of the glass. Her behaviour is so odd that I stiffen. She smiles and grabs the cigarette packet from the table. She takes out a cigarette which she sticks in her mouth, and takes out another which she offers to me. I take it. I keep it in my mouth, but I still need a light; meanwhile my companion is smoking like a chimney. She blows smoke in my face, lights my cigarette, and we sit smoking with our faces turned away from each other. When she has finished, she stubs out her cigarette on the table and stands up. She jumps up onto the table, crouches in a monkey position and looks right into my eyes. I stare back at her. Her hair, dyed orange, is styled in plaits like Pippi Longstocking. She looks very serious, but then she bursts into a smile so wide that she shows all her teeth, and I start to laugh. Her eyes are adorable, heavily made-up, but the visible gap between her front teeth makes her smile very comical. Without knowing it, she smiles like a stand-up comedian.

"HEY GIRL!"

Her voice is so loud and piercing that my body reacts. I start grinning and I give her a hug. I don't know why. I hug her just because I feel like it, then I grab her and lift her down from the table. We stand there, still holding each other tightly. When she lets go of me, she puts my jacket around her shoulders, grabs my hand and leads me out of the bar. She takes me to a pickup truck I didn't notice earlier and sits me down on the passenger seat. She gets into the pickup and turns to face me.

"Where to?"

Her smile is so wide that I start to laugh again. She sticks her tongue out at me.

"Kansas City, baby!" I shout by way of reply.

She gets so overexcited that she grips the wheel and pretends to race the car while she makes engine noises. I can hear that her car is on its last legs; it shudders and splutters when she starts it. It is red and tall. The pickup has an open deck filled with empty bottles.

"Oh, shit. Hang on a minute, I'll be back soon."

She jumps out and runs back to the bar. A few seconds later she returns, waving a bag of cannabis in front of my face. We laugh and drive off.

I discover that it is daytime and I put on my sunglasses because the sharp light bothers me. I don't know how long we have been driving, but at least we have left the city behind. The landscape around here is deserted. Except for our spontaneous giggling fits, we have yet to have a proper conversation. The sunshine is merciless. My chauffeur pulls over and jumps out of the pickup. I join her and discover that she has put down the back flap and is sitting on the deck of the pickup while she rolls a joint. I sit down next to her, waiting for her to pass it to me. I don't know if I have tried cannabis before, but I don't care. We get so high that our lungs turn black. We puff and we cough. She gets up and stands in front of me. She rests her hands on my knees and looks at me, very gravely.

"I'm Suffia."

Once more I'm startled.

"Who are you? Where do you come from?"

Her sudden curiosity jolts my thoughts so that I can give her a reply. Only I have completely forgotten where I'm from and so I offer up a guess instead.

"I'm Changhi Peng Pong from Japan!"

Suffia looks momentarily wrong-footed, then she flings out her arms and starts to dance. "Japan Japan Japan! Peng Pong Ding Dong!"

She doesn't laugh. I don't laugh.

"Hello, Ying Yang! It's very, very, very nice to meet you!"

For the first time, I erupt in bellyaching laughter and Suffia joins in. Our laughter is so powerful that we collapse on the ground and start to howl. Our eyes water. The cramps in our stomachs hurt so much that we burst into real tears before we start to laugh again. I roar with laughter until I can no longer breathe and it feels as if I am about to die. Not that I would mind.

When we have recovered, we get back in the pickup and take deep drags of the joint. I plug my iPod into the car and play Pink's new album, *The Truth About Love* and find the song "Blow Me (One Last Kiss)". We are on the road again with the windows rolled right the way down, and we join in the song: *"Have you had a shit day? WE'VE HAD A SHIT DAY!!!"* We sing along at the top of our shrill voices and drive faster. *"Blow me one last kiss!"*

We appear to have arrived at Chicago. The city is vast and it has grown dark without me noticing it. We stop at a petrol station; I go inside the shop to buy something to eat while Suffia fills up the pickup. I'm exploring the crisps and sweets section when someone taps me on the shoulder. I turn my head and nearly have a heart attack when I see her face.

"Are you from Greenland?"

The woman who has Greenlandic features looks at me in wonder. Before I have time to think about it, I nod. I would appear to be from Greenland.

"What are you doing here? Wow, I can't believe I've bumped into a fellow Greenlander! Who are you? Who are your parents?"

I panic so much that I snatch some food and drinks and make my escape while the woman tries to grab hold of me. When Suffia sees me come running, she opens the door to the pickup and starts to drive very slowly. She accelerates as I get in.

"GO GO GO GO!" I scream.

When we have driven some distance, we stop the car and light a joint while we howl with laughter.

"I'm not Ying Yang, Ding Dong! I'm Greenlandic!"

I say all the words I can get out; meanwhile Suffia's laughter grows louder.

"Where the fuck is GreenLAND?!"

I can barely remember our drive from Chicago to Kansas City, but my stomach muscles and my cheeks ache—apparently because we have been laughing all the time. I'm fairly sure that we have been smoking cannabis the whole time as well because my lungs sting and my eyelids are heavy. We drive past a large sign saying Kansas City and get out in the city centre. Here the buildings are also enormous, but they display themselves like great dinosaurs. This city seems filthier and less safe than the other cities. It is revolting. Suffia looks after me when I leave the car to do some shopping and she blows me a kiss. She starts shouting, "BLOW ME ONE LAST KISS!"

I shout the same back, kiss my hand and blow the kiss to Suffia. When I have done my shopping and am leaving the shop, I see that Suffia is about to drive off and I get a strange feeling. She calls out to me through the open window.

"GOODBYE!"

She turns a corner and waves as she disappears. I don't really want to her to go, but I find the situation funny because that is just what she is like. Suffia is Suffia. I laugh out loud at her for the last time.

I have left the big city behind and reached the old part of Kansas. The houses are made from wood and the roads are gravel tracks. The people are few and slow. I would appear to have walked the whole way and my stupid, post-operative knee hurts. My post-operative knee . . .

Following my operation, I stay at the surgical ward at Sana Hospital. I keep falling asleep because the poison is still coursing through my veins and the staff rouse me by shaking me gently. I'm taken through a big corridor in a bright white bed, wearing bright white clothes. I look at the hazy lights above me while they move me along. I feel fine. Smiling, I turn my face to the waiting room as I'm rolled past it. I check her beautiful but anxious eyes when she sees me and am reassured; a feeling of joy takes over my body. She gets up and accompanies me to the side ward. When we are left alone, she comes over to me, indescribably relieved, touches my head gently and kisses me. "I love you," she says. For more than one long month, she nurses me, cooks my food, entertains me, comforts me when I cry, helps me into bed, is with me, loves me. She never leaves me.

And now I'm alone . . .

My head hurts. My last memory is of the old part of Kansas. Perhaps I've had a fall. The clearer my eyesight becomes, the more I feel that I'm flying across a big road. Street lights appear and then disappear just as quickly, and my body feels cool. The sound of an engine hums in my ear and I turn my head to explore my surroundings. A man about forty years old is sitting behind the steering wheel, and I only wake up properly when I realize that he is staring at my thighs.

"Who are you?"

I try to look terrified even though I'm not.

"You can call me Jeff."

He winks at me, without smiling. Even though I feel very unsafe, I stay neutral. He wears a faded red cap with visible sweat stains around the headband. He is huge and has pitch-black hairs on his arms. I look more closely and I see that he also has long hairs on his fingers. His stubble bristles; he clearly hasn't shaved for days. His disgusting lips are so swollen that they might burst at any moment. He is truly hideous. I would really like to know how I got inside his truck, but I remain silent because I am scared of making him angry.

"Where are we going?" is all I say.

"Denver, Colorado."

He replies while he stares at my breasts. Apart from that, I don't think a lot about anything during our long drive, but I'm tormented by a hangover and feelings of emptiness and darkness. I'm in anguish. Finally I pluck up the courage to ask him what I'm doing here, but before I have time to open my mouth, he responds as if he could read my mind: "You were lying in the road and I picked you up so you wouldn't freeze to death. I was fairly sure you had no place to go."

I wonder what I was doing on the ground. I'm too exhausted to ask any more questions, so I switch off my thoughts and stare out of the window instead.

I come round when I feel too strong fingers squeeze my thigh. The man wakes me up; I appear to have fallen asleep and I remove his hand immediately.

"Easy now; I'm waking you up because we'll be there in the couple of hours."

So why wake me up now? I'm looking at him with fear and loathing when suddenly he turns his face to me. When he realizes that I'm staring at him, he winks at me a second time, and I feel both abused and destroyed. Utterly terrified, I cover myself with my jacket and divert all my energy into not nodding off again because the thought that he might touch me again terrifies me. I try to ignore the endless, long road. I count street lights instead and try my hardest not to think. The beast's foul smelling eau de cologne makes me nauseous and I keep the window open so as not to throw up. Thus we drive through a dark forest for what feels like forever. At times I try to remember something I think I have forgotten, but I can't identify what it is, so I go back to counting street lights. This lack of clarity brings on a painful headache which keeps getting worse, but as the houses start to rush by more and more often, I start to feel reassured. We drive past the sign saying Denver and vile Jeff heaves a deep sigh. Just before we reach the city centre, bloody Jeff turns off in another direction. Out of fear I tense every muscle so as to be prepared. He pulls up at a remote and deserted car park and rubs his hands.

"Thanks."

I have thanked him and am about to open the door when that bastard Jeff grabs my wrist and forces me to touch his stiff dick which is caged behind his trousers. Shocked, I try to get away from him, but his hold is strong and I don't succeed. Even though my heart is pounding, I try to act relaxed and strike up a conversation, something even I don't understand.

"I'm into women. I don't have sex with men. I've only ever been into women, ever since I was a child."

The idiot doesn't listen to my words and forces my hand closer to him.

"I'M GAY!"

I scream it at him and try to snatch back my hand. When I feel his grip loosen, I turn my head to his disgusting, filthy face. When I see a change in his facial expression, I get ready to save my life. His face turns red and his eyes become insanely angry.

"What? A fucking dyke? You're sick! SICK, SICK, SICK!"

His body is arched and his muscles tensed when I open the door to throw myself out in order to force him to let go of me. When he finally does, I fall a long drop from the high truck. I'm so concerned with making my escape that I don't feel anything at all when I hit the hard tarmac. All my energy goes into fleeing. It feels as if I'm running underwater; my legs are heavy as they are in dreams. I'm slow and exhausted.

"Come back so I can have you put in a mental institution!"

The devil has followed me and roars at me. In order to break away from the darkness, I run towards the light; at times I crawl on all fours. I don't look back and I fight to escape. I run out of strength and can move no further.

"Fucking dyke."

My energy returns when I discover to my horror that he is still behind me. With the last of my strength, I run to the entrance of a metal building. When I reach the automatic glass doors, I fling myself inside and crawl a few metres before I stop. A couple of people pass me and I am so relieved that my fear starts to fade. The monster doesn't come inside. I calm myself down and drag myself further inside the big building where I slump against a wall to recover. The place is full of all sorts of shops: clothing shops, a florist, toyshops, cafés and a bookshop. At the end of it all are escalators. I'm into women, it would appear. I wonder why? How did that happen?

We're sitting on a bench in the Nuuk Centre outside ITTU. We have shopped for dinner tonight and are eating French hot dogs from Café Mamaq. The shopping centre is fairly quiet, but every now and then people wander past us. She holds my hand and kisses my cheek. I can feel her joy and warmth and look forward to spending a lovely evening with her. She moves closer to me and whispers in my ear. Pure love makes me melt and I smile. As I think about her sweet words, I notice a group of giggling teenagers making remarks about us and I stare at them. I grow a little irritated at her welcome caressing of my back, but I don't do anything. Two women walk past Nønne Fashion and I turn my head towards them. One of the women sees us and whispers something to her friend. I follow them with my eyes. The friend slowly turns her face to us with a look of surprise. I feel deeply embarrassed. I let go of her lovely hand and quickly finish my hot dog so that we can get out of this place. I see an elderly, fragile man head in our direction. His bag groans with beer bottles. I look at him when I feel her warm hands on my cheeks. She turns my face towards hers and kisses me gently near my lips. I want to kiss her back. The man looks at us, furrows his brow and stops. He glares at us and shakes his head.

"Why don't you go home if you want to do that, it's too hideous to look at!"

Then he stomps off in disgust. A feeling of shame and inferiority overwhelms my common sense and I push her hand away from me.

"Stop it. Not here, it's too embarrassing!" I say and look at her. The joy drains from her face and is replaced with distress. Her beautiful eyes are veiled with tears and she stares down at the floor. I have hurt her deeply. I shouldn't be angry with her. She is a loving person. She is not someone I should be ashamed of, she is someone I should be proud

to show off. I should have gone over to those grinning, staring and prejudiced people and told them that my love for her cannot be changed and that I'm lucky that she has chosen me because I'm happy. I want to scream at the top of my lungs: "This is my girlfriend!" But I just get up and leave.

When I can no longer breathe, I run outside and into the city without stopping. I need to drown my blinding headache in strong alcohol. I count the passing cars as I run and slap my forehead when I get it wrong to make me count properly. Even though my body is exhausted and my lungs hurt, I keep moving and I don't stop until I reach the nearest bar. I go inside and order three shots of neat vodka and down them in quick succession. I start to relax. Every time my thoughts try to take over, I knock common sense into myself with vodka. I feel lighter and I sit down at the bar to enjoy a quiet beer. The bar is murky, lit only with dim red lights. The customers are few, but their loud talk is pleasing to my ears. I can make out someone in a corner and I'm taken aback. My heart aches when I recognize her, but I still can't work out who she is. Who is she again? Her long hair is dark and loose. Her beautiful body has impressive curves. Her back arches inwards while her buttocks stick out a little. Her legs are straight and I think they would be lovely to touch. I feel warm. Time passes and I give her a few looks while I order stronger drinks. When she turns around, her face is different from what I expected, but it's OK. I think it will do. As she walks up to me, I look away and pretend to ignore her. She places her hand on my back and moves her face very close to mine.

"Were you looking at me?" she asks.

Even though her voice is not what I expected then, it's all right.

"Yes."

I hope to score her quickly. She smiles and whispers to me. "Why?"

I smell her neck and whisper back to her. "Cause I want you."

She is still for a moment. Then she takes my hand and leads me to the lavatories. The moment we get inside, I turn her towards me and start to kiss her. We enter one of the cubicles and we paw and tear at each other like wild animals. My blood races. I come alive. I stroke her arse and her back. Her breathing deepens. I pin her against the wall and kiss her while I slip my hand under her T-shirt. Her breasts are not particularly big and they are lovely to touch. Her nipples, which I'm busy kissing, are hard. I move my hand from her breasts and down across her stomach. When I reach her belly button, she closes her eyes and starts to pant. I lead my hand away from her belly button and slip my fingertips inside the lining of her trousers. I move my fingers further down because I can wait no longer. Wet. My blood is pumping through my body. I close my eyes and everything inside me starts to burn. I plant wet kisses on her neck and her moaning grows louder. I look down and discover a tattoo on her stomach which I don't recognize. I feel dizzy and I steady myself by taking deep breaths. I feel her tremble violently and I remove my hand from her and support my back against the wall and my hands on my knees. She comes over to me and gives me wet kisses on my neck. I want to, but I just can't do it. I can't do it. I'm overcome by nausea, I push her away and I leave. I stumble through the crowd which has grown larger, looking for the exit. I get outside and I throw up for what seems like forever while I rest my hands against the wall. During a brief pause, I try desperately to drag oxygen into my lungs so as not to suffocate and then I start to throw up again. I still feel queasy, but appear to have puked up all my guts as nothing more comes out. My throat is burning. In order to get my breathing under control, I stand with my head lowered while I inhale deeply.

Someone touches my shoulder and I turn my head.

"Are you OK?"

The petite woman looks to be around fifty or maybe more. I nod while I carry on trying to breathe. She takes my arm and slowly leads me to her car. The tall black SUV is elegant and looks comfortable. She leaves me next to the car while she fetches something from the driver's seat. She returns with a bottle of water and helps me to drink from it. As my breathing stabilizes, distressing thoughts start to creep up on me again. I discover that I have feelings . . .

I go limp and I start to cry. The woman sits down next to me and puts her arms around me for a long time.

"Do you need something? How can I help you?"

Her voice is gentle and comforting. I can't give her an answer because I'm bawling my eyes out and I can't breathe. She holds me tight, refuses to let go. My sobbing is so convulsive that I have to force myself to stop. The woman dries my tears and waits patiently until I become lucid. Neither the pain in my throat nor my desperate sobs hurt me because my heart suffers more.

"Can you take me to San Francisco? Please, please, please?"

I burst into tears again. She embraces me in silence and strokes my hair.

"Yes, of course. I'm heading that way so I might as well take you, mightn't I?"

She comforts me. I nod my head and dry my eyes, hugely relieved. The big seats in the car are covered with light brown leather. The seat on which I sit is so soft that my body relaxes instantly.

I look at the woman, my saviour. She turns to me frequently with a concerned smile and I start to feel safe. The fine, fragrant car is almost silent and makes me sleepy. I abandon my efforts to count street lights.

"What's your name?" I ask out of curiosity.

"Danielle Michel," she replies kindly.

"Hello, Mrs Michel. Thank you very much for helping me."

I am on the verge of crying again, but I swallow my tears. She makes no reply, but touches my arm and smiles gently. She clears her throat and makes to speak. I don't mind.

"Where are you from?"

I am tempted to say that I am from Japan, but I can't lie to a person with such a big heart.

"I'm from Greenland."

I'm reminded of Suffia and am tempted to giggle, but when I can't manage it, I remain silent.

"Why are you so far away from home?"

She asks casually and even though I don't feel like telling her, I can no longer control my mouth.

"I've lost someone."

I can feel that Mrs Michel is struck by grief and struggles to find the words.

"Who?"

Her voice makes me feel so safe that I want to answer, but I can't recall anything.

"I can't remember," I reply without lying.

I am relieved that Mrs Michel doesn't think I am insane; instead she looks at me with understanding and unprejudiced eyes. The pain in my heart floats away. I realize that it is morning and that Mrs Michel has a calming effect on me, so I find the courage to look at her without worrying about it. From time to time she touches my arm to ask if I need something. I know perfectly well that there is something in my mind and heart that I need to explore and resolve, but right now I am at ease. We drive for a while in silence. We arrive at Salt Lake City and the many hours we have been driving feel like a short period of time. I am so comfortable that I stay in the car while Mrs Michel gets out to do some shopping.

She returns, hands me a cup of coffee from Starbucks and turns to me. "Sweetheart, what is Greenland like?"

She smiles faintly. I try in vain to think of an appropriate answer.

"It's cold," I then say.

We start the car and drive on. Mrs Michel's questions become more frequent which makes my body grow restless.

"What do you do in Greenland? When did you come to the States? Are you visiting someone in San Francisco?"

Every time I have to reply that I don't know and every time my heart beats faster. Why can't I give her an answer? Why can't I remember anything? What am I doing here? What am I doing in San Francisco? As I have not thought so profoundly for a long time, I struggle to come up with a reply. Just as we are about to cross a large bridge, a magical city appears and it dazzles me. My emotions intensify. Whether it is from joy or grief, I don't know. But I feel too much.

"SF"—San Francisco. When I see the big sign, I become nervous and my heart hurts. Mrs Michel senses my anxiety and takes my hand. She does not let go of me. A feeling of loss overwhelms me and I focus on my breathing so as not to panic. SF. Now I'm here.

The streets in the city centre have no specific directions. Up, down, right, forwards, left, down, up, backwards. It is undoubtedly an enchanted city. I know people call it "gay town". There are cable cars here, small, open trams that you see everywhere. You can follow tall buildings into infinity. Outside the windows, clothes have been hung out to dry next to the dried fish. People look down from the windows and admire the city from the top. I spot the great ocean which I have not seen for an eternity and am reminded of Greenland. I get a little homesick. Mrs Michel asks me to look at her and I become aware that she wants to tell me something.

"I have to move on. Go for a walk and get some fresh air. Search carefully for the things you repress and don't be afraid of them. You take care of yourself now."

She puts her arms around me, and even though I don't want her to leave, all I can do is let her go. My throat starts to well up.

"The things I repress?" I ask confused.

Mrs Michel looks at me, smiles faintly and drives off. I take a good look at my saviour before I turn around. What things?

SF. San Francisco is so unique that it can't be compared to anywhere else, and I decide to do something about my feelings for this city to fill the emptiness inside me. I enter a discreet tattoo parlour and wait to be served. A man with multiple tattoos on his arms comes over and shows me to a chair.

"How do you want to be tattooed?" he asks with a smile.

"A heart with SF inside it. I don't want it to be big."

While the tattooist gets ready to tattoo my wrist, I look at the people around me. A large man weighing around two hundred kilos sits on my left. He is having a naked woman tattooed on his arm and I'm pretty sure that tattoo is the only woman he will ever have. I turn to my right and see an attractive woman with short whitish-yellow hair. Now who does she remind me of? I jump when I feel a prick on my wrist and the tattooist gets to work. He doesn't take long and in a strange way the pain calms my body down. While he fetches me a Band-Aid, I look to the right again. When the woman turns to me, I can barely believe my own eyes and I stare at her unashamedly. Pink! Pink! Pink! I snap out of my dreamlike state and turn my gaze to her again. She is so beautiful that I can hardly believe it. She talks to her tattooist. She is clearly aware that she has been recognized and glances at me. She has noticed me! She is looking at me! Oh my God, oh my God, oh my God. I can hear a voice screaming inside me. Several of Pink's songs come back to me and I rediscover all the love which has been absent in me for so long and the feeling is so indescribably huge that it cannot be resisted. When she turns to me, I bow my head to her in gratitude. There is no doubt that Pink's music is the best guide I have in my life. When she sees me bow, she sends me a smile which I will treasure deep inside my heart forever. Pink. Who would have thought that I would see such a beautiful person? I pay the tattooist and take a last look at the woman with the wonderful voice when she suddenly waves to me by wriggling her fingers and my heart explodes. I can sense that Pink is looking at me with compassion and as I can't understand why, I just leave.

SF. Heart.

My tattoo has penetrated the skin properly and my body is less tense. I sit down on a small mound of green grass and light a cigarette. I pick up my iPod and play Pink's latest album, *The Truth About Love*. I gaze at the blue sea and try to put my chaotic feelings and thoughts in order. I have to knock some common sense into myself. What am I doing here?

"Right from the start, you were a thief, you stole my heart, and I, your willing victim." The song "Just Give Me a Reason" starts to play and some degree of lucidity seeps into my thoughts in such a terribly short space of time that I almost become fearful. I have come to my senses.

"Just Give Me a Reason" is playing in the background. The television is on, but silent. Our small kitchen has been left untouched and filthy. I have woken up feeling fraught and because of that I have a headache and I am crotchety. I heave a deep sigh and go to the kitchen to start washing up. She dries the dishes and smiles a little while I try not to get annoyed with her. I want to look at her lovely face without looking angry myself. When we have finished, I sit down on the sofa and spend a long time on Facebook to avoid talking to her. She sits on one of the chairs by the table and looks at me with devotion. I pull a face to offer her a kind of smile by way of acknowledgement. Today we have been together for three years and I'm still in love with her. I get butterflies in my stomach when she puts her arms around me. I always long for her to come home from college. I always look forward to lying next to her, holding her,

kissing her neck. When I tell her that I love her, I always mean it. I don't want to lose her, but I'm not OK. Even though our relationship is exciting and happy, something is wrong. I'm fine as long as I'm at home, but when I go out, it feels as if the whole town despises me and talks about me behind my back. I log off and go to my room to lie down for a little while. My lovely girlfriend enters and lies down next to me. Without making eye contact, I slip my arms around her and kiss her a few times "Fia, just look at me," she says. I make myself comfortable and she smiles and starts to caress my face. She gazes at me with her pretty eyes.

"Are you OK?"

I nod in order not to show my frustration. We lie in silence holding each other. "Fia . . ." She clears her throat to firm up her voice.

"Three years." I smile and she starts again.

"I love you, and you know it. You love me, I can feel it. When I think about my future, I always imagine spending it with you. You're so precious to me and I don't want to lose you. I can't imagine life without you." She smiles and continues. "If you feel the same way about me, I would like to marry you, make a home with you and have children." She kisses my cheek.

"Of course I feel the same way about you. If all goes well, I obviously want to live the rest of my life with you and have children. You're a part of my future because I have no chance of ever being happy unless you're with me." This is what I want to tell her, but I'm worried what other people might think. "Get married? Have children? You have to understand that our relationship will never be straightforward. Can you imagine what people would say if we were to marry? If we have a child, people will look down on her or him because she or he doesn't have a father. I'm telling you, our child will be bullied at school. He or she will have two bloody dykes for mothers, and that will be a shame." I don't pause to think before I launch into my rant. She looks shocked.

"If our child doesn't have a father, but gets plenty of love, feels safe and can talk openly to us, having only two mothers won't be a problem. I know that we would make good parents. I'm sure that we can offer a child everything it needs. Are you against marriage? Are you against making promises to each other, loving and respecting each other for the rest of our lives? You have to ignore what other people say and live your own life. Many people think that we're completely ordinary. Our relationship is no different from their relationships."

The truth of her words hits me hard and I snap. I get up and reply: "But I know that lots of people think of me as a freak!" She gets up, comes over to me and puts her arms around me, even though I shrug them off. "Fia. And so what? I don't want them getting in the way of our love. Don't let them stop you from being yourself." Her embrace reassures me, but I remove her arms and get ready to leave. "Where are you going?" she asks softly. "Out to buy fags," I reply angrily and leave. The rest of the evening I'm unapproachable. I walk away whenever she comes near me. I go outside to smoke when she tries to talk. My body grows tenser and I can no longer control my rage.

Everything comes back as images. A sofa. A 42-inch television. A big lamp. A double bed. A freezer. A MacBook Air. A PlayStation 3 and two games. I remember now that I sold it all except my iPod. Her mother's pale and red-eyed face appears when I close my eyes. Her grave. Sara being buried deep in the ground. Sara. Sara. Sara. I can't remember attending her funeral, but terrifying images flash up in my mind. Everything is dark, but her bright white coffin shows up horrifically and I can't make the disturbing sight go away. I remember the phone call. The words seem so fresh that it feels as if they were spoken only a few seconds ago. "Knocked down. Dead." Sara's last word, "Sorry", and her pretty face filled with grief repeat on a loop, tormenting my ears and eyes.

San Francisco's warm atmosphere is choking me. I can no longer bear to watch the otherwise fascinating people. The enchanted city turns into something ugly. I start to wish that someone would blow up the Golden Gate Bridge. I have to go. I need Sara because I'm going crazy. Sara. Sara. Sara. How do I find her? I want to search the entire city, but instead I go to a hotel because deep down I know that I won't find her anywhere. I throw my heavy body on the bed and I suffer. I don't care that children are starving to death in Africa; all I want is for Sara to come back. I don't care if World War Three breaks out; I would be content as long as Sara is by my side. I don't care if I die as long as I can touch Sara again. I'm dying because I can't go on living. I hear my heart beat, but I can't feel Sara's heart. Sara isn't here. She is gone. She is dead.

I have to fall asleep. I have to forget her. For the first time since her death, I remember going to bed. I'm cold. I'm in pain. I'm shaking. I'm insane. I'm alone in the world. I prefer not to wake up again. "Sara, come here. Sara, I'm sorry I threw you out. I'm sorry. Lie down next to me and warm me up. Lie down next to me and love me. Come back to me. I will always love you." I don't usually believe in God, but I pray to him with all my heart for help. I close my eyes. I try to recall the feeling of Sara's warm skin against my body. She is by my side. I can feel her breathing against my neck and my body feels safe. She is by my side. Her love embraces my heart. She is breathing. Her heart is beating. She is alive. I can see it. I believe it. I will fight unto death to preserve this magnificent love that I feel. I am no longer cold and I fall asleep.

I wake up. I can feel Sara in my heart. I want to be by her side for the rest of my life. I will love and take care of her for the rest of my life. I want to be with her for the rest of my life. Is there anything left of my life? Is there a rest of my life?

"Don't leave me," I beg Sara.

"I'm right here," Sara says.

I have probably lost my mind, but I don't care. Her voice calms me down. I'm no longer afraid, I open my eyes and all I can see is SF . . .

The small picture frame is sitting on the small table in our room. SF, heart. We carved it into a small log cabin in the mountains so that our love would last forever.

Sara. Fia. Heart. It is so reassuring that it brings me to my senses. I feel her hand near my heart and I grab it and I will never ever let it go. My heart is pounding. I turn around—I turn towards Sara. Her eyes sparkle, her cheeks are flushed, her beautiful face is alive. Her heart is beating. She is alive. She is alive, and I'm restored to life. I awake to life. I am alive. I feel her warmth, I embrace her wonderful body, I kiss her soft lips. I feel love and reassurance in my heart. My eyes fill with tears of joy and I say:

"Why don't we go to San Francisco?"

TRANSLATED BY CHARLOTTE BARSLUND

NOTES FROM A
BACKWOODS SAAMI CORE

SIGBJØRN SKÅDEN

NOTE 1

A creek.

The fireweed blossoms.

Nothing here is coincidental.

The fireweed is an intelligent plant that knows where the dirt is

rich on nitrogen.

Long roots fetch nourishment from the deep.

He who understands the fireweed can read off its stem

what is north and what is south.

Rarely do people know that the fireweed's blossoms also can

be white, like water lapping the stem of a moving boat.

NOTE 3

He's got a washing machine that's gone to hell. He takes out
the drum, cuts off the top and puts it on a rack. Now he's got
a grill. When he tears down the old shed, he builds a wind-
stopping wall out of the rubble.

NOTE 4

She looks at him smoking a fag. After a while she goes inside. She knits. A scarf with a message in Saami for mum. "Eadni, don leat máilmmi buorremus!" says the pattern. "Mum, you're the best in the world!" Only one word is misspelt.

NOTE 5

It's a few generations back. King-Jo stands on a hill overlooking the village. A mastodon of a man. He's heard that the Swedish king himself will pass here with his cortège on his way to the coast. Jo's brought two planks of wood onto this hill which has a good view in several directions. Now he just waits. Nobody in the village understands what he's doing. Until now they've called him only Jo.

Then Jo sees a long cortège approaching in the distant. It can only be the king. Jo has never laid hands on an instrument, but he's heard "God Save the King". He picks up the two planks and starts banging them to the beat of the song so hard that the sound echoes throughout the parish. He keeps on doing this until the king's cortège has passed and is out of sight. Then Jo walks down from the hill. Whether the Swedish king ever understood the tribute, nobody really knows.

NOTE 6

There's an inherited pride in not buying new stuff, but rather making what you need out of what you already have. Here we call it making one's own patent.

NOTE 7

Any car has potential value. Enough organ donors could in the end become a product. The organ-donor hoods remain lying around in the field encircling the house. No need to remove them, he says, they shimmer so nicely in the sun.

NOTE 10

His parents buy him new trainers while on holiday in Sweden. The shoes are blue and yellow. Among the kids in the village they are quickly nicknamed "the Swedish shoes". The Swedish shoes are made from a stiff, synthetic material that proves unsuitable for soccer. To shoot the ball is impossible, it's too painful. He can only lob it. In the course of that autumn and the following summer, until he finally grows out of the Swedish shoes, he develops a sophisticated lobbing technique. There is no situation he cannot lob his way out of. For all time he is the one who's lobbed the highest penalty on the calves' grazing field.

NOTE 12

Recipe for a boat trailer:

Buy a 30–40-year-old caravan.

Slash it all to smithereens with a chainsaw.

Dump everything apart from the undercarriage behind the barn.

NOTE 13

Greetings from the neighbour: Nothing colours the September sky like the sound of a chainsaw eating away at fibreglass and aluminium.

NOTE 14

The dead are here. With no drama, no conundrum, without being anything out of the ordinary, they are here.

NOTE 17

The floor of the community hall is about to cave in during the New Year's party. He's on the committee. Like all the others he's drunk out of his mind. He sees only two possible solutions to the problem.

Option 1: Tell the villagers to stop jumping to the beat.

Option 2: Phone his grandfather in the middle of the night and tell him to get over there with some building materials quick as hell so they can emergency-reinforce the floor foundation.

He chooses option 2.

NOTE 19

Down by a place where two rivers meet there is a meadow. If the time is right, he who passes here will hear infants crying. These are the unwanted newborns, left here to die by a desperate father or mother. Every seventh year these children return to the place where they were abandoned.

We call them *eahpádusak*, human apocrypha trapped between existing and never having existed. That is why they return. That is why they cry. Only by performing an ancient baptizing ritual may all be alleviated. Only then will it all be over.

NOTE 21

"I wash the dishes the Saami way," he says.

"How so?" says the anthropologist.

"It's in the wrist," he says. "But for people who are not so familiar with Saami culture it might seem like I do it exactly the same way as everyone else."

NOTE 23

My coffin is slender, skinned trunks of willow, tightly bound.

My coffin is old postal bags, split and sewn to a snug cocoon.

My coffin is nightfall and the following day.

My coffin is the particularly roomy ski-box I got so cheaply in Sweden.

My coffin is a boat, with no sail, no oars, and the sky open above me.

My coffin is the wind, and entrusted men carry me onto the mount.

NOTE 24

Much later they arrived at a place. They viewed the land.

"This looks rather OK," he says.

"Yeah," she says.

"We'll settle here," he says.

"Yeah," she says.

TRANSLATED BY THE AUTHOR

Author Biographies

Originally from Greenland, NAJA MARIE AIDT is a Danish poet and author with twenty-seven works in various genres to her name. She has received numerous honours, including the Danish Critics' Prize and the Nordic nations' most prestigious literary prize, the Nordic Council's Literature Prize, in 2008 for *Baboon*, and her work has been translated into ten languages. Her work has also been anthologized in the *Best European Fiction* series and has appeared in leading American journals. *Baboon* was published in the USA by Two Lines Press in 2014. Denise Newman won the PEN Translation Prize for her translation of *Baboon* in 2015. Naja Marie Aidt's first novel, *Rock, Paper, Scissors*, was published in August 2015 by Open Letter Books. She lives in Brooklyn, New York.

KJELL ASKILDSEN (born 1929 in Mandal, Norway) is one of the great Norwegian writers of the post-war era and a major figure in contemporary Scandinavian literature. Since his debut in 1953 he has published seven acclaimed short-story collections, as well as five novels. His latest book, the short-story collection *The Cost of Friendship*, was published in 2015. Askildsen has won the Swedish Academy's Nordic Prize, the national Brage Prize and the Norwegian Critics' Prize twice. His short stories have been translated into twenty-nine languages.

JOHAN BARGUM (born in 1943 in Helsinki, Finland) is a writer and director. He writes Swedish, Finland's second official language and had his first book, a collection of short stories (*Swartvitt*, "Black and white") published in 1965. He has mostly written short stories, but has also published novels and plays, some thirty works altogether. Films and television plays based on his work have been produced in Finland and Sweden, and his prose has been translated into several West and East European languages. His play *Are There Tigers in the Congo?* has been translated into more than twenty languages. Bargum has received many awards, among them the Pro Finlandia medal in 1996 and has been active in the cultural field as chairman of several organizations including the Finland-Swedish Authors Union. He is married, with two daughters and four grandchildren.

GUÐBERGUR BERGSSON (born in 1932 in Grindavik, Iceland) published his modernist novel *Tómas Jónsson metsölubók* in 1966 ("Tómas Jónsson Bestseller"), a cultural breakthrough in Icelandic literature. His novel *Svanurinn* (1991) (*The Swan*) secured his position as a major European novelist. Bergsson's books have been translated into many languages. He is also a prolific translator of world literature and has enriched Icelandic literature and culture with timeless masterpieces by Spanish, Portuguese and Latin American writers, including Cervantes's *Don Quixote*. He has been the recipient of several major prizes, including the Nordic Prize of the Swedish Academy in 2004. In 2010, he was awarded the Spanish Royal Cross (Orden de Merito civil).

HASSAN BLASIM was born in Baghdad in 1973, where he studied at the city's Academy of Cinematic Arts. In 1998, he was advised to leave Baghdad, as his documentary critiques of life under Saddam Hussein had put him at risk. He fled to Sulaymaniya (Iraqi Kurdistan), where he continued to make films, including the feature-length drama *Wounded Camera*, under the Kurdish pseudonym "Ouazad Osman". In 2004, after years of travelling illegally through Europe as a refugee, he finally settled in Finland. His first story to appear in print was for Comma's anthology *Madinah* (2008), edited by Joumana Haddad, which was followed by two commissioned collections, *The Madman of Freedom Square* (2009) and *The Iraqi Christ* (2013)—all translated into English by Jonathan Wright. The latter collection won the 2014 Independent Foreign Fiction Prize, and Hassan's stories have now been published in over twenty languages.

PER OLOV ENQUIST was born in 1934 in a small village in the northern part of Sweden. He is one of the most celebrated authors in Scandinavia, both as a novelist and a playwright. His novels have been translated into more than forty languages, and he is one of the most performed Scandinavian playwrights. Enquist is one of only two writers ever to have twice received the August Prize for fiction, the most prestigious Swedish literary prize: in 1999 with the novel *The Visit of the Royal Physician*, and in 2008 with his memoir novel *The Wandering Pine*.

FRODE GRYTTEN (born in 1960) made his debut in 1984 with the poetry collection *Start*. Since then he has written novels, short stories, poems and children's books. *Songs of the Beehive* won Norway's national book award, the Brage Prize, and was shortlisted for the Nordic Council's Literature Prize. His only thriller, *Floating Bear* (2005), won the prestigious Riverton Prize. Grytten's latest book, the short-story collection *Men No One Needs*, was published in 2016.

CARL JÓHAN JENSEN (born in Tórshavn in 1957) is one of the most original and provocative writers on the Faroese literary scene today. Poet and novelist Jensen is also a prominent figure in the public debate on culture and politics in the Faroe Islands. Since the early 1980s, he has produced seven volumes of poetry, four novels and a collection of essays, and he is a regular reviewer of the Faroese arts. He has twice been awarded the Faroese M.A. Jacobsen Literature Prize, and nominated five times for the prestigious Nordic Council's Literature Prize. His work has appeared in literary journals and anthologies in Denmark, Norway, Sweden, the Netherlands, Germany and the USA. Jensen's celebrated novel *Ó-: søgur um djevulskap* (2005) (working title in English: "Un-: Tales of Devilry") was published in Norwegian translation in 2010 and in Icelandic in 2013. He is currently completing his fifth novel, which is expected to be published in early 2018.

LINDA BOSTRÖM KNAUSGAARD (born 1972) is a Swedish poet and author, as well as a producer of documentaries for Swedish radio. In 1998 she made her debut with a collection of poetry entitled *Gör mig behaglig för såret*, and in 2011 she returned with *Grand Mal*, a critically acclaimed collection of short stories. Her first novel, *Helioskatastrofen*, published in English by World Editions as *The Helios Disaster* (2013), proved to be her international breakthrough. Some of her awards and nominations include: winner of the Mare Kandre Prize 2013; nominated for Svenska Dagbladets Literary Prize in 2016, for the prestigious August Prize in 2016, and for the International Dublin Literary Award 2016 for *Helioskatastrofen*.

NIVIAQ KORNELIUSSEN (born in 1990) grew up in Nanortalik, a small town in Southern Greenland. She went to California in 2007 as an exchange student, obtained Greenland's equivalent of GCSEs in Nuuk and moved to Denmark to study psychology. Because of the great success of her debut novel *HOMO sapienne* in 2014, she is now back in Nuuk writing and working on different cultural projects.

ROSA LIKSOM (born 1958 in Lapland, Finland) is a prize-winning writer and two-time candidate for the Nordic Council's Literature Prize. Her books have been translated into eighteen languages. She is also a renowned painter and film-maker. She is an expert on people who live in unconventional circumstances, on the borders of cultures. With "Passing Things" (2014), Rosa Liksom returns to very short prose, a genre she pioneered and a medium in which she is still an undisputed master.

ULLA-LENA LUNDBERG is an acclaimed and prize-winning Swedish-Finnish novelist and ethnologist. She was born in 1947 on Kökar in the autonomous Åland Islands, and drew on her upbringing there in *Ice*, her recent and most well-known novel. *Ice* won the prestigious Finlandia Prize in 2012 and was nominated for the Nordic Council's Literature Prize. It is published in the UK by Sort of Books in a translation by

Thomas Teal. Ulla-Lena Lundberg is the author of more than twenty works of fiction and non-fiction. She has travelled extensively, and has lived and worked in the USA, the UK, Japan, Africa and Siberia. She currently lives in Mariehamn, the only town in Åland. Her face has recently appeared on an Åland island stamp.

SÓLRÚN MICHELSEN (born 1948) made her debut in 1994 with a short-story collection for children, *Argjafrensar*, and has since published several books for children as well as poetry and other short-story collections. She was awarded the Faroese Children's Literature Award in 2002. In 2004 she published her first novel for adults, *Tema við slankum*, for which she was awarded the Faroese M.A. Jacobsen Literature Prize; it has been published in Denmark, Norway and Germany. Her latest novel, *Hinumegin er mars,* from 2013, is a gripping novel about a woman caring for her elderly mother who has dementia. The novel was nominated for the Nordic Council's Literature Prize in 2015 and was published in Denmark in February 2017.

MADAME NIELSEN is a Danish novelist, artist, performer, stage director and world history enactor; she is also a composer and chanteuse. She is the author of numerous literary works, including her novel trilogy, *The Suicide Mission* (2005), *The Sovereign* (2008), *Fall of the Great Satan* (2012), and most recently *The Endless Summer* (2014), the "Bildungsroman" *The Invasion* (2016) and *The Supreme Being* (2017). Her work has been translated into nine languages and has received several literary prizes. The autobiographical novel *My Encounters with the Great Authors of Our Nation* was published in 2013 under the name Claus Beck-Nielsen and was nominated for the Nordic Council's Literature Prize in 2014.

DORTHE NORS was born in 1970 and is one of the most original voices in contemporary Danish literature. She holds a degree in literature and art history from Aarhus University and has published four novels so far, in addition to a short-story collection, *Karate Chop*, and a novella, *Minna Needs Rehearsal Space*. Nors' short stories have appeared in numerous publications, including *Harper's Magazine* and the *Boston Review*, and she is the first Danish writer ever to have a story published in the *New Yorker*. In 2014, *Karate Chop* won the prestigious P.O. Enquist Literary Prize. *Karate Chop* and *Minna Needs Rehearsal Space* are both published by Pushkin Press.

KRISTÍN ÓMARSDÓTTIR was born in Reykjavík in 1962. Her debut work in 1987 was a play; and in the same year her first book of poetry was published. She has written novels, poems, short stories and plays, and in 2009 she won the literary prize Fjöruverðlaunin for her book of poetry *Sjáðu fegurð þína*. She received the "Griman", the Icelandic prize for best playwright of the year for her play *Segðu mér allt* in 2005. Three of her novels have been nominated for the Íslensku bókmenntaverðlaunin prize, and one, *Elskan mín ég dey* (1997), was nominated for the Nordic Council's Literature Prize. Her work has been published in Denmark, Sweden, the USA, France and the UK. She lives in Reykjavík.

SIGBJØRN SKÅDEN (born 1976) is a Saami-Norwegian writer from Skånland in North Norway. He writes in both Saami and Norwegian and made his debut in 2004 with the poetry collection *Skuovvadeddjiid gonagas* (*The King of Shoemakers*) which was nominated for the Nordic Council's Literature Prize. He has since published a second collection of poetry, a children's book and two novels, in addition to numerous works written for the stage or installation art projects. He was awarded the Young Artist of the Year Award at indigenous art festival Riddu Riđđu, has been the prologue writer for the Arctic Arts Festival and a keynote speaker at the indigenous forum of the Medellín Poetry Festival, Colombia. His latest book, the novel *Våke over dem som sover* (*Watch over Those Who Sleep*), was nominated for the Norwegian Broadaster's Listeners' Award and received the Havmann Award for best book by a North Norwegian writer.

SØRINE STEENHOLDT was born in 1986 and grew up in Paamiut, Greenland. She had a rather difficult childhood, which continues to influence her writing today. In 2012 she won a short-story competition that made her want to keep writing, and in 2015 her short-story collection *Zombieland* was published. She now lives in Nuuk with her daughter; she is engaged in many cultural projects and continues to write.

Copyright Acknowledgements

SCANDINAVIAN BOOKS

FROM PUSHKIN PRESS

MIRROR, SHOULDER, SIGNAL
Dorthe Nors

Translated by Misha Hoekstra

'Sonja is a thoroughly modern heroine… nothing at all like Bridget Jones. Comical and clever, with a knife-twist of uneasiness'

The Times

KARATE CHOP
Dorthe Nors

Translated by Martin Aitken

'Beautiful, faceted, haunting stories… Dorthe Nors is fantastic!'

Junot Díaz

MINNA NEEDS REHEARSAL SPACE
Dorthe Nors

Translated by Misha Hoekstra

'Darkly funny and incisive'

FT

MY CAT YUGOSLAVIA
Pajtim Statovci

Translated by David Hackston

'A strange, haunting, and utterly original exploration of displacement and desire… a marvel, a remarkable achievement'

The New York Times Book Review